W9-BXA-209

ADMIT TO MURDER

ADMIT TO MURDER

MARGARET YORKE

V I K I N G

30711 5541

VIKING
Published by the Penguin Group
Viking Penguin, a division of Penguin Books USA Inc.,
375 Hudson Street, New York, New York 10014, U.S.A.
Penguin Books Ltd, 27 Wrights Lane, London W8 5TZ, England
Penguin Books Australia Ltd, Ringwood, Victoria, Australia
Penguin Books Canada Ltd, 2801 John Street,
Markham, Ontario, Canada L3R 1B4
Penguin Books (N.Z.) Ltd, 182–190 Wairau Road,
Auckland 10, New Zealand

Penguin Books Ltd, Registered Offices:
Harmondsworth, Middlesex, England

First American Edition
Published in 1990 by Viking Penguin,
a division of Penguin Books USA Inc.

1   3   5   7   9   10   8   6   4   2

All the characters and events and
most of the places in this story are fictional.
Any resemblance to real people is coincidental.

LIBRARY OF CONGRESS CATALOGING IN PUBLICATION DATA
Yorke, Margaret.
Admit to murder/Margaret Yorke.
p.   cm.
ISBN 0-670-83224-3
I. Title.
PR6075.07A36   1990
823'.914—dc20   90-50054

Printed in the United States of America

All the world's a stage,
And all the men and women merely players;
They have their exits and their entrances;
And one man in his time plays many parts . . .

As You Like It, Shakespeare.

PART ONE

1

Prologue: 1976

She disappeared on a Wednesday night after the weekly practice of the Feringham Choral Society.

Norah Tyler, in her Pimlico flatlet, heard the news on the radio the following morning. The announcement was brief, merely stating that Louise Vaughan, aged twenty-four, had last been seen getting into her dark red Mini after the singers had ended their rehearsal of Fauré's *Requiem*, which they were to perform at Easter. She had not returned to the village of Selbury, five miles away, where she lived with her parents.

Tutting under her breath, Norah made her tea in the Crown Derby pot she always used. Two slices of bread already lay under the grill, and automatically she turned them at the precise moment when they were toasted just as she liked them. Butter, in a glass dish with its own silver knife, stood on the small table beneath the window. The morning sun made a pool of gold light across the pale linen cloth which was laid with delicate porcelain: cup, saucer and plate. Honey this morning, thought Norah, taking a pot from the cupboard, her movements precise. She liked things to be neat and orderly, and, when it lay in her power, they were. For ten years now she had been personal assistant to the managing director of an electronics factory which, with the development of new technology, was rapidly expanding. Norah's job had developed with it, and her salary had increased to match her responsibilities. She earned a good income and could afford to indulge her taste for modest luxuries.

As she made her small, routine movements, she allowed herself to absorb the shocking news she had heard. Louise was not an irresponsible girl. If her car had broken down or she had been delayed in some other fashion, she would telephone so that her parents did not become anxious. She must have had an accident, Norah decided, putting the toast in a small silver rack which old Mrs Warrington had given her one Christmas.

She sat down to eat her breakfast.

Wouldn't the police have traced her to a hospital by now, if that was the answer? Had something really dreadful occurred? Surely not. There would be a simple explanation.

She would telephone later from the office.

Norah first obtained permission from Mr Barratt. She never took advantage of her trusted position.

'I'm an old friend of the family,' she explained. 'It's most worrying.'

'Of course you must telephone, Miss Tyler,' Mr Barratt urged. He never called her anything else; both of them understood these subtleties, not like the young girls in the outer office where everyone was called by their first name as soon as they were engaged. Sometimes Mr Barratt thought it would be agreeable to have a voluptuous assistant wearing tight skirts and high heels and with long red hair, called Valerie, instead of Miss Tyler with her greying perm and her thin figure in the plain suits or skirts and shirts she always wore as she efficiently managed his affairs. But Valerie might not be able to spell and Miss Tyler could, and Valerie might marry or leave, and Miss Tyler had done neither. She was, in fact, the perfect secretary.

He never wondered about her private life and she never mentioned it; this would not have been suitable, in her view. But she knew a great deal about his, his wife and three daughters, their A levels and boy friends, and the Corfu villa the Barratts annually rented, Miss Tyler making all the arrangements.

This was the first time she had mentioned anything remotely personal, and during the afternoon he remembered to ask her if she had made her call.

'I haven't been able to get through,' she replied. 'The line's been engaged each time I've tried.'

'The girl will be all right,' he assured her, but he knew that if one of his daughters had vanished, he would have been nearly out of his mind.

'They'll find her car, if it was an accident,' Norah reasoned aloud. 'That is, if she was taken to hospital unconscious and unable to give her name. But of course, she'd have her bag with her – her driving licence and so on.'

'She might not,' said Mr Barratt, whose own daughters had large sacks they slung over their shoulders in which all sorts of things were kept but not papers denoting identity.

They returned to Mr Barratt's programme for briefing the next board meeting, and Norah put the Vaughans out of her mind until it was time to go home.

The thick black headlines screamed at her from the evening paper on the news-stand by the tube station. HEIRESS GOES MISSING, she read, and there was a blurred photograph of Louise, enlarged from a snapshot and unrecognisable, her fair hair blown across her face. She bought a copy.

Pressed among a mass of humanity strap-hanging homewards, Norah could not read the paper in the tube. She kept it until she was back in the flat, and broke with routine enough to sit down before taking off her good black coat.

Pretty fair-headed Louise Vaughan, 24, went missing after choir practice, Norah read. MOTHER'S VIGIL,

11

announced a line in thick type above a paragraph revealing that Louise should have been home by half-past ten, eleven at the latest, after the weekly rehearsal for the Easter concert to be given in Feringham Town Hall. *Her mother Susan Vaughan, 57, waited up in the large secluded mansion where Louise had her own flat in the west wing*, the report went on, and Norah learned that occasionally after a rehearsal Louise would go with friends for a drink but was never later than eleven. She might, it was hinted, have gone home with someone.

'Hmph!' Norah snorted aloud. Not Louise, not when her parents expected her. And flat in the west wing, indeed: what next? The house was certainly large, but scarcely a mansion, and Louise occupied the room which had been hers from childhood. It overlooked a rough patch of orchard where now the daffodils must be out, a mass of yellow under the apple trees which soon would be laden with blossom. Old Mr Warrington had kept bees there during the war and one had got tangled in Norah's hair. Mr Warrington had gently removed it and she had not been stung, but he had, and his hand had swelled up enormously. Some people did react like that, he told her, and warned her not to get between bees harvesting honey and their direct flight home to their hives.

She had never seen bees in hives, nor apple blossom, until she went to Selbury during the war as an evacuee and her life became linked with the family in the big house.

She took off her coat, hung it up, then tried the telephone again. This time, George Vaughan answered. Louise had not been found, he said; she had not been admitted to any hospital. Her car had turned up, however; it was parked in a side road on the new industrial estate in Feringham, with the keys in the dash. Her handbag was on the rear seat. They must be prepared for the worst, he told her, but of course there was hope. She might have been kidnapped, for instance, and this call must be kept short in case Louise, or her abductor, rang.

'That was Norah.'

George Vaughan returned to the drawing-room, where Susan was sitting by the fire. The day was fresh and bright, not cold, but she felt chilled through. Neither of them had slept, though in the end they had undressed and tried to relax in the silent darkness of their room, separated by the narrow gap between their twin beds. Both were thinking that this could not be real, it could not be happening, but Susan knew that tragedy could strike without warning. Hadn't she already had her share of it, she thought, staring at the lightening sky showing behind the curtains as dawn broke. Her first husband had been killed during the war, and their child, a boy, had died before he was one, a victim of what was now called cot-death syndrome. It had been a terrible time; the police had behaved as if she had killed him herself, even though she lived in Selbury House, her parents' home, and all agreed she had adored the baby.

Now the police were back, because another child had vanished. But she wasn't dead; Louise couldn't be dead. Susan shut her mind to the possibility.

'Norah?' Detective Inspector Scott, sitting on the other side of the hearth, looked up. The call would have been recorded; by this time the telephone had been tapped in case there was a ransom demand, although Scott and his chief superintendent thought it most unlikely. The parents, though comfortably off, were not in the really rich league, but kidnappers – and newspaper reporters – might think otherwise.

'Norah Tyler,' George explained. 'She's someone we've known for years.' It was always difficult to

13

explain Norah's role in their lives. 'She'd heard, of course, and wondered if there was any news.'

'If she's been kidnapped, how soon will we know?' asked Susan. Her voice was steady but her expression was strained and she mashed a handkerchief between her bony fingers.

'It's hard to say.' Scott had never been directly involved with a kidnapping. 'They might wait for a while to – er – ' he sought the appropriate expression, not wanting to raise false hopes but feeling that it was too soon to admit to the worst.

'To soften us up?' George suggested.

'Exactly,' said Scott.

'We're not rich enough,' Susan said.

'You live in a large house and you run an expensive car,' said Scott. George Vaughan drove a Rover 3500. 'Some people would consider you good for a touch.' He looked round the room. There were various pieces of furniture that were worth a bob or two: that bureau, for instance, with all the inlay; he didn't know what it was, Sheraton maybe, something like that, and those chairs were antique; you got an eye for that sort of thing, in his job. The sofa he sat in, however, needed re-springing and the chintz which covered it was faded. The house was not all that old; it had been built in the late 1920s by Mrs Vaughan's father, a prosperous manufacturer, something to do with biscuits, Scott believed. Her mother still lived here, in the lodge at the gates. At the moment she was on holiday in Madeira, where by now the news of her granddaughter's disappearance would have been broken to her. It had been decided that she could not be left exposed to the risk of discovering it herself from a newspaper or radio broadcast, and George had telephoned her companion, another elderly widow with whom she often went away. George had urged her to change no plans, for Louise might soon be found and the old ladies could do nothing if they returned; in fact she was better out of the way, one less person to worry about. He had promised to telephone as soon as there was anything to report.

While Scott sat with the parents, asking them about their daughter, Detective Sergeant Marsh and a woman officer were up in Louise's bedroom, seeking any clue to what might have happened. It was routine; they did not expect to find anything helpful, except perhaps an address book with details of friends not already mentioned by her parents.

The two officers appeared now, with tea on a tray.

'Thought you could do with a cup, Mrs Vaughan,' said Marsh, a sturdy young man with brown hair and a pair of shrewd blue eyes.

'Oh, how kind,' said Susan vaguely. Surely tea was over long ago? Someone had given her a biscuit. She hadn't wanted it but had tried to nibble some crumbs.

The woman officer could see that Mrs Vaughan was far too shaky to handle the teapot, so she picked it up.

'Shall I be mother?' she said, and began pouring.

Scott was glad of the intervention by the two younger officers. There was no right way of dealing with this type of case; days of suspense lay ahead, but he was certain that Louise was dead.

All day officers had been making inquiries around Feringham and in the village; Louise's Mini had been taken off to the laboratory for testing; searches had begun in the fields round the town and it might be decided to drag Feringham canal. The parents hadn't known much about their daughter's private life. They said she had no special boyfriend at present, though she occasionally spent the night in London, where she had once shared a flat with two other girls. She worked for a small publisher who specialized in books on art and natural history, and was an editor producing a series about alpine plants and the wild flowers of various areas. She had returned to live at home a year ago; it was easy to travel back and forth from Feringham station.

Her colleagues at work would have to be interviewed; the Met must be asked to help with that task. Scott didn't think the answer lay there unless someone obsessed with her had followed her and observed her habits. More important would be a close study of interviews with the rest of the Feringham Choral Society. By now most of them had been contacted and he would concentrate on the men; if she had given one of them a lift home, he might have tried something on and met resistance. Such things could escalate and end badly. If this were the answer, her car should provide some clues.

Much later that night, when reports had been collated and the chief superintendent had been brought up to date on what was so far known, which amounted to very little, Tom Francis, who had a pleasant baritone voice, received a visit from the police.

He lived in a four-year-old house in Coverton Park, a still-developing estate on the edge of Feringham. He was a computer programmer and had a wife, Anna, and two small children, a boy and a girl. He had been visited earlier, as soon as he returned from work, by a constable who had taken a statement confirming that he had attended the choral rehearsal the evening before, and volunteering the information that he and several others, including Louise, had walked together to where their cars were parked in the market square. A visit to The Swan had been discussed; they often called in there for a drink and a chat before going home.

'To wind down,' Tom said now, when Detective

Inspector Scott and Detective Sergeant Marsh called to ask him about his movements.

'Wind down?'

'The singing is stirring,' Tom answered. 'Gets the pulse going and all that. You know.'

Scott didn't: not really; but he nodded.

'So you went to The Swan last night?' That had not appeared in his statement.

'No, I didn't. Jennifer's got tonsillitis and I wanted to get back,' he said. 'My wife's a bit ragged round the edges after being up with her most of the night.'

'Did Louise go to The Swan?' No one had said that she did.

'No. She drove off alone,' Tom said.

'That's unusual? She normally joined in?'

'Oh yes.' She'd been very quiet, Tom had noticed, and hadn't looked very well, now he came to think about it. Still, that was irrelevant to the present inquiry.

'What's she like?' Scott sounded as if he really wanted to know.

'Very friendly,' said Tom. 'But not pushy. Shy, really, I suppose, until you get to know her.'

'Attractive?'

'Yes – yes, very,' Tom answered.

'So you found her attractive,' noted Scott, nodding to Marsh to make sure he was writing this down.

'Yes.' Tom sounded puzzled now.

'If you weren't married, would you have wanted to date her?'

'What a strange question!' Tom's bewilderment was obvious. 'I am married. It didn't arise.'

'But supposing?' Scott persisted.

'Well, maybe. Probably,' Tom decided.

'But you hadn't?'

'No.'

Scott kept at him, going over the time the rehearsal

17

ended and discovering that once, when his car was out of action, Louise had given Tom a lift home.

They knew this already. One of the other choir members had remembered the occasion and mentioned it in his own statement. He'd added that she'd done the same for him, another time.

The difference was that he had volunteered the information and Tom had not.

Tom Francis was taken back to the police station and questioned for as long as the law would allow, without being charged. This was years before the Police and Criminal Evidence Act imposed stricter limitations on such detention. The clothes he had worn on the night Louise disappeared were removed and sent for testing, and visible even to the naked eye were traces of blue wool that could have come from the sweater Louise had, allegedly, been wearing that night.

'How can you tell, since you haven't found her?' Tom demanded. 'It might just as well have come from Jennifer's dressing-gown. That's made of blue wool. Why don't you try testing that?'

The police declined this invitation. Tom had said that he went straight home but his wife, interviewed while he was being questioned, had told them that he did not return until eleven o'clock. She had not been alarmed because she thought he had gone, as usual after the practice, to The Swan, though he had said he would come home promptly. It seemed that twenty minutes to half an hour of his time was not accounted for, and he grew angry when asked to explain the discrepancy. He said he had filled the car up with petrol at the one garage which stayed open late, not wanting to be delayed in the morning, but inquiries failed to confirm this since he had paid cash and the duty cashier could not remember whether or not he had been a customer. The place was self-service and the staff barely looked up as they took the money.

After a few days, when Louise had still not been found and there were no more clues as to her fate, Tom was taken in again. Pushed hard enough, he might crack and admit to murder; then, once he'd confessed, he would reveal what he had done with his victim. Any further evidence needed for his conviction would soon be found when the body was examined. For by now everyone, even Louise's parents, was sure that this was a murder case.

But he did not confess.

They took his Cortina away for testing, but without Louise herself, it was impossible to prove that any traces found in the car were hers. They found what must be assumed to be her fingerprints in her room at Selbury House, on folders to do with her work, and her hairbrush and other possessions, but no matching prints were found in Tom's car. Blond hairs discovered on the upholstery probably came from the heads of his children.

As he had not been in The Swan and yet was late home, Tom's wife was curious about where he had been during the unexplained period of time that Wednesday evening.

'Getting petrol,' said Tom. 'I told the police that and I'm telling you. I didn't want to stop on the way in to work in the morning.'

But apart from the fact that filling the tank would not take more than ten minutes, Anna knew that it had been almost full that evening. She had used the car after Tom had come home from the office to go to the surgery to collect a prescription for Jennifer, nipping out while Tom had a quick meal before the choral society's meeting.

He couldn't have been having an affair with Louise, could he? Or wanting to, and she wouldn't? Or wanting out, and she wouldn't let him go? All these possibilities ran through Anna's mind. Her own life was so taken up with the children, and his day at the office was so long except on singing nights when he always managed to get home earlier, that they seemed to have little chance to talk together. Louise, unattached and attractive, might have presented some sort of temptation. But Tom would never have killed her. That was impossible, unless there had been a quarrel followed by some dreadful sort of accident.

Anna took to watching Tom, speculatively, wondering how many secrets he had. After all, she had a few herself; innocent ones, such as how she enjoyed her chats with the milkman when he called for the money. He was a cheery man who told her about his racing pigeons, which wouldn't have interested Tom; and there was the bank teller who always looked at her as if she were still available and worth more than a glance when he cashed her cheques.

Tom became very silent in the days that followed, during which no trace of Louise was found. She seemed to have totally vanished, although there were reports that she had been seen in Glasgow and in Liverpool, and even in Penzance. All these rumours had to be investigated; all led nowhere. There were the usual crank telephone calls from people alleging that they had killed her and dumped her body in various sites ranging from silos to reservoirs. Some of these allegations were explored; others were not. Meanwhile, anonymous letters arrived at the house, accusing Tom of murder. Although he had not been named in reports that a man was helping with inquiries, his identity had been discovered because of the frequent calls at his house by police and because of his absence from home. The letters were all local; no one outside the area could know who he was. Tom threw them away, but Anna rescued them from the wastepaper basket and brooded over them. She knew they came from evil or, at best, unbalanced people, but they had an effect on her. So did the sly looks and muttered comments of several neighbours.

Louise's grandmother returned from Madeira and resumed residence at the Lodge House, as it was now called. Re-wired, re-plumbed, and slightly extended, it had become a comfortable small house easily maintained by Mrs Gibson who came in daily from the village and, besides doing the cleaning, cooked lunch for herself and her employer and left something ready for supper. Mrs Warrington did very little for herself.

Her companion in Madeira had been Dorothy Spencer, the widow of a former Member of Parliament who had been knighted when he gave up his safe Conservative seat to make way for a younger and promising candidate. Lady Spencer had worked with Mrs Warrington in the WVS during the war and they were old sparring partners as well as friends. Though both were now in their eighties, they travelled up to London to matinées or exhibitions once or twice a month, lunching at Fortnum's or, occasionally, Brown's hotel. During the weeks after Louise disappeared Lady Spencer telephoned daily, and often came over to keep her old friend company. Both old ladies were filled with angry frustration because, powerful though each had been in her time, there was nothing that they could do either to make possible Louise's return or to discover what had happened to her. When search parties combed the fields round Feringham and later a wider area reaching a radius of ten or more miles, her father joined in, raking the hedgerows with sticks, stirring up heaps of dead leaves in the woods, prodding streams and culverts, coming home wet and exhausted but feeling that he was doing something active to help. Malcolm,

Louise's older adopted brother, named after his uncle who was killed in the war, went out with them too. He lived thirty miles away in Corton, where until he could find more lucrative work he drove a mini-cab, and he often spent the night at Selbury House, but when she disappeared he was driving a fare to Heathrow.

While the men were out, Susan stayed by the telephone in case there was news, occasionally reinforcing with tea and sandwiches the catering laid on by the police. She never went out without leaving someone else in the house to answer the telephone.

Soon, Norah was there to take over.

She took unpaid leave.

Louise's disappearance was still holding the interest of the major crime reporters, who conjectured about her fate and compared her case with that of other young women who were missing. With every day that passed, the chance of finding her alive diminished.

Norah had gone down to Spelbury the first weekend, leaving the office early and getting off the train at Feringham station just as Louise had done for so long.

George met her.

'I'm glad you've come,' he told her. 'You'll be company for Susan while we wait. I'm going out with the police, searching, whenever they'll let me. It's better than sitting about.'

He would have to go back to work soon, Norah thought. He was a director of Warrington's and still very active on the production side of the business.

They drove through the town and George took a detour to show her where Louise's car had been found, outside a factory that packaged toilet goods. The wide new street on the outskirts of Feringham was surfaced with shining macadam. Tall lamps were bright sentinels punctuating the pavement. At this hour of the evening, with all the works shut, there was no one about and no other car to be seen.

'I ask you, what was she doing down here?' George demanded. 'She'd no call whatever to come this way.'

'But wasn't the car dumped here? By whoever – ?' Norah let her question die.

'I suppose so.' George sighed and scraped the gears, making Norah wince, as he changed down to turn by the bus-stop. He was normally a very good driver who never abused any part of the machine. They drove back towards the centre of town, passing the new comprehensive school formed by the marriage of a grammar and a secondary modern school years before, and past rows of shops to the market square and the town hall, where the practices were held and where the concert would eventually take place. 'You see, it was nowhere near her way home,' George said.

'Haven't the police got any ideas about it?'

'They've been interviewing a man called Tom Francis,' said George. 'He sings with the choir. I suppose they're all suspect – all the men, that is. It must have been someone she knew, after all. She must have given a lift to someone who turned – well – ' He sighed. 'She wouldn't have picked up a stranger.'

'But someone she knew – she would have talked herself out of trouble,' said Norah. 'She's very sensible.'

'She's not very big,' said George. 'And a man's strength – she wouldn't be a match for it, if he was determined.'

'She'd have scratched him, though. Fought him off,' said Norah. 'He'd have scars.'

'I suppose the police have thought of that,' said George. He wrenched the steering-wheel viciously as they rounded a bend on the long winding road that led to Selbury.

'How's Mrs Warrington taking it?' Norah asked.

'She's only just got back from Madeira,' said George.

23

'We telephoned her there to let her know what had happened, but we insisted she stayed the fortnight. She was there with Dorothy Spencer. She's much calmer than I am.'

'She's seen it all before,' said Norah.

'Not murder,' said George, at last using the word everyone had so far been avoiding.

'Murder of a sort, surely?' said Norah. 'Both her sons killed. And her son-in-law.'

'Ah, but their deaths were a glorious sacrifice,' said George bitterly. 'Or so she can tell herself. Killed for King and country. She's had her share of sorrow, poor old lady. She shouldn't have to lose her granddaughter too.'

And why should I lose my lovely daughter, he was screaming inside his head.

They were entering Selbury now, passing a few outlying cottages which had once stood in isolation on the fringe of the village, but now the gaps between them were filled with modern houses. The village had grown to accommodate commuters and people who worked in local industries. George slowed at the speed restriction sign on the rise leading into the village. It was awkwardly placed and for years he had been trying to persuade the council to move it lower down, giving motorists more warning that the village lay beyond their horizon. There had been a bad accident when a car sped over the brow of the hill and knocked down a child running across the road. He had sustained various fractures and cuts. The inference was that unless someone were to be killed, the council would not shift the sign.

Now, Norah saw a raw gap gouged out of a bank at the side of the road; a skip stood there, and a pile of bricks.

'What's happening at Mrs Benham's house?' she asked.

'It's been sold and pulled down so that the site can be developed,' said George. 'Thirteen rabbit hutches are to go up instead.'

'Oh dear! What would she have said?' Mrs Benham had died two years before.

George made a sound which was an attempt at a laugh.

'She thought one of the family would live there,' he said. 'Didn't realise the commercial potential, I suppose.'

Mrs Benham had been a magistrate and had run the Girl Guides. Her large Edwardian house had stood in nearly two acres of garden where the Guides had camped and cooked sausages over fires, and where her own sons and daughters had played as children themselves.

'There's another colony springing up behind the Post Office,' said George.

'But that's agricultural land, isn't it? I thought you couldn't build on that.'

'It depends where you're standing when you look at it,' George replied. 'It can be called in-filling, and it's very profitable if you have land to sell. Feringham is growing all the time and people have to live somewhere, of course. Villages seem to have the choice of expanding or of dying – losing their school and their post offices and shops. We've got a new butcher in the village now, and Dobbs' Stores has changed hands and is on the up-and-up.'

Dobbs was the village grocery, which sold everything from cheese to shoelaces. Norah had spent her sweet coupons there during the war. Every time she returned to Selbury she remembered the first time she had seen it, brought in a bus to the village hall as a girl of thirteen, sent out of London for safety in 1939. The children had been as much selected by their future hosts as allocated by the billeting officer, and Norah

25

was a better bet than most. She was picked by the gardener's wife from the lodge at Selbury House, ear-marked already as a bigger girl useful for duties about the place. She was soon helping wash up at weekends and in the evenings, when the Warringtons' maids had gone to work in munitions factories. Susan was young then, and newly married. Norah thought she and her handsome husband in his army uniform were like people in the films. It was even quite film-like when Hugh Graham was killed at Dunkirk, before the birth of his son, though it was dreadfully sad.

She still felt some of that magic.

It was the waiting that was so hard.

'If only we knew,' said Susan, on the Sunday after-noon. 'If only we knew what we had to face.'

When Hugh was killed, she had known very soon that there was no hope; for her, there had been no weeks or months while he was posted officially missing before his death was confirmed. But there had been no body then, either: no funeral rites to observe. In time there had been a memorial service in the village church, attended by some of his surviving brother officers, and later she had married one of them.

A body was found in a river in Wales but it wasn't Louise. George was taken there in a police car to make sure. He looked at the pitiful collection of flesh and bones on the mortuary table and shook his head. This was someone else's tragedy.

Louise could be hundreds of miles away. Whoever had killed her could have taken her off in his own car, or one he had stolen, and dumped her anywhere in the country. While the search was centred around Fer-ingham, he would have had plenty of time to find a good hiding-place elsewhere.

'We may not get a lead until some other young

woman goes missing,' said Detective Inspector Scott on one of his visits to the house.

'Goes missing,' snorted Mrs Warrington. 'What an expression. Girls don't go missing, they disappear.'

She hid her grief under a fierce, autocratic manner. This time there had been no warning, no premonition, no awareness of particular risk. During the war she had been prepared, braced to face disaster, with mental plans about how to behave when it happened, and although part of her had died with each of her sons, on the surface life continued as usual. She had continued with her voluntary war work and had set an example of fortitude.

Susan was living at Selbury House when Hugh was killed. During the few weeks of their marriage, while he was with his Territorial regiment training on Salisbury Plain, they had rented a cottage near Warminster. As soon as he was posted abroad, she had gone home to wait for her baby. At that time life was still comfortable in the big house, even without the two maids. Mrs Johnson, the cook, who was in her fifties, remained; and Ford, the gardener, who had flat feet and poor sight, would not be passed fit for active service, so he continued to dig for victory in the large garden where fruit and vegetables already flourished. Mrs Ford undertook most of the cleaning and it was natural for Norah to help her. She was nearly fifteen when Hugh was killed and would soon be leaving school. Mrs Warrington had decided that she would shape into a useful little nursemaid for the coming baby. She was a biddable girl, not pretty, but pleasant-looking, with alert brown eyes and shining dark hair. Since living in Selbury she had grown and put on weight, and her face had a healthy glow; she had settled well and seemed to like the country, cheerfully helping a local farmer with the harvest in the long summer holiday that marked the Battle of Britain. The Fords had been lucky securing such a child; the Warringtons themselves had two small boys, one of whom wet his bed and constantly cried for his mother. It was Norah who, discovering their misery on the way to school, consoled them and helped them adjust until, after a few weeks of the phoney war, they both went back to London.

One of them was later killed in a bombing raid, and so were Norah's parents and her elder sister. After that there seemed nothing else for her to do but remain in Selbury until she was old enough to be called up.

After baby Harry died, Mr Warrington had advised Norah to stay on at school for another year. Since Mrs Ford would no longer be paid for her board, she could have one of the attic rooms in Selbury House and, in return, could make herself useful about the place in her spare time.

It had become a habit.

PART TWO

1

Norah

The radio alarm woke Norah at seven o'clock. Normally she slept well, but for the last weeks she had woken in the small hours and had lain in the darkness listening to the World Service, with the automatic cut-out adjusted so that it went off after an hour by which time, with luck, she would have fallen asleep again. Sometimes she started awake when a burst of music interrupted the even tones of the announcer relating news of famine, earthquake or terrorism, or analysing political events in some remote part of the globe. She let the sound wash over her, the volume low; if you listened too intently, interest kept you awake.

Susan had given her the radio for Christmas the year they moved into the Lodge House, after old Mrs Warrington's death at the age of ninety-one. Selbury House was put on the market and once again the Lodge House was refurbished. A second bathroom was installed above a study built on for George, who had now retired, and the kitchen, drawing-room and main bedroom were extended, turning it into a spacious house with three large bedrooms and a small one, and a quarter of an acre of garden.

Susan, who loved her garden, had taken to working in it obsessively after Louise's disappearance, clipping and pruning, planting and hoeing, until she was exhausted, reluctant, it seemed, to be in the house at all. One reason behind the move was George's hope that with less land around her, she would begin to spare herself, but Selbury House had become too large for them. Besides, they needed money; so much had been spent on Malcolm, settling his debts and saving him from bankruptcy when various ventures he started went wrong. After paying off his creditors when the house was sold, George had told him that this was the final reckoning and now he must take the consequences of any further folly.

Selbury House had been sold to a couple with two children. The husband worked in the City and the wife, alone while the children were away at school, had become bored and lonely. Village gossip said that one reason they had moved into the country was to steady her down as she had been having affairs in London; whatever the truth of that, they separated after less than two years and she demanded a generous settlement. Selbury House had been sold to provide it, and went to the highest bidder who gazumped a private buyer. The new owner was a property speculator who had hoped to build eighty houses in the grounds, but the planners permitted him to put up only ten. This he had done, and retained the land against a change of heart by the council. The house itself had been divided into two large flats and a small one in the main building, with another flat over what had been stables and were now extra garages for all the new inhabitants.

When the Vaughans realised what was happening to the place they were dismayed, and almost regretted what they had done, though there had really been little choice unless they let Malcolm go bankrupt and, as they saw it, defraud those to whom he owed money. It wasn't as if they had grandchildren to fill up the big house on regular visits; however, they had hoped that it would continue to be a family home.

Norah had pointed out that there might be grandchildren one day. Malcolm might yet have a family.

'Well, that doesn't look much like happening,' said Susan. 'Sad though it is to admit it.' As she spoke her thin face, with the fair skin etched by a network of broken veins, took on a forlorn expression. 'And anyway, if he does, I'll be too old to help take care of them.'

'Norah won't,' said George.

I won't be here, Norah said to herself. But four years later, here she still was and it was time to get up and tidy downstairs before breakfast, which democratically they all ate together in the kitchen. Norah, quick and neat in all she did, would clear away her own cup and saucer and plate as soon as she had finished her toast and marmalade, and leave husband and wife with the percolator and the newspapers while she went upstairs to make the beds in their two bedrooms, for since the move they no longer slept together.

Once I was personal assistant to a managing director, Norah thought to herself as she shook duvets – she had managed to modernise Susan and George that far – and plumped up pillows. Now I'm simply a housekeeper, a grand title, really, for what I do and no disgrace in itself, but I had risen in the world and now you could say that I'm back to my origins. Though not really; not when I'm on such intimate terms with my employers. The thought made her smile.

She had slid into it. Five years after Louise disappeared, Norah's firm was taken over by a large consortium and she was made redundant. Her compensation was generous and she was in no hurry to make plans. She went down to Selbury for a visit and had stayed there ever since.

She had fully intended to find another job or, because at her age good openings were limited, to set up on her own, but at Selbury House there was always plenty to do. Then old Mrs Warrington fell and broke her hip. After she came out of hospital, Norah moved into the Lodge House to look after her. Why engage a stranger when she was available, said the old lady, propped up in bed discussing what must be done. Besides, a woman from one of those agencies would be very expensive.

'Norah must be paid,' said George, who had been meaning to offer her something for doing his typing.

'Why?' Mrs Warrington saw no reason for such a step. 'She's part of the family now and one doesn't pay family members for their help. Besides, she gets her keep. And she had a pay-off, didn't she, when she stopped work? Anyway, she'll soon be eligible for her pension. She can't need much spending money.'

Susan was less shocked by these reactionary remarks than George, but she agreed that Norah must be recompensed to some extent. It was decided that they would stamp her insurance card for the remaining years when this would be necessary, and that she should be paid thirty pounds a week.

'There's no point in her having to pay tax,' Susan pointed out. 'And she'll get lots of perks.'

When Norah, who had been earning an excellent salary, was told of these decisions, she remembered the hours she had spent as a girl helping Mrs Ford wash up, polish floors, clean silver. She had peeled mounds of potatoes and had put eggs in waterglass for Mrs Johnson, the cook. She had bottled plums and dried apple slices, and she had, incidentally, become a very good cook herself, helping out when the family came home on leave and special celebratory meals were prepared.

Old Mrs Warrington had left her a thousand pounds in her will, and her garnet brooch as a keepsake. Norah had bought a car with the money, adding to it some of her own. Malcolm had found her a low-mileage secondhand VW Golf, economical to run and easy to park. It enabled her to achieve some freedom and she went away for occasional weekends at country hotels, something she had begun to enjoy in the last years of her time with Mr Barratt.

While she lived at the Lodge House there was no room for Malcolm, as he would never settle for the small room above the hall, where there was just space for a single bed and a chest of drawers. The Vaughans never had overnight guests now; indeed, they had rarely done so before the move, though occasionally Louise had had friends to stay. Their social life had dwindled since her disappearance. Susan's closest friend was Helen Cartwright, Lady Spencer's daughter, who had married a merchant banker and lived fifteen miles away, between Feringham and Malchester. The two had been at school together and were godmothers to each other's children.

Susan had expected to rebuild the family after she had married George. She had replaced her husband and she would have other children, lots of them, and in time would forget that one small baby who had been so smiling and happy and then was so suddenly dead. How could the police imagine she might have had something to do with that? In those days there had been a constable in the village and he had been very embarrassed at the implications of his visit, with a sergeant from Feringham, and the nature of their questions. It was impossible for Mrs Vaughan to have done such a thing, he had insisted. The sergeant had pointed out that she might have been in a state of distress because she was now a widow, and the constable had opined that this was very likely, but she would be comforted by having her baby. He knew this was the truth; he knew that Susan was devastated. In the end the coroner agreed with this view and the sorry inquiry was over. Susan was left with her grief and a tiny grave in the churchyard.

After her marriage to George, no new baby had arrived and so, eventually, they adopted one. Before the advent of the contraceptive pill and legal abortion there was no shortage of babies for adoption and they were considered a highly suitable couple. Malcolm was two weeks old when he came to them, and two years later Louise, their natural daughter, was born, but there were no other children after her.

Susan was disappointed. Four would have been nice, she thought; she had had easy pregnancies and gave birth without complications. They did not, however, adopt other children, for already Malcolm was proving to be a handful. At five years old, fully aware of the consequences of his action, he deliberately threw a stone through the drawing-room window when his grandmother was sitting at her desk writing letters. Mrs Warrington was cut, though not badly, by splintered glass. She would not believe that the child had deliberately aimed at her, but he was quite old enough to know that what he was doing was wrong. George would not spank him, but she did, until bright red marks showed on his plump white buttocks. Susan had been upset by her mother's action and had comforted Malcolm with kisses and cuddles.

Norah had not been at Selbury then, but she heard what had happened, just as she heard about everything of importance that went on, for Susan wrote to her at least once a month.

It was Susan who had helped her to advance herself in the world, and it was because of Susan that she had again become the family's prisoner.

Since Louise's disappearance, the population in Selbury had almost doubled, swollen by the arrival of young families in the smart new houses which had sprung up wherever a clutch could be inserted. There were some bungalows to attract the retired, but most of the newcomers were on their way up in the world of commerce – computer programmers, accountants, executives in companies either local or at some distance. The village lay six miles from a motorway junction and commuting was easy, making it an attractive area. The schools were good and there was a large branch of Sainsbury's in Feringham, but there was scant provision for young couples marrying within the parish; they were forced by high prices to move away.

Walking around the village with Bertie, the Vaughans' black Labrador, Norah would recall the days, not so long ago, when doors had been left unlocked because no opportunist thief could possibly be wandering about during the daylight hours, and she could remember when the telephone exchange was manually operated by Jessie Brown who would tell you that so-and-so, whom you wished to call, had just gone out and could be found at such-and-such a house up the road.

'Do you remember?' she used to say to Mrs Warrington, during their evening games of Scrabble; but it was she who indulged nostalgia, not the old lady. The past, which held Norah's days of innocence, was too painful for Mrs Warrington.

Louise's body had never been found, and after a while interest in the case died down. Other people vanished, were found or not, and horrible crimes were committed, taking the headlines. Sometimes, if an unidentified body were discovered in some remote area, there was speculation about Louise, and until dental records or other evidence proved that it was somebody else, the mystery would be resurrected. As the years passed it was accepted that she was dead, and the truth about what had happened would never be known unless the perpetrator were to commit another crime and be caught, when he might confess. Susan was torn between longing for this to happen, to put an end to her imaginings, and dread that another victim would succumb to the same assailant.

In the first weeks after it happened, Norah spent a lot of time at Selbury House doing what she could to help, which meant making sure that Susan and George, and Mrs Warrington at the Lodge House, were fed, and that someone was always there to answer the telephone. Later, when she returned to work, she came down every weekend and helped to answer the scores of letters the Vaughans received. Most were sympathetic; some were from clairvoyants and people who said they had dreamed about Louise and her fate. A few were damaging, vicious documents which accused the Vaughans of being heedless parents or, worse, alleged that Louise had had a secret life devoted to sexual promiscuity or drug-taking. After a time, George sorted the mail and left any envelopes which might contain such communications for Norah to weed out. Norah would cart them to the end of the garden to burn, enjoying stirring the angry words into cleansing flame. What made people write such vile accusations? The same sort of motives that spurred others to physical violence, perhaps.

Things had gradually died down. George took early retirement so that Susan was less alone. He stood for the district council, seeing it as his duty to put something into the life of the area, but he found the work wearing and often grew discouraged, though he fought hard to retain school dinners and prevent over-urbanisation. Susan spent more and more time in the garden; she would dig up huge areas and plant them with shrubs, then change her plans and root them all out, grassing them over again. She made ponds and a connecting stream, George helping her when he could in an attempt to prevent her from exhausting herself, but it was her way of coping with what had happened and when she was physically worn out she did not think about Louise. Later, encouraged by her friend Helen Cartwright, who thought such activities more appropriate than excessive manual labour, she joined a fine arts group and, apart from attending their lectures, went to exhibitions and visited galleries in London. She also helped raise funds for various charities.

Susan was out a great deal, and the housework was done by two visiting daily women who each came for three mornings a week, overlapping on one day to combine for major tasks. There was still fruit to be picked and made into jam, vegetables to be frozen, and the cooking to be done. Once a keen cook who had enjoyed running her home efficiently, Susan had lost interest in anything to do with it. She ate very little herself, and became very thin. Life, for her, had become something to be endured and had lost all its pleasure.

After her enforced retirement, Norah gradually took over what was being neglected, and more. She typed George's council correspondence. When repairs were necessary, she obtained estimates and supervised the resulting work. She painted several rooms herself and she found someone to mend frayed curtains and make new chair covers. She sorted Louise's clothes, which was something neither parent could face because to get rid of them was so final; Norah packed them in polythene bags and labelled them clearly. One day they could be sent to Oxfam.

As a girl, Norah had worked hard in Selbury House, eager to pay for her food and her keep, but she had never resented it for she loved to look in at the window of life in the big house.

'Norah will do that,' people said when an errand had to be run or some extra job done. Mr Warrington, who went daily to the works, where output now had to conform with food rationing and its limitations, sometimes gave her a ten-shilling note as a bonus.

Things hadn't changed a great deal, Norah thought, as she accepted the terms she was offered many years later, well aware that by working for one of the agencies to which Mrs Warrington would have had to turn if she had refused, she could have earned a great deal more.

'You must have plenty of time off,' Mrs Warrington had told her. 'And use the car whenever you want to go out.'

She thinks she's being generous, Norah thought. She considers me lucky to live here, in this house that is really rather inconvenient with its coke-fired Aga and ancient Hoover. She thinks being at her beck and call is a privilege.

'You'll have a little income, won't you, from your golden handshake,' Mrs Warrington had added. 'And if you sell your flat, you can invest that money.'

It was true. Norah had seen that if she gave up her home she was, in effect, surrendering, but she did it all the same. It was not practical to leave the place empty and if she sub-let she might have difficulty getting tenants out. She could always buy her way back into the property market again.

But after she sold the flat, prices soared, and unless she moved to Scotland or the remotest tip of Cornwall, she could not rehouse herself for the same amount.

She had settled down, devising little routines to give herself comfort and maintain a degree of independence. She insisted on having the big spare bedroom at the lodge, not the tiny boxroom Mrs Warrington thought would do, and she used some of her own furniture in it; her china and other possessions were packed in tea-chests in the loft against the time when she made her escape at last. Before long it seemed obvious that this would be only when Mrs Warrington died, for with every year that passed it became less possible to abandon her. Norah would take her on little drives in the car and to lunch with Lady Spencer, going off on her own to the local pub and collecting her later. Unlike Mrs Warrington, Lady Spencer had learned to cook and was a dab hand at omelettes and chicken *suprême*. Mrs Warrington had discovered that if you were unable to do something, such as cooking, for yourself, there would always be someone else to do it for you; and now she had Norah, with Mrs Gibson still coming in to do most of the cleaning but reduced in her weekly hours.

Sometimes Lady Spencer came to lunch at the Lodge House, and Norah would give the old ladies chops and creamed spinach and Duchesse potatoes, followed by *crème brulée* or strawberry fool. They liked grilled trout, or sole *Véronique*, if such occasions coincided with the weekly visit of the fishmonger's van to the village square. She enjoyed preparing these feasts and had heard Lady Spencer tell her friend how lucky she was to have such a treasure.

'Well, she owes us a lot, you know,' Mrs Warrington said. 'But for our family, she would still be living in the East End of London and would probably have married some oaf who would have beaten her black and blue and given her eight children.'

Lady Spencer had laughed at this and told her old friend she was a disgraceful snob. Why shouldn't Norah have married a kindly tradesman who would have looked after her well?

'No reason at all, I suppose, except that she had a nose for trouble when she was young,' said Mrs Warrington.

'It takes two, you know,' Lady Spencer had remarked.

Norah herself sometimes played the 'What if I'd done something else?' game. What if she had remained in London, never set off on that September morning with her bag of emergency rations and one change of clothes, her gas-mask over her shoulder?

She'd be dead, of course. She would have been killed with the rest of her family when a bomb wiped out

41

their house. Instead of this, she had had a rewarding career and subsequently had been usefully occupied in such ways as driving old Mrs Warrington's elderly Maxi to collect the groceries and visit the chemist. After lunch she would take the old lady out for a drive, and if it was warm enough they would park the car and stroll on the common above Feringham, looking down at the growing town, the outcrop of factories, the place where Louise had met her death. Norah felt herself to be no longer personally vulnerable, unlike Mrs Warrington and her family who had been stalked by tragedy over the years.

One day, there would be serious trouble with Malcolm. Only influence had kept him out of court when he had picked a fight in The Grapes in Feringham soon after Louise had vanished. He had laid out a youth who had, he alleged, provoked him. Money had passed then, Norah knew, and it had smoothed his path many times since, though, as far as she was aware, violence had not been involved again.

As a small boy, he had been fearless and bold, and charming to look at, with dark curls and pale blue eyes. He had grown into a big, handsome man with a highly aggressive nature but without the intelligence to direct his energy into profitable directions. He had one broken marriage behind him, for which failure Susan blamed his pale, shy ex-wife Gwynneth. Luckily there had been no children to have their lives torn apart by the separation.

When Louise disappeared he had just returned from four years in Australia, but he was not officially living at home though he frequently arrived without warning, even quite late at night, announcing that he wanted to stay. This continued through the following years and sometimes he stayed for weeks at a time, when he had been turned out of lodgings for non-payment of rent or had broken with the current girl-friend. He moved in with various young women who had their own flats or houses, and sooner or later he moved out again. Norah marvelled that there always seemed to be someone new who would take him in, but surely the supply of gullible females must one day run out? Susan lamented over him, consumed with guilt because she felt his failures reflected on her and his upbringing, convinced that if he could only find the elusive Miss Right who would understand him, he would gain confidence in himself and find the proper direction for the ability she felt he must have.

He had always been jealous of Louise, imagining that she had replaced him in their parents' affections and, when he understood the difference between them – that he was adopted and she was not – resenting it even more.

'But we chose you,' Susan would say, hugging him as he wriggled on her lap, not wanting to attend to some story she had been reading. 'Louise just arrived.'

Louise, however, did well at school; she was small, fair and pretty, everyone's idea of a dream daughter, and George adored her. Malcolm seized every chance he could find, when no adult was about, to torment her, pulling her hair, teasing her, hiding and even breaking her toys. Once, Norah saw him lift her, struggling and screaming, out of a window above the stables and deposit her on the flat roof over the garage outside. He closed the window so that she could not climb back. Norah rescued her and told George what had happened. George did not believe in beating children but he was so angry with Malcolm that he could think of no other appropriate punishment and the boy was still young enough to be laid over his knee and thrashed with his hand. Two days later Malcolm shut Louise in an outhouse and she was there for half an hour before Ford, the gardener, heard her cries and released her.

This time, Malcolm's punishment was to dig a large

patch of vegetable garden instead of going on a long-planned seaside picnic with some other children.

'I didn't want to go on the silly picnic anyway,' said Malcolm. Physically strong, he dug up the patch of ground very rapidly and afterwards went off to the shed in the paddock to smoke, something he had lately taken to doing. He threw his cigarette end into some hay in the corner and burnt the place down.

George could not prove he had caused the fire, but he knew. So did Norah, who had been staying for a few days during these events. She sometimes came down in the school holidays, helping Susan buy clothes the children needed for the next term and stitching on name tapes, even taking them to the dentist. Susan found it hard to believe that Malcolm had been so naughty, and though she did not excuse him for what he had done to Louise, she told George that Louise must in some way have provoked him. But even she was relieved when the new term began and he went back to his boarding-school. Louise did not go away until much later when she was sent to her mother's old school in Surrey, where she acquired seven O-levels and two modest As. Then she went to stay with a family in France, on and off for over a year. She had always been good at languages and she ended up speaking excellent if not totally fluent French.

Malcolm survived his prep school, but he was asked to leave his public school after a year. It seemed that he had started a fire in the games pavilion. The evidence, circumstantial though it was, convinced George, though not Susan, of his guilt. Shortly before the blaze was discovered, Malcolm was seen leaving the building and, when he was later questioned, there were matches in his pocket. After this he was sent to a school with less ambitious academic aims and a wide curriculum combined with a loose system of discipline. He and another boy got drunk one night on beer they had bought unchallenged on a trip to the nearby town. They became involved in a fight with some local youths, one of whom had been badly cut and bruised. The police were called to the affray, but all the boys escaped with a caution.

George decided that this school was too lax in its approach to be right for Malcolm, even if they agreed to keep him after this episode. Desperate, he made extensive inquiries and discovered a place in Yorkshire which catered for difficult boys and concentrated on physically demanding activities. Here Malcolm learned rock-climbing, canoeing and sailing, and worked on the farm attached to the place. George began to hope that he could be sent to an agricultural college and in due course, perhaps, be set up with a smallholding or even a farm of his own. He also learned motor mechanics, at which he was brilliant, and there was scope to drive old bangers restored by the boys around the large grounds.

He was often in trouble even here, provoking fights, but there were other large and aggressive boys, and nothing happened which could not be handled by them or the staff. If this place couldn't sort Malcolm out, George decided, then nowhere could. In the past, wild boys like him had made excellent fighting soldiers, but there was now no war for him to take part in. Perhaps he would join the army, however.

Malcolm did not do that. He did not care for regimentation.

He had brought little joy to his parents, thought Norah. She knew he resented her position in the Lodge House and her occupation of what he thought should be kept as his room for his various homeless spells between girl-friends. He had attended his grandmother's funeral looking very correct in his dark suit with his black tie, his springy curls brushed down, and he played the part of the grieving grandson to perfection. Mrs Warrington had left him her books, hoping, she said in her will, that he would profit by reading them.

What good were sets of Dickens and Scott and the Georgian poets to Malcolm? He read the sports columns of newspapers, and the racing news to decide how to place the bets with which at intervals he sought to restore his fortunes, but little else. Even so, he took the trouble to consult several second-hand booksellers in order to obtain the best possible price when he sold them. He did not realise enough from his inheritance even to take his current girl-friend to the Bahamas.

What a chance he had had in life, Norah thought, and how he had messed it up. He had cost George and Susan a fortune in getting him out of trouble.

How much was due to heredity and how much to environment? What had his true parents been like? Norah knew that her own were hard-working and honest; her father had been a baker's roundsman and her mother, once in service – they met when he called at the house where she worked – had later had a job as an office cleaner. The two of them had dove-tailed their hours so that there was always someone at home for their daughters, who had been much loved. Susan and her brothers, though, had been packed off to boarding-school and had grown up with a number of inhibitions quite foreign to Norah. The educational pattern had been followed with Malcolm and Louise.

Norah had kept a keen eye on the conversion of Selbury House and at first she had entertained a fantasy of buying the smallest flat for herself, thus regaining her independence whilst still being close to Susan and George. But if she staked herself to that out of her small capital, with a mortgage, she would no longer be able to run a car or take her annual foreign holidays, for she was realistic enough to know that at her age she was unlikely to find a well-paid job in the area. She was trapped in a gentle web of mutual dependence, for without Susan and George she would be quite alone.

She made friends with the builders, walking up to the house with Bertie, the Labrador, and introducing herself to the foreman.

The earth gaped raw where a giant grab had torn out a track to form a side entrance away from the Lodge House. Huge tyre marks dented the loamy soil and uprooted shrubs lay on their sides, their leaves dropping. Here were the laurestinus and lilac, the syringa and mahonia, the various berberis plants with their spectacular foliage and prickly stems that had grown undisturbed for years, shielding the garden which they enclosed from the weather and from the curious gaze of passers-by. Here, Norah had helped to cut holly boughs to deck the house at Christmas. There, beyond the site of Susan's water garden, now demolished, lay the orchard, most of it to be preserved as the property of one of the new occupiers, but the mistletoe-bearing apple tree that had so amazed her when she first came to the place had been cut down. A huge JCB was parked near where there had been a small pond with goldfish lurking beneath the water-lilies. In the bitterly cold first winter of the war they had been frozen into blocks of ice, but two of them had miraculously revived when Mrs Warrington had chipped them out, brought them into the house and thawed them. Tough little creatures, they had later repopulated the pond. No trace of this remained.

Heaps of scooped-up soil lay in mounds at the side of the fresh approach to where the new houses would be built after the main conversion was done, and several workmen stood about while a man holding a large plan discussed it with one of them. The site manager, Norah decided, and so it turned out.

47

She walked past them and gazed at the house where it stood in the bright spring sunshine, its brickwork looking raw because plants that had covered it had been pulled out to allow for new external doors. The big wisteria had gone. Norah felt a pang; Susan had cherished it over the years. Perhaps it would rise again from the roots. She had not inspected the plans at the county offices, and nor had Susan, unable to bear the thought of what was to be done to the place, but George had, in case there was anything to which they should object. He was in an awkward position about this, since he was now on the council and as a close neighbour had an interest, and was relieved to find that the details were not unpleasing, though it was a pity that so much of the mature garden would be lost. The new houses were to be set some distance from the original building and were not being packed densely together; each would have a reasonable plot of its own. The high-density building would follow when the rest of the land was developed, as must inevitably happen in time.

One of the workmen saw Norah and made a move towards her.

She immediately addressed the man holding the plan.

'I hope I'm not trespassing,' she said. 'I was interested in what you are doing here. I used to live in the house.'

'Oh, good morning,' said the man, who wore a Barbour jacket above corduroy trousers and mud-encrusted wellington boots. 'You'll be Mrs Vaughan.'

'No. My name's Norah Tyler. I'm Mrs Vaughan's housekeeper,' said Norah. 'I've known this place since I was thirteen years old.'

'Have you really? This must be a shock to you, then,' said the man. 'Seeing the mess we're making, I mean. But when it's finished it will be quite attractive, you'll find, and bang up to date. Everything of the best. Go in and have a look round, if you like. Now's your chance, before anyone moves in.'

'Are some of them sold yet, then?'

'They all are,' said the man. 'They're so convenient, you see.'

Norah had not been into the house during the interval when the couple from London had lived in it, so she had not seen the alterations they had made, but Susan had described the purple walls in the study, the bilious ochre oval bath in what had been the main bathroom. The kitchen had been stripped of its Aga and turned into something starkly white which had made her think of a hospital operating theatre.

Now Norah discovered that in place of that former kitchen and the scullery where as a girl she had so often washed up in a papier-maché bowl in the large porcelain sink, there were a bathroom, bedroom and living-room. A space where the coal had been kept had become a small kitchen. The rest of the house had been similarly transformed and some of the apartments were quite large; all were equipped with top quality fittings, as the site manager had told her.

Who would move in? Would they be happy? Were there ghosts here who needed to be exorcised? Did Louise's spirit come back, looking for sanctuary, and what would such a sad spectre think about all the changes?

Norah shivered, as if a goose had walked over her own grave. So many people had died.

Old Mrs Warrington had grown physically frail in the last years of her life but her mind had been alert to the end. As her sight began to fail, she had liked Norah to read to her and even after so many years would correct what she heard as a slovenly vowel sound. George had bought her a Walkman and the tapes of several classics but she preferred to hear

49

Norah, liking the company, and pretended she could not work the set, which was quite untrue.

'It takes up a lot of your time,' George grumbled to Norah.

'I don't mind,' Norah replied. 'It's quite restful, though I get a bit croaky after an hour or so. After all, she has more or less educated me and I owe her something.'

'That's been paid back long ago,' said George.

Ah, thought Norah, but there's more to it than you know. Mostly, now, she was able to shut her mind to that dreadful time, but its consequences had shaped the rest of her life. It was Susan who had insisted that she must get away and make a fresh start, helping her leave the factory and join the ATS. Norah had remained in the service for five years, during which time she had acquired secretarial and accounting skills, risen to sergeant, and finally had been offered a commission.

Susan had urged her to take the opportunity. It would give her a chance to see the world. If she'd done so, she might have ended up with high rank and a generous pension, but she had decided that she wanted to put down roots.

Her training had helped her to a good secretarial post in London, and, changing jobs several times before settling with Mr Barratt, she had gradually acquired some possessions along with her mortgage. She had had only one serious love affair after that bitter experience when she became pregnant at the age of seventeen.

She was doing the ironing in the kitchen of the Lodge House when the doorbell rang one afternoon. She had appropriated Mrs Warrington's Walkman and tapes and was tuned in to *Our Mutual Friend*, so that she did not hear the bell, and the caller had come round to the back door before she realised that there was a visitor.

She looked up from the ironing-board as a shadow fell across the kitchen window, and unplugged herself to see who was there.

A large man in his forties stood bulkily filling up most of the door-frame.

'I rang the front doorbell but could get no answer,' he said.

'Well?' Primed by tales of con men disguised as officials to prey on the elderly, Norah squared up to him, working out that she was unlikely to win in a test of strength over closing the door.

'You don't remember me, Miss Tyler, I can see,' said the visitor. 'Marsh is my name. I'm a Detective Superintendent now and just back in this division.' He took a police warrant card from his pocket and showed it to her.

'Oh – Sergeant – no, Mr Marsh – I'm sorry. I remember you, of course, but I didn't recognise you,' Norah said, her mind flitting back to the dark-haired sergeant who had spent months investigating Louise's disappearance. The man in front of her was balding, thickset but not paunchy, with deep lines on his rather pale face. 'You've changed,' she said, and added, 'So have I, I expect. Won't you come in?'

Detective Superintendent Marsh came into the large kitchen with its wide windows, oak fitments, geranium cuttings on the sills and green oil-fired Aga.

'Changed a bit, hasn't it? The kitchen wasn't as big as this in the old lady's time, if I remember correctly.'

'No. It was all enlarged after she died,' Norah explained.

'Ah. When was that, now?' asked Marsh.

'Four years ago,' said Norah, switching off the iron. A sweet smell of freshly pressed linen gently rose to meet Marsh's nose as he entered. His sense of smell had sharpened since he gave up smoking.

'She must have been getting on.'

'Ninety-one,' said Norah.

'A remarkable old lady,' said Marsh. 'She took all that amazingly well.'

'Her generation was brought up not to show emotion,' said Norah, who had found some of that training brushing off on herself. 'It doesn't mean that she felt it any the less. Would you like some tea, Mr Marsh?'

Why had he come? Was there news after all this time? Was there another poor, decayed body to go and inspect? Surely a superintendent wouldn't call in person about that? It would be a telephone call first, then a sergeant, or at most an inspector. Wouldn't it? Or perhaps this time they were sure it was Louise, and Marsh, having worked on the case before, wanted to break the news himself. She remained outwardly calm. The man would explain when he was ready.

'Thank you,' said Marsh, accepting the tea.

'Do sit down,' said Norah, adding, 'I hope you don't mind the kitchen. It's warmer in here than in the sitting-room. The fire's not lit yet in there.'

'The kitchen's the heart of the house, I always say,' said Marsh, lowering his bulk on to one of the oak-framed chairs by the big square table and watching while Norah put the kettle on and found cups and saucers. She was still a slim woman, in her dark pleated skirt and maroon sweater. She wore low-heeled black pumps and pale ribbed tights. He recalled that she had always been bandbox neat. When he had returned to take charge of the CID in the area, one of his first actions had been to ask what had been happening to the Vaughans, but now there were not many officers left in Feringham who remembered the case, as the senior detectives involved had retired and others had

52

moved to different divisions. This afternoon, with for once some time to spare, he had decided to go to Selbury and find out for himself how the family had survived the years. 'I went up to the big house,' he went on. 'I expected to find Mr and Mrs Vaughan still living there.'

'You had a surprise, then,' Norah stated, pouring water into the teapot to warm it.

'Yes. Well, I suppose it was a big place for just the two of them. There's quite a colony up there now, I discovered. There were some children tearing about on cycles having a great time. There was a son, though, I remember. Still, he'd be married and gone. He lived at Cornton then, didn't he? Came out on some of the searches.'

'That's right,' Norah said. 'He's living in Malchester now but he isn't married.'

'And you're visiting again?'

'No. I'm here permanently now,' said Norah. 'Or sort of. I was made redundant and came for a visit, and stayed on.'

'I see.'

Marsh had not taken a great deal of notice of her, years ago. She had clearly had nothing to do with the girl's disappearance and he had thought her some sort of distant relative until, from the case reports, he had learned otherwise.

'Is there news, Mr Marsh? Is that why you're here?' Norah briskly poured boiling water into the pot as she spoke.

'No, I'm afraid not. I've just come back to the district and thought I'd take a look round the village,' Marsh explained. 'I've often thought about that poor girl and wished we'd managed to find her.'

'There have been many more disappearances since then,' said Norah. She opened a decorative jar and put biscuits from it on to a plate.

'Ah,' said Marsh. 'This is nice.' The china was good, there was a tiny pot of winter jasmine on the table, and Norah had put a silver teaspoon in his saucer. 'It's a lot more elegant than what we get at the station. Two sugars, please.'

Norah poured out.

'Do help yourself to a biscuit,' she said.

They were custard creams, which George adored.

'My favourites,' said Marsh. 'Thanks.' He seemed to remember her producing tea at intervals during the investigation, always in a quiet, self-effacing way, yet somehow exuding efficiency. She was, he realised, a confident woman. 'What do you think about it all now?' he asked. 'Have the parents adjusted?'

He did not ask if they had got over it. No one could get over a daughter's violent death.

'They've survived,' she replied. 'Her mother has changed completely. She spends very little time in the house. She works in the garden or goes to art exhibitions or lectures.'

'And has nightmares,' said Marsh.

'Yes, sometimes,' said Norah. 'She's never stopped blaming herself for what happened, though how she could have prevented it, I don't know. You can't chain up an adult young woman.'

'No. I was surprised she was still living at home,' said Marsh.

'Well, she had shared a flat with some friends for a while, but she got rather tired and thin and I think her parents persuaded her to come home again. I used to see her in London sometimes – I lived there then – and she didn't really enjoy the social life her flatmates liked.'

'There was no special boy-friend, I recollect.'

'No.'

'Poor girl. She was in the wrong place at the wrong

time,' said Marsh. 'Maybe someone asked her the way and got fresh and took it from there.'

'You gave that young Tom Francis a grilling,' Norah reminded him.

'Well, he was a likely suspect. It's usually someone known to a victim who kills her, and he did have some time unaccounted for that evening.'

'You remember the case very well,' said Norah.

'I do, because it was so frustrating,' said Marsh.

'Poor Tom had been seeing someone else. Someone in the choir, as it turned out, but they'd been very discreet. She was married, too. They'd met that night to end their affair. His wife found out, of course, after he'd been questioned so much. It broke up their marriage.'

'Oh dear. I'm sorry about that,' said Marsh.

'Yes. If she hadn't, it might have all blown over and they'd still be together, not adding to the divorce statistics,' said Norah, who blamed the police for what had happened.

'There were children,' said Marsh.

'Yes. One was only a baby then,' said Norah. 'I don't condone what he did,' she added. 'But their whole world broke up.'

'You never married, Miss Tyler?' asked Marsh.

'No.' Norah pressed her lips together. There was no need to tell him about the long liaison she had had with a man she had met through her work, who at first had said he would leave his wife and marry her. After some years, she had realised that the time would never be right for the break to be made and it would not happen. Later, growing bored with each other, they had ended the affair by mutual consent. She had never regretted the experience, and she was glad, now, that his children had been spared the pain of their parents separating. Two years ago, on a trip to London, she had seen him, quite by chance, with his wife; they were

55

going into Fortnum and Mason as she went past on her way to Hatchards to buy a book for George's birthday. Out of curiosity, she had followed them into the store and had seen them discussing some purchase in the grocery department. They had looked rather old, but sleek and content, and she assumed that they were. They never saw her, and she looked rather old, too, she had decided, going back into the street without any regrets. 'A lot of men have patches in their lives when they seem to need two women,' she said. 'One for excitement, and a workaday model for domesticity.'

'That's true,' said Marsh.

'Are you married?' she asked him.

'Not any more,' he said. 'It's difficult for wives, with the job. I've got two children, though,' he added. 'A girl and a boy, ten and eight. I see them whenever I can. It's all quite amiable, really.' Sometimes he thought it would be easier if it were not: if he and Lynn could be so friendly now, why couldn't they have got over their troubles and stayed together? She'd been lonely, of course. She'd got some fellow in tow, a furniture salesman, but he hadn't moved in with her and there was no talk of marriage. Marsh didn't know what the children would make of having a stepfather, and he wasn't at all keen on the idea himself except that it would mean he could stop paying her maintenance.

'I'm sorry things didn't work out,' she said. 'Are you going to reopen the file on Louise?'

'It's never been really closed,' he replied. 'Just left in a sort of pending file. We won't be doing anything unless some fresh evidence turns up.'

'Like a body, you mean,' Norah said.

'That's right.'

'There have been one or two,' she said. 'Mr Vaughan has gone to look at them. It's been horrible for him.'

'I'm sure. He's retired, then? They told me that at the big house.'

'Yes, but he keeps very busy with village affairs,' said Norah. 'And he's on the county council.'

'The brother thought Louise would come back, didn't he?' Marsh said, taking another biscuit. It was nice sitting here in the warm and chatting as if they were old friends. In a way you could say that they were. 'He thought she'd had a row with someone and would turn up again when she'd cooled down.'

'Yes, he did, but that was a silly idea, said Norah. 'Louise wasn't like that. Besides, how could she have managed without any money? The police never seriously considered it, I believe.'

'Not on the evidence,' said Marsh. 'And who was the quarrel with, anyway? She got on well with everyone in the choir who knew her, and all the singers were checked out.'

'The one person she might have wanted to get away from was Malcolm,' said Norah. 'He hadn't been back from Australia long, and they'd never got on together, but he wasn't living at home and she seldom saw him, so that couldn't have been a serious problem.'

'No. Well, I'm afraid we're unlikely to find the answer now,' said Marsh. 'Unless whoever did it is arrested for something else and confesses. That's about the only hope.'

'That will be too late to help her parents,' said Norah.

'If it happens at all,' agreed Marsh. 'I'd like to know who it was, all the same, and see that he got put away. He was a tall chap. We know because he'd put the seat of her car right back.'

'I hadn't heard that,' said Norah, surprised. Louise's parents had kept the car for two years, but at last they had sold it and given the money to a children's charity.

'There's no secret about it,' said Marsh. 'It was all in the reports, though perhaps it didn't get into the papers. Would you give me Mr Malcolm Vaughan's address? You said he's living in Malchester. I might have a word with him in case at this distance in time he remembers something that didn't seem important then.'

'I doubt if he will,' said Norah. 'He's running a secondhand car business in Sebastopol Road, called Vaughan's Reliable Cars, and he's living with a young woman. I can't remember the address but I'll just look it up.' She rose and left the room, soon returning with a piece of paper on which the name and address were neatly printed. She gave it to Marsh. 'I don't suppose he'll be very pleased to see you,' she added. 'He's put all the past behind him.'

2

Malcolm

Malcolm Vaughan had always known he was special. His mother had often told him so as she tried to teach him to read or helped him assemble his model train. He enjoyed playing with that, especially when it crashed going too fast round a bend. She bought him Dinky toys which she allowed him to park all round the drawing-room fireplace on the carpet. She told him the pattern on the Persian rug by the hearth was marked into roads and towns, but he could never see it himself. Her brothers had arranged their toy cars on it, using it as landscape, she had explained, and seemed disappointed when he did not understand. To him the lines were like a series of car parks.

Later, when he overheard his grandmother talking to Lady Spencer, he learned he was not so special.

'How does one know what characteristics they've inherited?' Mrs Warrington asked. 'It might be just the shape of a nose or the colour of their hair, but what about other things, other tendencies? Adoption's a risky business.'

'It was a wonderful chance for the boy, though,' said Lady Spencer. 'Coming into a family like this should be the making of him. I admire Susan for taking it on.'

'What's adoption?' Malcolm had asked a teacher at the small private kindergarten he was then attending, and she, unaware of the significance of the question, had explained.

It was months before he asked Susan if she had gone to the same hospital to adopt him as when she had collected Louise. He remembered that; she had been in bed for a while and he had been taken to see her and the small, pretty baby who had looked like a doll.

'But Louise isn't adopted, darling,' said Susan, and then realised what the question implied. She had turned quite pale but had grasped the nettle. 'You're very special. I've always told you that and I would have explained it properly when you were a little older. I can see I shall have to try to explain it now.' She took a deep breath and plunged. 'No baby came along after Daddy and I were married, and we wanted a boy so much. Sometimes babies come to people who can't look after them, and they go to live with families who want them a great deal. We chose you from among lots of other babies.' She cuddled his sturdy body close and kissed his springy dark curls, so unlike her own fine, straight hair which she had lightly permed to give it some body, and different, too, from George's black thatch. She began to tell it like a story, how the day was fine and sunny, and they had gone in Daddy's big car because it was more comfortable than her small one, and there he had lain in his cot looking appealingly up at them, only two weeks old. The sun had been shining when they left with him, all wrapped up in a very soft shawl, and they had been so happy.

Malcolm wriggled about as she related this tale; it seemed to apply to somebody else, and years passed before he understood the difference between him and Louise. Susan could not think how he had learned about himself, and supposed there might have been talk in the village which had somehow got back to him. She had always been resolved that he should never have cause to feel inferior to Louise, and she spent a great deal of effort and energy attempting to compensate for failing to be his natural mother.

A year later Malcolm joined together the long hair of two girls who sat in front of him at school. The teacher found it impossible to undo the knot he had somehow managed to tie before one of the girls felt what was happening and jerked her head away, pulling the connection tight. Scissors were required to separate the pair. For this offence, Malcolm was kept in at playtime and made to write lines.

He enjoyed the attention he attracted by this piece of mischief. Some of the little boys thought he had been funny and bold, and the small girls began to avoid him, whispering behind their hands and shrinking away whenever he came near them. Never good at his lessons, he devised ways of avoiding boredom by carving his initials on his desk, reading comics, and, when detected, swaggering up to receive his punishment which, as time went on, involved being kept in after school so that his mother knew what was going on. Susan pleaded with him to work harder and at home tried hard to help him learn his tables and read.

His misdeeds were undetected at the prep school where he was sent as a boarder at the age of eight. Tall for his age, and solidly built, he was good at football and the other physical activities which the school encouraged. He joined the Cubs, and when a tent went on fire one afternoon, was never suspected of being responsible. He had earlier found a master's cigarette lighter lying in the grass, where it had been accidentally dropped, and thought it would be fun to make a blaze and see the other boys run. No one was hurt, and Malcolm hid the lighter in a hole in a tree in the copse; it might come in useful again. The episode was written off as a freak accident, and when the term ended Malcolm retrieved the lighter and took it home. He sold it to a boy in Selbury village for a pound, a great deal of money then.

When a very small boy fell into the swimming-pool and alleged that he had been pushed, since Malcolm, the only other boy about, had leaped in after him and hauled him out, the victim was assumed to be romancing. Both were rebuked for being near the pool at an unsupervised time, but Malcolm was praised for his presence of mind.

Other things happened. A master walking in the copse received a crack on the head from a stone. It knocked him out for a few moments, long enough for Malcolm, perched up a neighbouring tree armed with a catapult – strictly forbidden – to escape without being seen. Then he began gambling, taking bets on whether he could climb out of the dormitory window and walk all round the roof and back, a feat another boy had attempted the previous term, ending up being caught by the headmaster. Years before, went the legend, a boy had fallen from the roof and been killed, trying the same thing. Malcolm succeeded and won a shilling from every boy who was part of the dare.

Other bets followed, involving less risk: whether a certain boy would win a particular prize; how many times the vicar would say 'And now finally' in his sermon on Sunday; who would win various matches with other schools. Sometimes he won and sometimes he lost, but he was elated when his bets came off; it was money for nothing.

His first sexual experience was with a girl who worked as a maid at his final school, where he had learned so much about cars, and that came about as a result of a bet that he would produce her panties, sure proof of conquest. He won the bet but did not reveal that the girl had not been compliant; she had struggled and had been left weeping and bruised but intact. She had allowed various boys certain liberties in return for rewards of a financial nature but had permitted nothing below the belt. When Malcolm, now a big, strong boy, offered her five pounds for the trophy – he would clear a good profit with what had been staked and had no need to achieve anything more – she agreed only when he caught her by the wrist and twisted her arm. To the girl, surrendering the panties seemed the easiest way to escape and she would avoid him in future, but, with the prize in his hand and titillated by the look of fear on her sharp, pertly pretty face, Malcolm sought more. It was only his lack of expertise and her agility that saved her from actual rape. She did not report the incident because she should not have been taking money for such favours as she had hitherto granted, but after that she gave in her notice and left the school.

Malcolm made a good tale out of the event but what he had most enjoyed was his sense of power. Later, he found prostitutes, and then, working on a farm in Wales where he had gone at George's insistence after other career ideas had failed, he had met a meek, pretty girl who kept him at arm's length and it seemed to him that the best plan now was to marry. At that time the age of majority was twenty-one, and as soon as he reached it they went off to the registrar's office together. Gwynneth's parents had, at first, protested, advising the couple to wait, but their objections collapsed when Malcolm subjected them to the full battery of his charm. It was clear, too, that he came from a moneyed background and had an assured future. He made out that he was gaining experience from a variety of jobs before joining the family firm, though the truth was that no family member would be employed there unless he or she were of outstanding ability.

Gwynneth spent a good deal of her honeymoon in tears while Malcolm was drinking too much in the bar of the hotel in Corfu where they were staying. She lay on the beach in her bikini while he went swimming, and her fair skin soon grew red and sore. Sometimes she splashed in the shallows, but she could barely swim and Malcolm made no effort to help her become more confident although the clear, calm water was ideal for such practice. He talked to other people he met on the beach or in the hotel, mostly men; she pretended to read a paperback novel she had found on a shelf in the foyer, but she was too wretched to take in much of the story. He seemed entirely different from the person she had known – or thought she knew – before they came away, and in bed he was rough and demanding; none of this was what she had expected, and they had nothing to say to one another. Perhaps things would improve when they went home and perhaps she would get used to what must be endured. She could not understand why people raved about sex when to her it was painful.

They settled down to raise chickens on a small-holding near Hereford financed by Malcolm's parents, to whom he had presented his bride with some pride; an acquisition he had obtained without their aid. Susan and George had liked Gwynneth, although they thought her excessively timid and later admitted to one another that perhaps a wiser choice would have been a girl with more self-possession. Still, that might come with time. Gwynneth had at first been frightened of them and of the style in which, as it seemed to her, they lived. She was afraid, too, that they would be angry about the secret wedding, which they were told of only weeks later. But they had been kind and friendly, and Malcolm had been on his best behaviour during the visit, drinking moderately and finishing with her very quickly in bed. That haste was the one thing that made it bearable; she gritted her teeth and lay rigid until it was over.

The marriage lasted for less than two years, during which time the poultry farm lost money and the couple ran into debt. Malcolm would go off on drinking bouts and would place bets on horses in the hope of putting things right. When he came home, angry and frustrated, Gwynneth was at his mercy. The farm was isolated, and when Malcolm had taken the Land Rover, she was marooned. Then one day an old school friend came to see her, found her moving about the kitchen as stiffly as an old woman and noticed a bruise on her arm. Out came the whole story and when Malcolm returned that evening, Gwynneth had gone.

He went home to give his version of events before Gwynneth had a chance to spread hers. He alleged that she was unfaithful and did nothing to help with the chickens. At that time divorce was not possible until after three years of marriage, but Gwynneth immediately sought a judicial separation and a financial settlement, charging Malcolm with physical and mental cruelty. The Vaughans paid her off with the farm and a capital sum on the understanding that later she would sue for divorce on other grounds. There had been a distressing interview at her parents' house, where she was living, when George and Susan had driven over in an attempt to bring about a reconciliation.

Gwynneth was waiting for them with a solicitor at her side, a short, middle-aged man with steel-rimmed spectacles, determined to do well for his client. It was made very clear that at the first hint of opposition to Gwynneth's demands, the fact that Malcolm had knocked her about causing bruises noticed by neighbours, had been before magistrates on a charge of drunken driving for which he had been lucky not to lose his licence, and was in debt, would become public knowledge. Indeed, it was possible that she might be given special permission for an early divorce before three years were up, said the solicitor, chancing his arm.

George and Susan had been routed. They drove home in silent despair, until at last Susan spoke.

'Of course she drove him to it,' she said. 'She's such a milksop. Those great spaniel eyes and all that sad hair hanging down her back.'

Gwynneth had had a different effect on George. He had shared the sentiments clearly felt by the solicitor, wanting to wrap her, figuratively speaking, in blankets, tell her not to worry and he would see that Malcolm never hurt her again. She was no sophisticated actress assuming a wounded little girl role; she had been genuinely hurt, both mentally and physically. He had known, when Malcolm brought her to Selbury, that she would never be able to deal with him.

'The boy's a bully,' he had answered. 'He bullied small girls at school, he bullied Louise, and he bullied Gwynneth. If he'd picked a big, robust girl who would swear at him and give as good as he handed out, it might have been different.'

'But he'd never be drawn to a girl like that,' said Susan. 'I expect he lost patience with Gwynneth's whingeing.'

It was as close as she would come to criticising Malcolm. Both snatched at the idea of a trip to Australia as a remedy, and George had arranged an introduction to a sheep farmer who might give Malcolm work. With any luck he would like the life enough to stay there, George had thought. While he was away life at home had been much easier, though Susan had fretted because Malcolm wrote so seldom. George remarked that no news was good news, and earned a reproof for being callous. During Malcolm's absence, Gwynneth's uncontested divorce petition on the grounds of desertion was granted.

'Why can't he take himself to Leeds or preferably John O'Groats?' George had remarked to Norah soon after Malcolm's return. They were having dinner together in London, something they did from time to time, very discreetly.

'It's Susan who draws him back. He's as besotted with her as she is with him,' said Norah.

'Besotted? Is that what you think?' George asked.

'Well, obsessed, if you prefer,' Norah said.

'I think that's a truer description,' said George. 'Poor Susan. She still thinks he'll settle down one day, but how much longer do we have to wait?'

When George was Malcolm's age, he was commanding a company in France, following D-Day.

Norah shared George's concern, and she understood Susan's feelings of guilt because Malcolm had turned out so unsatisfactorily. Susan was sure that his upbringing must be somehow to blame; perhaps, when sent away to boarding-school, he had felt rejected. Norah did not think it was as simple as that; traits ran in families and little was known about Malcolm's antecedents; he might have rogue genes.

Some months after Louise's disappearance he found a job as sales manager in a garage. This lasted until there was trouble over money paid as deposits on new cars and never received by the company. Unknown to George, Susan bailed him out to prevent him being charged with embezzling the firm's funds. Then she helped him to open a motor accessory shop, which was not the career she would have chosen for him but seemed suited to his abilities; it was clear that he was unlikely to succeed while working for somebody else. Grateful, he promised never to cause her another day's anxiety.

At the time, George told Norah that he was sure the venture would fail and regretted that remittance men were a thing of the past.

'You can't just write him off, George, like a bad debt,' Norah protested. 'After all, he is your son.'

'But he's not,' said George, and added, 'Thank God.'

The accessory shop lasted three years before it went under, leaving Malcolm on the verge of bankruptcy. Once again, Susan saved him and paid off his creditors.

Now he was running a second-hand car business in Malchester. Nobody dared to ask how it was doing.

Between times he had tried other things, including selling double-glazing, but nothing had lasted. He worked on cars he bought, and sold them in good condition; there was some visible turnover, and if he had asked for money recently, Susan had never told either George or Norah.

More than two weeks after his visit to Selbury, Detective Superintendent Marsh went to see Malcolm. He had had no time to spare before for a case which was inactive and might never be officially investigated again.

He drove past Vaughan's Reliable Cars in the dusk of early evening. Three vehicles – a Porsche Carrera, an old Jaguar XJ6 and a Maestro saloon with a D registration number – were parked on the forecourt outside a large barn-like building. The Jaguar and the Maestro had price labels attached to their windscreens, and invitations to pay in easy stages were written below the totals. Lights were on in the building, and Marsh, after parking alongside the Maestro, pulled open the sliding door to enter. Inside, he saw a blue Metro elevated on a mechanical hoist and an elderly Triumph Vitesse, with its bonnet raised, beside the lift. A big man in green overalls was adjusting something on the engine of the Vitesse. Pop music played loudly.

'Mr Vaughan?' Marsh inquired.

'Right.' Malcolm extracted his upper torso from the car's vitals and turned to switch off the portable radio which stood nearby. He turned upon Marsh a smile which someone less cynical than the superintendent might have found disarming. He had pale blue eyes in a rather florid face that was already puffy round the jowls. How old was he? About thirty-eight? He looked more. A drinker's face, Marsh decided. 'This old girl will soon be ready for sale.' Malcolm indicated the engine he had been working on. 'She'll be good for many more miles when I've finished with her.'

'Do them all up, do you, before selling?' asked Marsh.

'Too right,' said Malcolm, who sometimes affected an Australian accent, and indeed other accents from time to time when attempting to make some sort of impact on a new acquaintance. 'What can I do for you? Are you interested in something I've got on show or do you want to sell? Part exchange can be arranged.'

'No.' Marsh was not tempted to feign interest in one of the cars. He produced his warrant card. 'My name's Marsh. Detective Superintendent Marsh,' he said. 'Twelve years ago, when I was a detective sergeant, I was on the investigation after your sister went missing, and now that I'm back in the area I'm making a few checks on those involved.'

'Oh, are you?' Malcolm was not able to mask his suprise. 'I thought all that was over now,' he said.

'No case is ever over until it's solved, Mr Vaughan,' said Marsh.

'Isn't it? Well, you'd better come into the office,' said Malcolm. 'Though there's nothing I can add to what I said at the time. I wasn't living in Selbury then. I had my own place at Cornton.'

He picked up the handset of a portable telephone which lay on the workbench beside him and led the way into a small room opening off the workshop. Marsh had expected a shabby cubicle with tatty filing-cabinets and a scratched desk, but the area was classily furnished with a desk whose melamine top resembled mahogany and was only slightly dusty. Behind it was a padded revolving chair and there was a comfortable, if small, upright armchair facing it, for a client.

'Tea?' offered Malcolm. 'Or coffee? I'd better not suggest anything stronger,' he added as he replaced the telephone on its base.

'Coffee, please,' said Marsh. 'Milk, if you have it, but no sugar.' He did not really want it, but was curious to see how Malcolm would prepare it. There was no equipment in sight.

Malcolm opened a door at the rear of the office. It led into a lobby where there was a sink and worktop along one wall. Marsh saw an electric jug-type kettle. Malcolm opened a cupboard and took out two mugs, a jar of instant coffee and a carton of milk.

'I've got no fridge here,' he said. 'But I've got other things – there's a shower beyond that door.' He nodded towards the rear of the area. 'I get pretty grubby working and need to clean up,' he explained.

'Ah,' said Vaughan. 'Very convenient.'

'Yes,' agreed Malcolm, returning with the coffee. He set one mug down opposite Marsh and took a gulp from the other before seating himself in his swivel chair. 'And what is it you want to know?' he asked. His manner was easy and as assured as though he had just poured Marsh a Scotch in a well-ordered drawing-room.

'I'd like to know how you've spent the years since Louise went missing,' said Marsh. 'And whether there's anything about her disappearance which, with hindsight, you think might be helpful in finding out what happened to her.'

'Does that mean you're opening the case again?'

'No. As I said, I'm just bringing myself up to date because I've returned to the area,' said Marsh. 'There could be some trivial detail – possibly the name of a friend who wasn't mentioned before – a remark she'd made – just a little thing, perhaps, but significant and overlooked at the time.'

'You can't expect me to remember everything that happened so long ago,' said Malcolm. 'As I said in my statement, I'd last seen her the weekend before, when I was at the house. She seemed all right then.'

'She was all right until she went missing,' said Vaughan drily. 'You were not living at Selbury then.'

'No. I'd come back from Australia a couple of months earlier and hadn't found work that really suited me,' said Malcolm. He fixed Marsh with a frank, honest gaze as he spoke.

Marsh gazed steadily back, unimpressed.

'You were driving a taxi,' he stated. 'Is that correct?'

'More a mini-cab, really,' said Malcolm. 'Just helping a friend who was short-staffed. My father wasn't too keen, to tell you the truth. He thought it rather down-market for me, but I was providing a service. What's wrong with that?'

'What indeed?' Marsh concurred. 'You had a fare that night?'

'Yes. I told the police at the time. I had a run out to Heathrow,' said Malcolm.

'And you were living in Cornton, in a flat in Thames Road?'

'Right.'

'Where are you living now, Mr Vaughan?' Marsh had the address because Norah had given it to him, and he knew, because he had asked his department to check, that the householder was a Mrs Brenda Carter, who ran an employment bureau from a small office in a narrow street behind the abbey.

Malcolm glibly gave the address.

'And do you own the house, Mr Vaughan?'

'I pay the mortgage,' Malcolm replied. 'It's my girl-friend's place. She's divorced – no kids. I met her when she needed a car.' He wore on his face the smile that had charmed Brenda then.

'And the lady's name?' asked Marsh.

'None of this has got anything to do with her,' Malcolm protested.

'Of course not,' said Marsh. 'Still, I need to keep

71

records up to date. It's no secret, is it, if you're living there openly? She's not on social security, is she?'

'Certainly not,' said Malcolm. 'She runs her own business.' He supplied Brenda's name.

'And you've no theories about what happened to your sister?'

'No. She must have been stopped by someone who attacked her,' said Malcolm. 'That's what everyone thought, isn't it?'

'Would she have stopped for a stranger?'

'I don't suppose so, but he might have got into the car when she stopped at the traffic light,' Malcolm suggested. 'She wouldn't have locked it.'

'Hm.' Marsh could not remember discussing this possibility. 'But there were no signs of struggle in the car,' he said.

'Well, maybe they got out to argue,' said Malcolm. 'How should I know?'

'You were fond of your sister?'

'Of course I was. Well, we had the odd row – brothers and sisters do quarrel, don't they?' Malcolm said. 'She could be obstinate at times.' He stood up and took his empty mug through to the sink where he rinsed it and set it on the drainer to dry. How pernickety he was, clearing it away so promptly, thought Marsh.

'What did you and Louise quarrel about?' he asked, when Malcolm returned.

'Oh, I don't know. It's so long ago,' said Malcolm. 'She thought our mother favoured me and was jealous,' he said. 'Of course, I was the son, you see. Mothers like their sons.'

'Did she get on with your wife?' inquired Marsh.

'My wife? God, that's going back a bit,' said Malcolm. He had almost forgotten Gwynneth's existence. 'I don't know if they met. Louise was living in London then.'

'What's your view on why she returned to live at home?'

Malcolm shrugged.

'George kept nagging at her to come back. Thought she wasn't safe in London, with dozens of lecherous blokes after her,' he said.

'And were there dozens?'

'I doubt it.'

'What about her mother?'

'Oh, Susan thought she should stay in town. Thought it was the best place to find some nob to marry,' said Malcolm. 'It was top priority, that, with Susan. Getting her married. That was the pattern, you see. She'd done it – married when she was very young, and found another husband fast enough after the first one died. It was what happened then. Girls had to find some guy to take them on, provide a meal ticket for life and get them off their father's hands.'

'Did Louise go along with that?'

'No. She wanted something romantic,' said Malcolm. 'Well, girls do, don't they? Till they get some sense and learn what it's all about.'

'And what is it all about?' asked Marsh with interest.

'Bed, of course. Sex, if you'd rather call it that,' said Malcolm. 'That's what makes the world go round, and some of them aren't too keen.'

'Do you think Louise was one who wasn't?'

'How should I know? She was supposed to be a virgin, wasn't she?'

'And you don't think she was?'

'No. She'd been having it off with a bloke for years,' said Malcolm.

Marsh tried not to show his excitement at this revelation. Here was what he was hoping for: a new observation.

'Was she?' he asked. 'Who with? Do you know?'

'His name was Richard Blacker,' said Malcolm.

73

'Really? You didn't mention this at the time,' Marsh pointed out.

'No. Well, he couldn't have had anything to do with it, and there was no point in spreading scandal about her if she was dead,' said Malcolm. 'He was married, you see.'

'How can you be so sure he wasn't involved?'

'They'd broken up. That was why she came back to live at home,' said Malcolm. 'Susan and George didn't know about it. It would have fairly cracked up George if he'd found out.'

'Ah. What did he do, this Richard Blacker?' asked Marsh.

'Something in advertising, I think,' said Malcolm.

You don't just think: you damn well know, Marsh reflected.

'She told you about it, did she?' he asked.

'Of course. What are brothers for?' answered Malcolm.

But that was not how he had learned about the affair.

He escorted Marsh to the forecourt, saw him into his Cavalier, remarked that it was a useful car and offered to find him something with a little more dash any time he felt like a change, then sketched a waving salute as the superintendent drove off. Traffic was building up towards the rush hour now as people started to leave their offices and the shops closed. It was a fine evening, though windy; November had been unusually dry this year, with bright, sunny days and skies massed with huge, billowing shadowy clouds.

Back in his office, Malcolm found he was sweating. He had not expected interest in Louise to resurface after so long, not unless she were to be found. He mopped his face with a piece torn from a roll of paper towel and threw the crumpled stuff into the waste-bin beside his desk. His hands were shaking and he needed a drink. He took a bottle of Scotch out of the kitchen cupboard and poured himself a stiff tot. He wouldn't go back to the workshop now, except to lock up; what he needed was Brenda. He'd take her somewhere special tonight, treat them both to an extra good meal. She was no cook and nor was he, so they often ate out, and he enjoyed being seen with an attractive woman as much as eating a gourmet meal. Brenda always looked smart; she said it was important in her job, and he agreed. If you didn't look good, people didn't respect you.

Brenda was tough. She'd had a struggle, setting up the business, and she was hard enough to take a high fee for what she did. She was physically strong, too, and played badminton twice a week. She didn't go weepy over a bit of rough stuff when that happened but gave as good as she got, and he had found that a turn-on at first. Now it was more of a challenge. He'd liked being able to make that stupid Gwynneth cry, and other girls he'd been with, but he had never seen Brenda shed a tear.

He took off his overalls and had a quick shower. Brenda hated the smell of engine oil, which she said clung to him if he came home without showering, so he had had the fitment installed. It was useful, making it easy, when he was taking cars to prospective buyers, to freshen up first. Dressed in a dark suit, with an expensive shirt and a silk tie, he made a favourable impression on those he was meeting for the first time. The cars he sold were in good condition. Sometimes he cannibalised two to make one vehicle out of the best parts of both, and he enjoyed working on really old cars, almost veterans; there was satisfaction in making an engine run sweetly and cogs mesh smoothly toge-ther. The trouble was that it took time, while the bills piled up; his desk was full of them, and his rent was owing.

Brenda had been surprised to discover how tidy he was and wondered where he had learned his neat ways. His memory took him back to when he was five or six, and for some reason Norah Tyler was staying at Selbury House. She came for occasional weekends and would sometimes stay with the children while George and Susan went out. In those days they frequently went to lunch parties or to play tennis, and in winter George would go shooting; Susan used to accompany the guns, enjoying the day in the open air.

They had treated Norah as an unpaid mother's help, he thought, looking back, and wondered why she let them make use of her like that. Probably she enjoyed being able to say that she was off to visit her smart friends in the country and liked showing off photographs of the large house. He and Louise behaved well in her care; she had a knack of promoting harmony between them and could interest them in various ways which both enjoyed. She played games with them and, when they were old enough, took them on bicycle rides round the lanes; there was much less traffic then than now. But she had been extremely tidy and had made them fold their clothes and put their toys away after use. He remembered her making him clean up the sandpit. It was full of old patty-tins, buried wooden spades and discarded cars. She had provided him with a large-meshed garden sieve obtained from Ford, the gardener, to go through the pile of sand, rescuing buried treasure. Louise had not had to help.

Malcolm forgot that she was only three or four at the time, and that he had, when Norah was not in sight, thrown sand at his sister and been given the task as a punishment. Later, at school, being tidy had been a way of safeguarding his possessions: knowing just where he had put them meant that he was on sure ground if another boy borrowed something and deserved a bloody nose. Perhaps he owed some of this to Norah, but later, in prison in Sydney, he had had to be tidy, though no one over here knew about that.

'Aren't you curious about your real parents?'

Brenda had asked Malcolm that after she had been taken to Selbury Lodge for lunch one Sunday. Until then, she had not known that he was adopted, but afterwards she had commented that he was not very like either of his parents.

Malcolm had found that telling people he was adopted worked to his advantage with women. They were filled with pity at the notion of his being abandoned as an infant; one of his girl friends had devised a script with his desperate mother seeking a safe place for her infant and dumping it on a hospital doorstep, with a note attached to its hand-knitted shawl praying that the child might prove to be the answer to an unhappy couple's prayers. Malcolm could not believe that the scenario attached to his birth was like that; he remembered Susan's tale of their selection of him, implying that it was made from among a wide choice of babies. He decided, however, not to reveal this conviction.

'They could be anyone, you know,' Brenda said. 'You can find out, Malcolm.'

'What difference does it make?' Malcolm said. 'They didn't want me. Susan did. That's all that counts. She'd had this other kid that died, from her first husband. I suppose she thought I'd look like him. Maybe I do look like her first husband. Hugh, his name was.' He had never thought of this before.

Brenda liked the idea of romance attached to his origins, and the mystery explained things that didn't quite fit together. His manners in public were every-

77

thing you would expect from someone with his background, but he could lose his temper and his control in seconds, and he was happiest among people who did little talking but engaged in some shared activity like drinking, playing darts or gambling. A lot of people, she thought, and especially men, were like that, while most women enjoyed a good natter.

'I know a girl who traced her real mother,' she told him. 'She – the mother – had married and got other children. My friend didn't just barge in. She rang up and made a date to meet at a café. This old lady came in. Well, she seemed old. But she was nice – said she'd always wondered about my friend and thought of her on her birthday. She'd told her husband about it and it was all right and now my friend has a whole new family. Your real mother probably thinks of you on your birthday.'

'Well, she'll have to get on with it, then, won't she?' said Malcolm. 'She can find me, if she wants.'

'She can't. It's the other way round – the children trace the parents. They gave up all their rights at the time of the adoption.'

'Oh.'

'It could be hard for the adoptive parents, having the real ones muscling in when they've done all the work of rearing the kid,' Brenda said. 'What about Norah? Do you fancy her as your mother?'

'Norah? Don't make me laugh,' said Malcolm, not looking the least bit amused. 'She's never had any kids.'

'How can you be sure about that? She's not married, it's true, and single parents were bad news in her day. Wouldn't it be quite likely she'd give her baby to friends to adopt, if she had one? You could do that sort of thing then. Nowadays there are all sorts of rules.'

'It's a theory, but it didn't happen like that,' said Malcolm. The idea was repellent. He remembered Norah's stern words to him when, as a child, he had transgressed, and she was less than warm to him when they met now.

'What do you know about her? How did she get in with your parents?'

'Oh, she's always been around,' said Malcolm. 'She came to the village during the war to get away from the bombs. She was only a kid then – an evacuee. Her parents were killed in a bombing raid and she more or less stayed on. Later she went into the army and after that she had a job in London.'

'So why did she give it up?'

'It gave her up,' said Malcolm. 'Booted her out. So she came running back to the Vaughans expecting to be rescued.'

'Well, maybe they rescued her before,' said Brenda, though she had formed the opinion that any rescuing at the Lodge was being done by, and not to Norah.

'They certainly taught her to drop her Cockney accent and all that sort of thing,' said Malcolm. 'She's on to a good racket now, living free and all that.' And occupying the room that should rightfully be his.

'If you want to stay in Selbury, you can buy a place of your own,' George had said when the big house was sold.

'Where do I get the money?' Malcolm had asked, and George had replied that he hoped Malcolm would not apply to Susan.

Not normally perceptive, Malcolm had noticed that latterly George had stopped referring to Susan as 'your mother' when mentioning her to him.

They had sounded surprised when he had telephoned to say he would be bringing Brenda over, and they had said that he could not do so on the first date he suggested because they were going out themselves. He had been quite annoyed by this rebuff. However, they had been friendly to Brenda when the occasion finally arrived. Norah, who had sat at the table with them

79

unlike a real housekeeper who would, in Malcolm's opinion, have known her place, had shown interest in the employment agency, asking about temporary positions and wages, so much so that George had said, 'Are you going to look for a job, Norah?'

She had laughed and said, 'You never know.'

She had cooked the lunch, of course: roast lamb with peas and new potatoes and treacle pudding, his favourite, with fruit salad for those who preferred something less substantial. Brenda had been amused to learn that Malcolm liked steamed puddings. They were never available at any of the restaurants where the couple ate; on the rare occasions when they ate at home it was usually convenience food from Marks and Spencer, cooked in the microwave.

Since this conversation Malcolm had begun to wonder about his real mother, but not enough to want to trace her. After all, she'd given him away, hadn't she? Could she really have been Norah?

Brenda had enjoyed her day at Selbury and felt she understood Malcolm better now. It wasn't easy, past forty as she was, to find an unattached man, and she did not like living without one. Malcolm was presentable and she was not dependent on him in any way, which kept him guessing and meant she could turn him out of her house if she tired of him. So far, whenever he had lost his temper, she had been able to bring him to heel.

She would get rid of him when she found someone interesting enough or attractive enough to take his place. Meanwhile, it would be amusing if he could be persuaded to trace his real parents. In his place, she couldn't have borne not to know.

Malcolm hated being alone, unless he was working on a car when he became absorbed in what he was doing.

80

Even then, except when he was tuning an engine and needed to listen to what it was doing, he liked a background of pop music.

When he went home after Marsh's visit to the workshop, Brenda was out. He was annoyed. She had said nothing this morning about being late. If he'd known, he'd have gone somewhere himself instead of coming straight back. Malcolm never admitted a need for reassurance, for to do so was to be weak, and he was strong. He did not understand that his talk with Marsh had unsettled him, just that the silence in the empty house was oppressive. He turned on the radio while he looked in the fridge for something to eat. The freezer section held various processed meals but he had an urge for a steak, a large one, red and juicy. He would go out and get one.

He had already showered and had run a razor over his face; Brenda didn't like even a hint of stubble, which she said scratched her skin and gave her a rash. Now he took time to change his shirt, slick down his dark curls and select a new silk tie before he went out to look for company, drink and food, in that order.

At The Bull he found some acquaintances in the bar. If asked, he would have described them as his friends, but he knew very little about any of them though they often met in various bars, especially this one. Some were, like him, displaced persons with difficult or broken marriages; others were sales representatives working away from home. The few who had merely looked in for a drink on the way home or to complete some business discussion soon left. Malcolm, his craving for steak alleviated by alcohol, continued with the rest to drink and tell tall tales to impress one another. Malcolm did his share, enlarging on his experiences in Australia where he made out that he had been very successful and ignoring any questioner who wondered aloud why, in that case, he had returned to England.

He had some good stories about sheep that went down well with an uncritical audience. Four of the group at last moved on from the bar into the restaurant and Malcolm went with them. They were all noisy and spuriously cheery. One man tried chatting up the waitress and another told her not to believe a word he said. She took no notice of either; she was used to all sorts and there was help at hand if things went too far. They all had prawn cocktails and large sirloin steaks, and four bottles of burgundy between the five of them, followed by brandy.

Three of the men proclaimed their need to relieve themselves and went out to the washroom from which they failed to return. When the bill came, the fourth man followed and Malcolm was left to pay.

He decided to treat it as a joke. He'd get even another time, do the same thing when he got the chance. In a way it was his own fault; he liked to make expansive gestures and imply that money flowed from his fingertips, often buying rounds of drinks outside his turn and saying just leave it to him about meals. It made him feel good. But at the moment he owed money all round and could get no more credit. Two cars he had recently sold had not yet been fully paid for and he had bought the Vitesse to keep stock turning over. In an attempt to clear some of his debts, he had staked three hundred pounds on a bet on an outside chance two days before and it had not come off. He was in debt to the tune of over forty thousand pounds, and now he was adding two hundred more to the total as he wrote a cheque against non-existent funds.

The best thing would be to go bankrupt. Then he could write everything off. Too bad about those to whom he owed money. He could start again, float a new business in someone else's name – Brenda's, for instance. He took a bottle of whisky home with him.

Brenda had not returned, so he opened it and turned

on the television. A film was showing. Cars screeched round corners, and palm trees bordered a brilliant blue sea in the distance. Malcolm sprawled in an armchair gazing at the screen, not taking in what he saw. He needed it to deaden the silence and give him the illusion of company.

Suppose he found his real mother? Would she help him now? Would things suddenly go right for him if they met? Not if Brenda was right and it was Norah. He thrust the distasteful idea away. Anyway, none of this was his fault; it was all down to the failure that Susan and George had made of his education and training. Why hadn't he been sent to an engineering college, for instance?

He remembered the day he went to his preparatory school, in his grey shorts and maroon blazer and cap, delivered by Susan at a large building bigger even than Selbury House and where every boy was a stranger. She had gone off without saying goodbye while he was being shown the train room where there was a huge electric lay-out. It was an hour before he discovered that she had abandoned him.

He decided not to cry. Two other new boys had lapsed into tears and had been regarded with scorn by others. Instead, he fostered an inner truculence and the following day had a fight with the boy meant to be his 'shepherd', which meant teaching him the rules and how to find his way about. There had been no provocation; Malcolm just turned on the other boy and punched him, taking him completely by surprise and giving him a bloody nose.

A different shepherd was appointed after this incident, a bigger one. The headmaster had not known what to make of the episode since the original shepherd had shielded his charge from blame, alleging that he had bumped his nose on a door, but there had been an independent witness, an under-matron walking across the playing-field some distance away, too far to see more than that Malcolm had struck the first blow. Provocative words might have been uttered first, though it seemed unlikely since the shepherd was of a placid disposition.

Malcolm soon established a reputation among the boys as one not to be crossed because he struck at once, and he was bigger and stronger than most of his contemporaries.

He had lost none of his aggression, and his impulse, still, was to strike out at anyone who used words or anything else to attack or taunt him.

Norah had always been somewhere about in the background, perhaps not seen for months but turning up after Christmas or at Easter and often staying as much as a week in the summer.

'She's like a poor relation,' he had once heard old Mrs Warrington, his grandmother, say when she and her friend Lady Spencer were watching Louise and a friend play tennis. Malcolm, lying in the long grass beyond the shrubs bordering the tennis court, had been smoking, the light wind taking the fumes away from the two old ladies. Then Lady Spencer lit up, saying that the smoke would keep the midges off. This was to counter Mrs Warrington's disapproval, for Lady Spencer had a persistent cough and frequent attacks of bronchitis but would not give up what she called her one vice. 'She's always with us but in her case useful,' Mrs Warrington had added, referring to Norah.

'Where would she be without you all?' murmured Lady Spencer.

'She's certainly done well. She's got a very good job,' said his grandmother.

'Yes. Considering that unfortunate business, it's all worked out for the best,' agreed Lady Spencer.

'I sometimes wonder if we did the right thing,' Malcolm had heard his grandmother remark.

What about, Malcolm had wondered, eyeing the girls in their short pleated skirts and little white pants. Louise's legs were thin; the other girl was plumper, with a round behind revealed when she spun about.

'Well, she couldn't keep it,' Lady Spencer said. 'A girl of her age with an illegitimate baby and no means of support.'

'She never married,' his grandmother said.

'No, but nowadays marriage isn't everything. A girl can be independent and have a career and she has done that. It wasn't the same in our day.'

Years later, sitting alone by the television set in Brenda's small house, Malcolm suddenly remembered that afternoon and what he had overheard. At the time he had been more interested in peeping than listening. He would have been about fifteen years old.

'Adoption was the right answer,' his grandmother said, and then Lady Spencer began coughing, obscuring any subsequent comment. When her attack was over they started to talk about something else.

Why hadn't he thought more about what they were saying? Why hadn't the meaning of it sunk in? Well, he was remembering it now, all right, and the blood began to pound in his head as he saw what it could imply: just what Brenda had idly suggested. Without her words he might have never cottoned on to the truth.

For it must be that: it made sense of so many things.

What was he going to do about it, now that he knew?

3

Susan

She would lie in her small bed, which had half sides to prevent her rolling out on to the floor in her sleep, and watch the shadows cast by the dying fire. There would be fearsome shapes on the cornice and ceiling, the pointed hats of witches and the gnarled noses of gnomes, but the glowing caverns among the coals were more friendly, with warm grottoes full of gold or hidden treasure or peopled by happy pixies. Every morning Mabel, the under-housemaid, lit the fire before Susan got up, coming in with bucket and brushes to sweep out the dead ash from the night before and kindle new flames which soon crackled up the chimney. Susan would sit up in bed with the thick eiderdown pulled close against the cold, watching her, and they would chat. Mabel told tales of a fox with an earth in Selbury Copse and how he had crept out at night to kill Mrs Betts' chickens, leaving only feathers and bits of bone behind him. Or she would recount the latest adventures of her own brother who had run away to sea and sent postcards from places like Buenos Aires and Panama, making his life sound unbelievably romantic. These interludes would be ended by Nanny, who would come into the room briskly clapping her hands and saying, 'Now come along, Mabel, you haven't all day to waste chattering. Joyce is looking for you downstairs.' Joyce was the head housemaid under whose instructions Mabel carried out the more menial household tasks such as doing the grates, polishing brasses and cleaning shoes. She would carry the brass cans of hot water up to the bedrooms, and Joyce herself would take one into mother in the big bedroom overlooking the gardens. Father's dressing-room was next door and he had his own brass can. Mabel brought the nursery hot water, and later, breakfast to the day nursery.

Looking back, Susan would marvel, half ashamed, at all the chores undertaken by Mabel, and her myriad laden journeys up and down stairs, but the large house could not have been run without the help of its staff. That was before central heating was installed and when there were only two bathrooms, one upstairs for the family, and another with a bath covered with a board when not in use in a small room opening off the scullery for the use of the servants. Later, that had become a laundry room equipped with washing-machine and iron; now it was part of Myra Slavoksy's flat. In those days before the war, when Susan was a child, Selbury House had been full of activity and housed at least ten people. She and her brothers, and their parents, were dependent on others to keep things running smoothly and themselves fed and warm. Her mother never even made up the drawing-room fire herself; Mabel would enter at intervals during the day to add coal. The washing had all been done by hand with a scrubbing board and large blocks of yellow soap, then put through a mangle to wring out the excess water. She had enjoyed watching this being done; the rollers would flatten the linen, part-ironing it in the process. She couldn't remember when Joyce got her first Hoover but she had not forgotten the machine itself, made of dull chrome with a black bag. Presumably before its arrival Joyce had used brush and dustpan to clean the carpets, or more likely it was Mabel who went down on hands and knees. Susan had an impression that used tea-leaves were scattered first to bring up the dust. All this work was done before the family came down for breakfast, an array of kedgeree, scrambled egg and bacon, arranged on hot plates kept warm by heaters running on methylated spirits, and served in silver dishes. Nowadays it was generally thought that Joyce and Mabel and their fellows had been grossly exploited, and in some households that was certainly true; their pay was low and the hours long. But in other families they were happy, well fed, and surrounded by friends. Good employers felt responsible for their staff, looked after them, saw that they were cared for if they were ill and finally gave them pensions. Paternalism was considered a dirty word today, but it had not been entirely a bad thing; it involved thinking of other people as a duty.

How they worked, though. If mother and father went out to dinner, Joyce or the parlourmaid waited up for their return, no matter how late that might be. Mabel's lot was improved when a bootboy was taken on; he fetched coals for the fires and did other odd jobs besides cleaning the shoes. Susan and her brothers saw very little of their father, who went up to town every day on the train from Feringham, returning in the evening just before Nanny came to take them up to bed after their time with Mother in the drawing-room. Later, Malcolm stayed downstairs for an extra half hour, and in the final term before he went off to prep school he had dinner in the dining room twice a week.

Malcolm was the eldest. Then came Susan, and finally David. She remembered being pushed out in the big pram with him. David, in woollen jacket and bonnet, sat up beneath the hood, and if her legs grew tired after walking, she would be lifted into the pram to sit facing him, with her feet in a well in the centre. If you stamped, it gave out a hollow sound. Life was cosy and safe. Nanny would take them to look for primroses and to see young lambs at the farm where Joe Simpson, with his dog, would come and talk and would show them new calves and piglets. Nanny always lingered when Joe was around. He was a widower whose wife had died when their third child was born; later he married Nanny and they had two more children. Visiting them was, after that, a rare but wonderful treat; Susan loved sitting in the large kitchen drinking milk fresh from the cow and eating scones or biscuits Nanny had baked.

Mother had been seriously displeased when Nanny departed.

'What does she want to get married for now?' she had grumbled. 'She's too old. She was settled here.'

'She's only thirty-one,' Father had said from behind his paper.

Susan, playing with her Noah's ark on the floor, went on pairing the model animals ready to parade them to safety. She liked the zebras best, with their smart stripes. All the animals were made of real skin, soft to the touch, the hairs silky.

'Well, she should have more sense,' said Mother.

'Don't you recommend matrimony, my dear?' Father asked.

'For some, yes, and younger women,' said Mother. 'But she'll regret it. She'll have to work very hard.'

'And I suppose she didn't do that here?' Father was smiling, teasing Mother. 'You're just cross at losing an excellent nanny.'

'I'll never find another as good,' Mother had lamented, and it was true. David was still only four, and he and the new nanny got on well enough, but Susan did not care for her ways, which involved having bows in her hair which were pulled so tight that they hurt, and curling-rags at night. She couldn't sleep, tied up like Ameliaranne Stiggins. Luckily Father made some observation about her surprising new curls and the rags were abandoned.

Curling-irons came next. Bidden to a party, she would be put into her white organdie dress with the pink satin sash, white socks, and her bronze pumps held on by elastic crossed over her insteps, and Nanny would crimp her hair with tongs. There would be a singeing smell as the ends were twisted into ringlets.

Malcolm used to laugh at this process but he was sympathetic.

'I should cut it off,' he advised one day. 'If it was short she couldn't do it to you.' He had a running feud with Nanny, who administered Californian Syrup of Figs once a week. Malcolm, back from prep school for the holidays, found the stuff nauseating and refused to submit, skilfully sicking it up all over Nanny's clean uniform dress, after which she contented herself with painfully scrubbing behind his ears and putting him on the rule of silence at meals whenever she had the least excuse.

He had enthusiastically helped Susan cut off her hair, finding a pair of sharp scissors and holding the strands so that she could do the actual hacking herself. Susan snipped a fringe across her forehead, like the pages in fairy tale illustrations, and Malcolm neatened its jagged edge so that it ended up very short, well above her eyebrows.

That night they were both sent to bed with no supper and Nanny beat Malcolm with the back of a hairbrush on his bare buttocks, finding the strength to hold down his wriggling, protesting form. She was just about to beat Susan too when Father walked into the nursery. He so rarely did this that it came as a total shock to all the occupants, including David, who was standing with his thumb in his mouth wondering if he would be next.

Nanny was sent out of the room and they never saw her again. Mabel, deputed to get them up the next day, reported that she had been despatched with her trunk and her bags.

'Sent off, bag and baggage,' she told them with glee.

90

'Gave herself airs, she did. Been in a lord's family, or so she said, and thought trade a come-down. Well, she'll not get into any other lord's place after this.'

Susan thought Mabel meant something to do with Our Lord in Heaven and was mystified.

'Never mind, dears. Forget the silly old thing,' Mabel advised. 'I'm going to be looking after you until they find someone else.'

Halcyon days now began, for Mabel, who by this time was nineteen, proved so good at her job that she slid into being their permanent nanny and a new under-housemaid was taken on in her place. Mabel worked harder than Nanny had done, still carrying their meals upstairs and doing the nursery fires as well as the washing, ironing and mending, but she found time to play with them and tell them stories, and it was she who took them to visit their old nanny, now Mrs Simpson, at the farm. She left in the end to marry the Spencers' chauffeur and after that there were no more nannies. A nursery governess arrived and some other children joined them for lessons until David went off to school. After that Susan and the Spencer girls shared a different governess who came daily to the Spencers' house; the boot boy, Alfred Ford, now a man, had been taught to drive and he took her over in the Austin. Later still, after central heating and a new plumbing system had been installed, with two more bathrooms upstairs and basins in the bedrooms, he became the under-gardener until finally, when the war began, he was the head gardener with a boy under him who cleaned the shoes and washed the cars.

Susan herself went off to boarding-school in the end, with the Spencer girls. There were only a hundred pupils, who lived in a large house on the South Downs overlooking the Channel. The air was bracing, the food plain but nourishing, and the tuition moderate, with an emphasis on equipping the girls for life as the wives of successful men. Few girls achieved academic distinction, but most were happy enough at the school.

As they grew older, Susan and her brothers had ridden their bicycles for miles round the country lanes near Selbury. They were allowed a lot of freedom. The boys would cycle to Feringham to buy parts for their bikes, or sweets, and to go to the cinema. She rode her pony over the fields alone. Neither of the boys had liked riding and Father was no horseman.

'I wasn't born to it,' he would say, with a smile, but he offered his children the opportunity to try a variety of sporting activities.

Susan and Dapple used to canter along the headlands of ploughed fields, jump the stooks of corn after the harvest, wander down woodland paths. She loved the golden late summer days with the stubble pale against the brown earth when ploughing began. In spring the woods would be full of primroses and bluebells, with the fluff of catkin and pussy willow softening the brown of the hedgerows. Sometimes Susan would meet the Spencer girls, all of them with sandwiches in their pockets, and they would have a picnic lunch before riding home. The worst calamity that ever befell them was when Helen Spencer's pony stumbled one day, tipping Helen over his ears so that she hit her head on the ground and sustained mild concussion, sitting up and talking nonsense afterwards. Pamela Spencer had stayed with her sister, and their two ponies, reins looped over a handy tree, had stood docilely by while Susan rode dramatically off to the nearest house to telephone for help. Not a serious mishap, and an innocent adventure: nowadays few householders would welcome someone wanting to telephone in an emergency, fearing confidence tricksters seeking to steal from them. You still saw children out riding alone, but all in hard hats essential with so much traffic about; that had not been a hazard before the war.

Louise had had a pony too, and had enjoyed riding until she was about fifteen, when she had gradually lost interest; but Malcolm, like his uncles, had never been keen.

When her thoughts turned to Malcolm, Susan always felt as if a great weight sat on her chest. He had been such a lovely little boy, lively and physically strong, and not really naughty, she still excused, until he began pulling Louise's hair and hiding her toys to tease her and make her cry. Even that was just what boys did; Susan's brothers had teased her too, but never with malice. Louise had always been better with words than Malcolm, and Susan suspected that as she grew older she had verbally provoked his attacks.

Now only Malcolm was left. Her brothers, and Hugh and her first little baby had all gone, then Louise. Susan felt that her earlier bereavements had made it easier for her to accept Louise's death, though not its manner, than it had been for George. What she found hard was to be in the house where she kept expecting to see Louise, just as for years she had expected one or other of her brothers to come walking in or to be sitting in the drawing-room, or striding about in the garden. This was what people meant when they said they saw ghosts, she decided, and she could cope with it out of doors, so gardening became her solace. This helped life with George, too; they did not have to spend long hours together if she kept active with other things. A gulf had opened between them as they found they could not discuss what might have happened to Louise, for her fate was too terrible to imagine. George could not bring himself to talk about it, while Susan, at first, wanted to pour out her theories and fears.

Norah had been wonderful then. She had known just what to say and when to let her weep. Susan believed that without her support, she would have gone out of her mind. Norah had been there at all the other bad times, too, though she was still at school when Hugh was killed. Her being made redundant had, in the end, worked out well for them all. True, she had had ideas about setting up in some way on her own, but Mother's accident had put paid to that.

'Of course Norah will look after me,' Mother had said. 'Look at what we've done for her. She'll be glad to, and it will be doing her a kindness. Where else would she go, after all? Whom has she to turn to but us?'

Mother had still equated putting a roof over someone's head in return for long hours of work with doing them a favour. She herself had been careful never to learn to cook, though she could heat up the dishes Mrs Gibson left ready for supper and had been known to make tea and to open packets of biscuits. She had always been able to find someone to look after her.

Susan, grown old herself, with fine wrinkles lining her thin skin and with her faded, almost white hair once again cropped short though now in a neat cap close to her skull, could remember Norah arriving to live with the Fords, and the two little boys who had been sent to Selbury House. The boys, six and four years old, brothers, had not wanted to be parted and her mother had handed them over to Joyce to be housed in an attic and cared for by the maids. Norah had taken a sisterly interest in them and often came up to the house to play with them and see that they were behaving themselves, as she put it. The three children had all found country life very strange, and the boys had been awed by the size of the house they were living in. Norah, though, had been fascinated by it, by the life and the people within.

'It's so quiet,' one of the boys had said, missing the daily sound of traffic, the big red buses passing by, but he had liked seeing cows in the fields and had been amazed to learn that milk had a source other than bottles. Norah, older and more experienced, had been to the country before, on day trips with her parents and sister. Her mother had come down to see her whenever she could afford the fare, and had been ambitious for her daughters. Susan's mother, losing Joyce and the under-housemaid to war work, never, as it turned out, to be replaced, and left with only Mrs Johnson the cook, had offered Norah's sister a place in the house, but she had already found a job as an office girl in the City.

Then she was killed, and her parents, too.

Norah, hitherto a bright, funny girl who made shrewd, forthright remarks, became silent and withdrawn. Mrs Ford kept her busy after school, work being the best remedy for grief. She had begun to read a great deal, borrowing books from the public library in Feringham, and she had worked hard at school. In the few short weeks of his life, she had helped Susan with baby Harry and had several times wheeled him out in his pram. Then, all at once, that had ended.

Susan had been working for some months as a VAD nurse at Feringham Hospital, where there were now whole wards full of wounded servicemen as well as civilian patients, by the time Norah left school and started at the factory. Sometimes, depending on their shifts, they travelled in together. Norah, just sixteen, was a pleasant concerned companion for Susan who still felt stunned by her double loss. Norah was bereft too; her whole family had been killed, though at the time Susan forgot that. She remembered it now, looking back.

From time to time Susan's brothers came home on snatched leaves. Often they would bring a girl friend down or go off to a party somewhere; both had sports cars and carefully hoarded petrol coupons. It was odd to reflect that both Father and Mother were relatively young then. Father, only fifty-two, was asked to advise a government department on fuel economy in factories and said he had become an honorary civil servant. He often stayed overnight in town and firewatched for incendiary bombs, sometimes extinguishing them with a stirrup-pump. Mother presided over the village First Aid Post, for which a room in the house was set aside, and she helped with the WVS, directing the rehousing of bombed-out people, and she gave first aid lectures to groups of women. Everyone was busy.

Bombs fell on Selbury.

Susan was in the garden one day, before Harry was born. She was mourning his father, unable to believe that her handsome young husband would never return, but she was sustained by the young life within her, nature asserting its claims. There was a droning sound overhead at a little distance and, hearing faint bangs, she looked up to see several planes flying quite low. The small white cotton-wool puffs of anti-aircraft fire around them told her that they were enemy bombers, but she felt entirely calm, watching them with interest, not fear. Months later a stick of three bombs unloaded at random by a Heinkel or Junkers unable to reach its target fell in the village. One landed on a cowshed, which was empty, one in the road at the top of the hill entering the village, and the third in a field. All left craters in the ground to be marvelled at until filled in. The village had been very lucky to escape without real damage or death.

People tended to think that quiet places like Selbury had escaped the worst of the war, and in many ways so they had, not exposed to direct intensive bombing and with gardens in which to grow vegetables and keep chickens to bolster the rations; but the war memorial in the square bore a long list of names of the dead, including Susan's two brothers and Hugh, who by marrying her became an honorary resident.

Susan had lived in Selbury nearly all her life, apart from the time spent away at school and the year in Switzerland where she had skied, learned some French, a little cooking and dressmaking, and had passed the time pleasantly until she was old enough to be launched into society with a view to getting married as soon as possible.

It was all we thought of then, she remembered, and to be single at twenty-two was to be on the shelf. She and the other girls would discuss their ideal men, how many children they would have, where they would live, and so on. Some were to be presented at court, with three feathers attached to their heads and long satin dresses with trains. Susan had had no wish to be among them although Lady Spencer, it seemed, had offered to present her with Helen, Pamela having made her curtsey the previous year. Mother had not been presented herself and privately agreed with Father that it was all a lot of humbug. Susan had had a dance, however: a fine affair at the house, with a band, and even Father, writing the cheque, had said that it hadn't been a bad evening at all.

We were indeed born with silver spoons in our mouths, Susan thought, and she had continued to live a quietly comfortable life with kind George, adapting to the changing conditions without any great hardship, becoming a good cook herself as help grew more difficult to find but never left coping alone. She had enjoyed entertaining for Malcolm and Louise when they were children, giving parties with conjurors or film shows, and later there had been modest dances, the big house once again fully used. Did people still have dances or was it all discos now?

If only Malcolm would marry again, have children and settle down. This girl – well, woman – he was living with seemed nice enough, pretty and bright and efficient, and obviously older than Malcolm. She had arrived to lunch dressed smartly in a black skirt and long scarlet jacket, with an emerald silk blouse, and she wore very high-heeled shoes which Susan had been brought up to think was not done in the country; it had made showing her round the garden a hazard. Some of Selbury's new residents could be seen teetering along in spike heels under slacks, propelling their children in plastic cocoons inside pushchairs, often with enormous dogs in tow. Times had certainly changed. Brenda must have found the Lodge House ordinary enough; doubtless her parents lived in something similar. She would have been impressed by Selbury House, however, Susan was sure. It had taken her some time to get used to less space.

In the big house, there was plenty of room to get away from people if you had quarrelled or felt unsociable. How dreadful it must be to live in a tiny house with two or three children always on top of you, thought Susan, stretching out in her single bed at the Lodge. It was a relief to be alone at night. Some people never slept alone in their lives, sharing with siblings as children, then marrying, and perhaps only on their own when widowed. George had had his dressing-room at Selbury House and had slept in it more and more often after Louise disappeared.

They lived a very quiet life now. Newcomers to the village gave drinks parties and invited each other to dinner, and there were a number of widows who entertained one another to luncheon, but the Vaughans kept apart from this although, had Susan wished to take part in the cutlet-for-cutlet routine, the food would have been Norah's responsibility. But she would have thought it a waste of time and money, except on special occasions, and might have rebelled. She seemed content enough, going once a week in the winter to learn French

98

at adult education classes in Feringham and playing her language tapes on the headset that had been Mrs Warrington's, and spending time at Selbury House with Myra Slavosky and some of the other residents. Myra had escaped from Estonia ahead of the Russian advance, had married twice and made money from buying old houses, renovating them and then moving on, finally opening a dress shop in Feringham where occasionally, when other staff failed, Norah helped out on odd days. Susan was not sure if the husbands had died or were merely discarded. She found Myra rather noisy and foreign; she spoke fluent English with an accent which George thought attractive. Norah had met her when out walking Bertie and had managed to track down someone to clean the flat which Myra, as a working woman, said she had no time to do. Myra occasionally came in for a drink in the evening, more as Norah's guest than theirs; George enjoyed hearing her tales of her youth on a vast estate with two lakes and a small forest.

Susan had feared, when her mother died, that Norah would leave. She was only fifty-eight then, fit and slim, though she was plumper now. She had been quite a plump schoolgirl, with shining eyes and a lot of vitality. Susan could remember her running across the big garden, laughing for the sheer joy of being alive. They had been stupid not to see how attractive she was as she grew older, and of course she was always about, part of the scenery. No wonder David had lost his foolish young head over her and of course she responded.

At the time, Mother, in her anguish because David had already been reported missing, believed killed, had angrily alleged that Norah had deceitfully trapped him, but Susan and Father had known that this was not true. Poor Norah had been devastated and had quickly begun to look very ill. She had truly loved David, with all the devotion of a very young girl in her first romance, and had thought that he loved her. To do him justice, he probably said that he did and may have believed what he said, though how could such an unsuitable attachment have lasted? It would have been difficult for any susceptible girl to resist him once he turned his blandishments in her direction. He had been so handsome and full of laughter, blue-eyed and fair-haired, with a cleft in his chin, a Flight Lieutenant in Bomber Command.

It was Susan who had taken care of Norah when it was all over, advising her and finally helping her to join the ATS and get right away to make a new life. It was Susan, too, who had kept in touch and who, after quite a few years had passed, had suggested a visit. By then she had made her mother concede that David had been as much to blame as Norah.

Father, even while shocked by his new bereavement, had been angry because David had been so careless.

'Getting her in pod – wholly irresponsible,' he had said, with touching faith in the contraceptive arrangements then available.

Susan had wondered if perhaps Father had someone in London during those war years when he so often spent the night in town, or wasn't there time amid all the bombs? She, a chaste widow living at home, could presumably have lived differently if she had wanted to do so, with opportunities at the hospital if she had sought them, but she had never felt such an urge. Sex had not been important to her, even in the first happy weeks of her marriage to Hugh when they made love in the thatched cottage near Warminster where Harry was conceived. If Hugh had not died, how would they have got on, living together for over forty years? She sometimes wondered if he would have been as kind and as gentle as George had turned out to be. A woman, even one with money, needed a partner, for life was geared to people in pairs.

Louise would have accepted the conventions and married some nice man, a barrister or a merchant banker, perhaps, if no suitor with land and a fortune came along. She would have seen the advantages of family life over a career spent doing the bidding of some testy employer in the name of independence. She would have had money of her own when Susan herself died, even after the depletions on her capital made by inflation and Malcolm's demands. Indeed, if she had lived and had children, Susan might not have felt obliged to help him so much in recent years. As her will stood at present, he would inherit whatever was left, though the house and the income from the remaining capital would be George's during his lifetime, if he survived her.

She should look at her will again.

She was going to London soon; perhaps she should see her solicitor then.

4

George

Not a day went past without George thinking of Louise. He treasured photographs of her at every stage in her life from an infant a few days old to one taken in the garden at Selbury House the summer before she disappeared. The sun had been in her eyes and she had her hand up, shading them, laughing at him. Every year on her birthday he remembered how old she would have been and wondered how her life would have developed, had she been spared to enjoy it. It was hard to imagine her at thirty-six, which by this time would have been her age. Probably she would be married with two or three children. He knew she had had some sort of unhappy romantic experience while she was living in London but she had, he believed, recovered from that and eventually would have met someone who would have been able to make her happy. With luck they might be living not too far away and would often come over at weekends. Susan would have enjoyed a grandmother's role; in his opinion she had been a perfect mother, endlessly patient and good at playing imaginative games, though Malcolm hadn't been able to make much of them apart from being a fearsome pirate with a bandana round his head and a patch over one eye. Malcolm had liked the tree house, built in an oak-tree and reached by a rope ladder, but if Louise was up there he would twist the ladder round the tree so that she could not come down and go off, marooning her, or he would not let her climb up if he was aloft. Once he had made her walk the plank. He had taken a board up and balanced it across the platform forming the house, wedging it under a strut. Then he had forced Louise, trembling with fright and crying, to walk along it towards the end which extended over the long grass below. The height was not great, perhaps ten feet, but even so, if she had fallen she could have been badly hurt.

Ford had heard her screams, hurried up the rope ladder, plucked her to safety and given Malcolm a clip round the ear which had made his head ring. The boy had protested that he was only testing her and of course he would have allowed her to walk back to safety.

'It was like in *Peter Pan*,' he said. The children had been taken to see the play at Christmas. 'She's a silly coward to cry.'

Ford, reporting the incident to George, confessed to hitting Malcolm. George said they would keep that fact to themselves since, with such a witness, Malcolm was unlikely to complain to Susan.

After that, Louise never went up to the tree house again and Malcolm, sole possessor of the territory, was very pleased with himself. He kept a store of fruit there, and if she passed within range he would bombard her, calling her an enemy alien. She soon learned to keep away and Malcolm discovered the power that grew from creating fear.

When he went away to school, Louise's life became easier, but it was clear that the boy resented her being at home when he was absent. He was very jealous when Susan gave her attention to anyone else. Trying to find excuses for him, George recognised that he felt he was a second-best, a substitute son. Other adopting families might have met the same problem, George supposed, but he knew that very often the arrangement worked most happily. Perhaps it was simply in Malcolm's nature to seek causes for resentment. George might as well have been jealous of Susan's first husband, but he wasn't; he had liked Hugh, a cheerful man with an extrovert personality who had died bravely fighting a rearguard action and had been awarded a posthumous Military Cross for his courage. George had visited the cottage near Warminster where Hugh and Susan had spent their short married life and had thought, even then, that they were playing at keeping house; it was all a sort of tender game, snatched at before disaster overtook them. Like Norah, he saw them as a fairy-tale couple, a handsome prince and a beautiful princess who had not anticipated a dark side to life. Susan should not have had to face so much tragedy; she needed love and protection and that was really all he had to offer her when she agreed to marry him. He was fourteen months younger than she was and had left school only a year before the war began. He had spent the interval teaching in a school near his home in Somerset and was planning to take it up as a career. After he was demobilised, he was offered a job by his new father-in-law and he flung himself conscientiously into learning the business from the bottom up. In time, as a director, he earned a good salary, but he had no capital of his own. With hindsight, he could see that Susan, after her comfortable upbringing, might not have appreciated life on a schoolmaster's salary, but he had not thought about that at the time, nor of the problems that could come from a wife having a higher income, whatever its source, than her husband.

After the war housing was scarce, and while George was still in the Army, stationed at Catterick during the last months of his service, they rented a cottage on the edge of the moors. For Susan it was a reincarnation of her first marriage, but the pregnancy she had longed for did not follow. George sometimes wondered if she had married him merely as a means of replacing her lost child, although he knew she was fond of him. She would make love with muted passion, affectionately, but he could never really arouse her. Her deepest feelings were stirred by Malcolm and Louise, an entirely different sort of emotion.

George would not allow disappointment a place in his thoughts. He put a great deal of effort into his job, working very hard to justify his appointment which could have been classified as nepotism. By this time they were living in a small house in Woking, from which he commuted by train. George had bought it on a mortgage and with two thousand pounds he had recently inherited from his grandfather. When Mr Warrington died and Susan's mother suggested that they return to Selbury House, George, whilst not eager to live under the same roof as his mother-in-law, saw that this was what Susan wanted and agreed. He spent the money raised from the sale of the Woking house on modernisation. It was several years before Ford retired and it became Mrs Warrington's own idea that she should remove herself to the Lodge.

George had married a wife with money but he had kept his pride and his self-esteem and had, on the whole, lived a happy life. He and Susan never quarrelled. Since his retirement, on a generous pension, George had become treasurer of the Parochial Church Council and had eventually felt obliged, for want of other promising candidates, to stand for the District Council. He needed to be busy and he had time for the work required, although he deplored the intrusion of party politics into local government. He scored a personal success by winning, although standing as an Independent. The few original village families remaining in Selbury trusted him, and he convinced enough of the newcomers of his suitability for election. Since then he had worked conscientiously to improve what he could and protest at what he could not alter, but he was often depressed when cuts were imposed where, in his opinion, more money should be allotted, and he fought a vigorous though unsuccessful battle for the retention of school meals in the district. Children who had started out for the day on only cereal, if that, needed a hot meal with meat and vegetables at midday, he said. Normally mild and calm, he raged when a child who lived one hundred yards inside the boundary imposed for free bussing to school was denied a seat though the coach daily passed and had space inside.

It was Norah who listened to these tales of frustration and those that ended more satisfactorily, and who helped him arrange meetings with planning officers and collect grievances and complaints.

They had been occasional lovers for years.

Louise's death had been a dreadful watershed in George's life and he would have traded everything for her safe return. He had worried about her when she lived in London, where she had shared a flat with a Spencer granddaughter and another girl with whom she had been at school. She became very thin and had lost her characteristic giggle, which he supposed were the consequences of growing up, but both manifestations saddened him. After her year in France she had been to a secretarial college and at first did temporary work until she got a post with a literary agent. She found this interesting, and when an opportunity arose, had moved on to a small, specialist publishing house where she eventually became an assistant editor. The books they produced about wild-life and country lore, all beautifully illustrated, appealed to her, for she had always enjoyed being out of doors. The firm had subsidised these publications by producing a range of definitive textbooks, but some years after her disappearance it had been taken over by a bigger firm and although the series she had been editing was completed, the list was now less esoteric.

Although George kept urging her to live at home, for it was perfectly easy to travel up daily, as he did, and she had friends with whom she could stay the night if there was a late party, she resisted, and when she changed her mind it seemed a sudden decision. If he had let her be, encouraged her to stay in London, she might still be alive for she would not have become a member of the Feringham Choral Society. She would have travelled on the tube, or walked from her car to her flat along an ill-lit street with muggers in the shadows, but she might not have been in the wrong place at the wrong time, which was the only explanation for her fate.

She had talked a lot about her work, enthusing over some of the books she worked on, lamenting that she had also to read unsolicited submissions which were usually useless. The firm commissioned much of its work and she found working with authors rewarding as she watched the projects grow. She had to find artists to illustrate particular books and she began to have a feeling for the fine arts which she had lacked before, much as her mother had done more recently; though Mrs Warrington, daughter of a prosperous industrialist and married to another, had been a great haunter of antique shops and had acquired some beautiful and valuable pieces to replace the unexciting, functional furniture with which Selbury House was originally equipped.

George himself, son of a country parson, had grown up with good solid Victorian woodwork around him, large, sagging chairs covered in faded floral linen, and a study full of books. His father, an impoverished younger son, had been a kindly scholar steeped in ancient history which he spent as much time studying as he could possibly spare from the supervision of his flock.

Your environment shaped you. George had learned

107

certain values from his own. Why had this not worked with Malcolm? All his life, the boy had been nothing but a worry. George could admit this to himself, and to Norah too, though never to Susan. He suspected that she was still helping him financially, even after they had agreed never to do so again. There had been reason behind paying his creditors; George, too, did not want them to be ruined simply because Malcolm was, at best, feckless. George knew from their tax returns that Susan's investments had decreased, but he never questioned her about them. It was her business, and she had a stockbroker to guide her. She had mentioned that she had given money to the charities in which she took an interest, and that was her affair as well.

The girl, Brenda, who was living with Malcolm at the moment – or rather, with whom he was living, which was a different matter altogether – would tire of him in time. She was too bright to put up with his drinking and his improvidence, although it was a fact that many otherwise sensible women made endless excuses for wastrel men and inexplicably tolerated their behaviour.

One thing that had improved with time was Malcolm's attitude to Louise. His childish jealousy of her had been obvious, but later he had seemed eager for her company. When they were young adults he had asked her to go with him to various parties and had been genuinely disappointed when, after agreeing several times, she refused further invitations. As a young man he had run with a wild crowd. They had torn about the countryside in fast cars on scavenging and treasure hunts and other chases, ending in some pub or other where they drank too much. Sometimes they had patronised dinner dances at hotels. The company was too rowdy for Louise; this was not her scene, and

Susan was right when she insisted that marriage and a family would have made her happy.

All that was required was that she should meet someone worthy of her, perhaps even agreeable enough for George to approve. He knew that he was biased; perhaps fathers always were.

He could not bear to think of what must have happened in her final hours and prayed that it had been quickly over. He would always wonder, and he was never going to know.

When George returned from a discussion in the graveyard about removing the tombstones to make mowing easier – George was against it, though he favoured levelling the graves – he found an unknown man in the kitchen with Norah. Learning that it was Detective Superintendent Marsh, he was taken by surprise.

He remembered the younger Marsh. Heart thumping, he took a deep breath to steady himself as Norah said, 'There's no news, George. Mr Marsh has come back to Feringham and called just to make contact.'

'I'm sorry if my presence is disturbing,' said Marsh, who could see very well that it was. He repeated what he had told Norah – that he had never forgotten the case and his regret that it had gone unsolved.

'You did all you could,' said George, sure that this was true. He would never forget the searches, the broadcasts, the newspaper appeals. 'Of course, that was before *Crime Watch* and *Police Five*, all the things on television that can help you now.'

'They're good ways of alerting the public,' Marsh responded. 'Sometimes they shock other villains into shopping those they know about. Then there are all the new scientific developments, like DNA fingerprinting. That makes it much harder for – ' he had been going to say rapists, but it would be crude to be so blunt to this man. 'For villains to get off,' he ended.

'If you ever find Louise, it will be too late for that,' said George, understanding perfectly.

'I'm afraid so, sir.'

'You'll see a lot of changes here,' said George, taking another chair at the table. Norah had made fresh tea when he came in and now poured him out a cup which she put beside him silently. 'Thank you,' he said to her. She had never seen his perfect manners fail.

'Yes. Selbury has grown,' agreed Marsh.

'It'll join Feringham if the developers have their way,' said George.

'And how is Mrs Vaughan?' asked Marsh.

'Very busy,' George replied. 'She does charity work and attends art lectures, and she's always been a most enthusiastic gardener.' He looked at the policeman. 'It stops her thinking, or that's how I understand it,' he added.

'Well, it's hard to come to terms with things,' said Marsh. 'But what about your son?'

'Yes – well, a son moves away, doesn't he? Makes his own life.' George could find little to say about Malcolm.

'You had a dog,' said Marsh.

'Yes. A black Labrador. We had another – his son – until a few weeks ago. He was run over in the village and we've decided not to replace him,' George replied. 'There's a lot of traffic in the lane and Bertie had managed to escape.' He'd been in pursuit of a bitch at one of the new houses up the road, his ardour leading him to snatch his chance when Susan was in the garden, planting bulbs. She had not seen him slinking off. George missed him, but Susan had not seemed particularly affected. After all, what was a dog, after losing a daughter?

'I see.'

'You don't need to speak to my wife, do you? She's in London at an exhibition, and I'm not sure which train she's catching back.' George spoke defensively; he did not want Marsh upsetting Susan.

'No. This is an unofficial visit – almost social, you might say,' said Marsh, who had learned all he needed to know from Norah.

'I'm glad you called, Superintendent,' said George. 'I'm glad you remember Louise.'

When Marsh had gone, George sat on at the table. Norah poured him another cup of tea and he absent-mindedly helped himself to a biscuit.

'Perhaps I drove her into the clutches of whoever that scoundrel was,' he said.

'Whatever do you mean?' demanded Norah, pausing as she bent to put the superintendent's cup and saucer in the dishwasher.

'I loved her almost too much,' George said. 'Just to see her every day – to see her growing up so pretty and so clever – she meant the world to me.'

'There's nothing wrong in that,' said Norah. 'Most fathers feel the same about their daughters.'

'I'd have cheerfully killed that man – the one who did it,' George declared. 'I'd rend him limb from limb if I could find him.'

'Mr Warrington felt like that about Susan,' said Norah. 'He hated Hitler for making her a widow. Other women lost their husbands and it was sad, but for his daughter it was something else. He was pleased about you, though,' she recalled. 'Thought you were kind and would treat her well.'

George had to laugh at this, and the way she spoke, looking at him speculatively, smiling.

'What a lot you know about us all,' he said.

'Too much, I sometimes think,' she said, and sighed.

111

'What was David really like?' he asked her. 'Susan seems to think he was just a happy-go-lucky boy.'

Norah found it easy to answer calmly.

'That was how he seemed,' she said. 'Living to the full while he could. How else could they cope, those boys? They were like undertakers, making jokes all the time because their days were so fraught.'

'Do undertakers do that?'

'I believe so,' Norah said. 'My uncle worked for one and that was his opinion. The other brother was different,' she went on. 'Malcolm was the first. He was more serious – his mother's prop and stay. David was her baby.' She was silent for a moment and then added, 'I never saw her shed a tear, not in all the years I knew her. I suppose she wept in private.'

Norah had cried.

When Susan had told Mrs Warrington what had happened to her, Norah was sent for and, terrified and heartbroken, she had sobbed resoundingly. Mrs Warrington had steepled her fingers together and decided what should be done. Norah was too sick in heart and sick in body to do other than submit.

'I'll light the fire,' she said now. 'It'll soon warm up in there. Go and do the crossword until it's time for the news. I've got stuck with it.'

'You bully me,' he told her, smiling, a balding man with strands of greying hair brushed across his pale scalp, blue eyes and a strong, straight nose, still handsome. Norah knew that he wouldn't have stood a chance with Susan unless he had been good-looking.

112

5

Susan

Susan went to the Henry Moore exhibition at the Royal Academy in the afternoon. She had travelled to London by an early train for her appointment with her solicitor, and when their discussion was over had looked in a desultory way at skirts in Simpson's, trying one on but deciding that it was too expensive. She never used to consider a good skirt an extravagance; they lasted for years. She would think about it, she told the assistant, and walked along to Fortnum's for lunch. Afterwards, she went into Hatchards and looked at the latest books produced by Louise's former employers. She bought nothing.

The days she spent in London were oases in the desert of what life had now become. On neutral ground, in some gallery or museum, she could make her mind a blank and simply assess visually what she saw before her. She seldom remembered detail, but she was soothed by the impersonality of paintings or sculpture for they were not flesh and blood. Moore's curving lines were pleasing to gaze at, whatever the subject; she sat on a bench in front of one of his groups and thought about nothing. She had found a way to exist.

Moving had helped her. She no longer saw ghosts round every corner, friendly ones though they had been. At first she had feared that her mother's dominating presence would haunt the Lodge House, but it was magically erased by the new building work. The extensions, the complete re-decoration throughout, had expunged images of the thin, hawk-nosed old woman

113

in her high-backed chair endlessly crocheting. In her final months her eyesight had failed but she still crocheted, making large loose shawls for starving Africans when she could no longer do more intricate work.

She had lost both her sons and never complained aloud. When Louise disappeared, she had reacted with anger. She was angry that the girl had somehow put herself in jeopardy and angry that Feringham, once a peaceful market town, could harbour such menace.

When Susan was a girl, white slavery had been a much dreaded peril, and Mabel had fed her tales of revenge wrought by disenchanted servants or nurses who allowed their charges to be wafted away, never to be seen again. Now, other dangers threatened young women. The worst had already happened to Louise, and Susan was no longer vulnerable, except over Malcolm. Why had she been unable to help him discover the best in himself, find his true direction? His failure had to be hers.

When her own little son had died, she had blamed herself. Even when the inquest had decided that he had died by misadventure and the police had stopped behaving as if they thought she had smothered him, guilt had been mixed with her grief, but in those days you pulled yourself together and got on with your life, as her mother had firmly told her. Susan had plunged into her nursing, working hard and with long hours on duty, often harrowed by the suffering she saw, but always returning home at the end of her shift to sleep in her comfortable room, with the house kept quiet by day when she was on night duty.

What she had wanted most was another baby to hold, a soft little form to clasp against her, silken hair to brush her cheek, a petal mouth to smile at her, little chortling laughs. She had not looked beyond this to the growing child, the difficult adolescent. She had married George because he was kind, patently adored her just

114

as Hugh had done, and was attractive in his dark, sturdy way, quite unlike Hugh. He brought her more physical pleasure than Hugh had managed in their short time together, but as the years went on she found that merely agreeable, nothing more, and in the end it became a bore. Once, when she was about fourteen and staying briefly with the Spencers, she had seen Lady Spencer and her husband, Sir Giles, walking through the coppice that formed part of their land and where, in spring, the ground was strewn with bluebells and primroses which gave off a heady scent. The two were arm in arm, and Lady Spencer was listening earnestly to something Sir Giles was saying. Suddenly they stopped and, to her amazement, kissed one another ardently, clasped together there in the woodland, unaware of Susan who had been picking primroses nearby. She had felt her whole body blushing as, intruder that she was upon such a private moment, she shrank back against the nearest tree, crouching as still as a statue until they moved on. They had not seen her.

She had never seen her own parents exchange more than a peck on the cheek, and even now could not imagine them having an intimate life.

When Norah had got into trouble, she and Mother had been of one mind. David's reputation must be protected now that he was dead and could not decide himself what ought to be done.

'It will be my grandchild,' Mother had said, just once, and had added, 'No matter.'

It was she who, after the decision was made, had discovered the name of a doctor from Lady Spencer, who had many sources of information.

Once it was dealt with, they had not discussed it again.

*

Malcolm had been a pretty little baby, with his quiff of dark hair and his large blue eyes. Small strong fists had clutched Susan's finger; sturdy legs had thrust against her as he sucked hungrily at his bottle.

He had never snuggled close in quite the same way as little Harry had done. It wasn't in his power, at first, to detach himself, but as he grew bigger he would push away from her, disengage himself, hold his head back and stare at her as if to say, 'What made you do it? Why me?' and she would have to charm him back into accepting her.

It was still like that, she thought, as she travelled home in the train after her day in London, except when he was in trouble and then he turned to her at once. She had made up her mind that this must stop.

While Louise was living at home, Susan had worried only intermittently about Malcolm in Australia. That had been a happy time, though she had wished that Louise would enjoy more of a social life. Feringham's Choral Society seemed a strange choice of activity to Susan. Sometimes Louise joined in the dinner parties her mother gave, but more often she elected to eat in her room, saying she must work on a manuscript. Now and then, if Susan had been shopping in London, she and George had met Louise after work, taken her out to an early meal and then to a theatre, all three driving home afterwards, for George would take his car up on those days. They would stop at the station on the way back to collect Louise's Mini.

Since her disappearance, Susan and George had almost stopped going out at night, except for occasional evenings spent at the Cartwrights', or perhaps a charity event they felt obliged to attend. When Norah began looking after Mrs Warrington, George had sometimes suggested a night in town and he had even secured seats for *Phantom of the Opera* for Susan's birthday; both alleged that they enjoyed these excursions, but they would have been just as content staying at home. It made each of them feel, however, that they were attempting a normal life.

Every summer they took the car to France or Italy, staying in small hotels in out-of-the-way places, visiting châteaux and galleries and tasting the wine. Neither expected too much from the other, and these expeditions were a gentle success, resting them both and providing a change of scene.

Norah took holidays, too; continuing the custom begun when she started to earn a good salary, she went off on some cultural tour, shepherded by a knowledge-able guide around Tuscany, or to Verona for the opera, or to Vienna or Salzburg. She set off alone but always seemed to find someone congenial to talk to and received Christmas cards even now from acquaintances met on such trips. She spent a lot on these journeys, and Susan told George she thought they were a gross extravagance.

'Darling, you think nothing of tripping round the Louvre or the Uffizi. Why shouldn't Norah do it too? She'll enjoy it all quite as much as you, and she'll learn more, since she starts off without your knowledge.'

'Yes, you're right. I'm a meanie,' said Susan. 'I still can't forget that shabby little girl with her hair tied in bunches and not an "H" to her name.'

'Think of Michael Caine,' advised George. 'He's done all right for an evacuee.'

'But the voice,' Susan objected.

'He can talk just like your old dad if he wants to,' said George. 'Or like me, if you prefer. Anyway, Norah owes her polish to you. You got her to join the ATS and start her climb.'

'Yes,' Susan agreed. 'She'd have stayed on in that factory otherwise, working a lathe or whatever it was that she did.'

It had not been straightforward, since Norah was

already doing war work in the factory, but medical advice that she should be employed out of doors had made the change possible.

Susan still sometimes imagined that when she returned from one of her days in London, Louise would have come back. There she would be, her mother dreamed, sitting by the fire with George while Norah made up a bed for her in the little spare room and filled a hot-water bottle, found her a nightdress and cooked her a meal. She would look just the same, with her fair hair brushed straight or held in a plait. She would have escaped unscathed from bondage in some dreadful bordello, avoiding a fate worse than death because her innocence would have led the madam to employ her as a book-keeper or in some other harmless guise; or she would have been married to a Middle Eastern potentate who had respected her and treated her kindly, finally, in response to her pleas, allowing her to escape. In wilder scripts she would have been involved in espionage ever since she began working in London, and had been wafted off behind the Iron Curtain on a mission of such secrecy that no reassuring cover story to explain her absence had been devised. She had been caught and imprisoned and only now was released.

These fantasies were a comfort, and after indulging one it was an anti-climax to come home and find George and Norah alone. He would always hear her car and come out to close the garage door after her, carry her parcels when there were some, and ask how her day had gone.

Tonight George told her about Marsh's visit, reminding her of the young sergeant who had spent so much time with them twelve years before. He and Norah had discussed whether to tell her or not, and had decided that they must in case she ran across Marsh herself and was unprepared.

118

'They're not starting it all up again, are they?' she asked.

'No.'

'Though maybe they'd find out something, if they did,' she said. 'If they went round talking to everyone they interviewed then.'

George thought it likely that Marsh would do exactly that. Some had moved from the area, like Tim Francis. His ex-wife, who had remarried, still lived in Feringham; she worked in one of the banks. The children must be growing up, he supposed – no, there had been a baby who would still be only about thirteen.

'I don't think anything new will turn up now,' he told Susan. How could it?

Unless, even after all this time, her body was discovered.

Susan had not seen Malcolm for some weeks, nor heard from him. When he was silent, she felt it was always the lull before the storm and would only be ended with a plea for help. Occasionally, when her anxiety became too great to bear, she went to his workshop to see him.

He always seemed pleased to see her, would stop whatever he was doing, switch off the radio, kiss her warmly and lead her into the office where he would make her a cup of Lapsang Souchong tea, which he kept especially for her. There was always a lemon, too. He was admirably organised there, with his sink and his shower and his portable telephone, and his paperwork so orderly that none of it was in view. It did not occur to her that a great muddle lay inside the drawers of his desk, a confusion of final demands and even a writ. She would see his superficial tidiness as evidence of ability never developed and tell herself, yet again, that all he needed was to find the right opportunity and he would be a success.

The day after her trip to London and Marsh's visit to Selbury, she went to the workshop. The doors were closed and a paper attached stated that he was with a customer and would be back at four o'clock.

The drive over had taken her nearly an hour. Susan decided to look round the shops and visit the abbey. She often did that when she came to Malchester, sitting quietly in a pew being soothed, as in an art gallery, by the beauty of the ancient building, the long fluted columns and high vaulted roof, with perhaps the organist practising and great rolling chords echoing round her.

She wished she could have retained the unquestioning childhood belief that had been fed into her along with porridge and cod-liver oil and malt. Father and Mother had regularly gone to church, and when she was five she joined them, though at that age she was not expected to sit through the sermon; taking her out gave Mother an excuse to leave too. School had continued the indoctrination, with prayers night and morning read by the headmistress who stood before the assembled girls in her gown, the rest of the staff on either side.

All that conviction had been destroyed in the war, though for years she had gone through the motions, still attending Matins on Sundays because she could not face explaining her defection to her mother. Now, she went because it was expected of her. Sometimes she wondered if the vicar was there only for the same reason.

In the abbey she was able to accept that Louise was dead. Here, she could think of her without pain, know that whatever torment her last hours had brought was over and nothing worse lay ahead. The building itself somehow made these thoughts possible. Susan would imagine the ancient masons toiling with no modern aids, hauling every stone into place, chipping away as they carved the decorations. So much that was wonderful had been achieved in the name of Christianity – so many fine buildings and such marvellous music – but there had been so much slaughter, too, such lack of toleration. Life was a lonely journey, and people needed a goal, a cause to believe in. There had always been gods of one sort or another to praise or placate; now people worshipped their status, their car, a political party, football, or some crusade such as opposing blood sports. Susan herself no longer had any aim beyond cherishing her garden.

She dozed a little, sitting there, while a clutch of late tourists walked round talking together in reverent whispers and a sacristan in his long black gown padded by. It was quite warm; the place was efficiently heated.

After a while she roused herself, left the abbey and went to a nearby café for tea. There were still two old-fashioned tea shops in the centre of Malchester, where other towns now offered only Wimpy bars and the like. Here, the Cobweb was thriving and today it was warm and busy. Susan sat with her tea studying the other customers. What sort of homes were they returning to? How many had faced or were facing tragedy, or had it yet to come? She often had such thoughts now, and would walk along a street looking at the passers-by and imagining them all weighed down by some dire form of stress. Once, in a rare moment of communication, she had told George this and he had tried to comfort her, telling her that in the end most people adjusted to their pain though it might never be healed. She must not, he adjured, go round believing that everyone's heart was breaking.

Since that conversation he had started devising surprise treats. He would suddenly say they were going to Paris for the weekend, or would bring her a present, a piece of porcelain he had found in an antique shop and hoped she would like, or a plant for the garden. On

121

other days, he would produce a special bottle of some good wine for dinner, or suggest an extra glass of sherry. She went along with his efforts, pretending to be cheerful.

If only Malcolm could be successful and, if possible, happy, she thought she could throw off this black cloud. As it was, like water dripping on a stone, the anxiety wore her down.

When she returned to the workshop he was still out, although it was nearly five o'clock. The note was still attached to the door. There was no point in waiting; he might not come back that night.

What did it matter what work he did, as long as he made an honest living? She knew he did not sell dud cars; look how hard he worked on them, taking a long time to move them because he would not sell unless he was satisfied with their condition. If she gave up believing in him, who else would? She had to trust him, though sometimes he made that very difficult.

She had never been able to forget that long-ago night when he had been at Selbury House unknown to her. Since his recent return from Australia, although supposedly living in Cornton, he often turned up without warning and of course he had a key. Restless because of a bad dream, she had gone down to the kitchen to make herself a cup of tea, moving very softly so as not to disturb George and leaving their bedroom in darkness.

He had stirred slightly when she left, but he had not woken; he was a sound sleeper. She had tiptoed along the passage to the head of the stairs, not a great distance, and as she reached for the light switch she heard a faint sound. She snapped on the light and caught a movement from the corner of her eye: a dark figure stood outside the door of Louise's room, one hand on the knob, and she thought that the sound she had heard was the door closing.

As she stared, almost giving a shriek of fright, the figure had moved towards her, gliding smoothly, and she saw that it was Malcolm. She was trembling as he reached her and he put his arm round her.

'What a fright I gave you! Sorry,' he said. He held her arm and went down the stairs with her, set her in a chair and put on the kettle. 'I thought I'd crept in without waking anyone,' he added. 'I had a late run out to Oxford with a fare and decided to drop off here instead of going all the way back to Cornton tonight.'

'Oh yes,' said Susan. 'I see. Lucky Daddy hadn't put the bolts across.' She always referred to George like this to Malcolm and Louise.

While Malcolm was in Australia, George had always bolted every outer door at bedtime. Since Malcolm's return, he had twice had to come down to let Malcolm in when he had suddenly decided to spent the night, so the front door was now left on the Yale.

'Yes,' said Malcolm, smiling.

While they both had tea, he told her about several amusing fares he had had. Then they went upstairs again. She watched him go past Louise's door to his own room, further along the landing and on the other side.

Why had he been outside her door, with his hand on the knob? Again and again she had pictured the scene and it was always the same, the stationary figure, frozen, it seemed, and the hand on the knob. Had she really heard him closing the door?

Brothers could innocently enter their sisters' rooms, but such visits were not usual when the siblings were in their twenties and it was the middle of the night. Adopted brothers and sisters, reaching adult years, might, however, regard themselves as outside the bounds of incest, and it was true; technically they were.

She had never mentioned the incident to a soul, and

123

over the years she had tried, without success, to forget it.

Two days afterwards, Louise had vanished.

As she drove home it began to rain, not hard, but in a misty drizzle. Susan turned on the wipers and stared past their hypnotising swish at the oncoming traffic. Lights were on now, and she peered ahead, anxious about cyclists difficult to see in the shadows. She had always had excellent, rather long sight, and disliked having to wear spectacles for driving; it was less easy, now, to judge distance in the darkness.

The car heater sent comforting waves of warmth round her legs and she began to look forward to reaching home, for she was tired. Anxiety was very exhausting. Would Norah be in, or would she be enjoying the social round she seemed to be developing? Perhaps Myra was entertaining tonight; it wasn't her French class evening. Susan pretended to herself to be glad when she and George were left alone. Norah always left the dinner ready, either a casserole in the oven or something to grill, or to heat in the microwave which George had bought during Norah's last holiday. Susan had lost all interest in cooking, which she had once enjoyed, and in Norah's absence George often made the few preparations necessary and loaded the dishwasher afterwards.

Mother had been dreadful, refusing to install one or allow her to have it done when Norah began looking after her.

'A machine costs money,' she had declared. 'And I've heard they're expensive to run. Besides, there are only two of us to wash up for.'

But there were often more, when Mother's surviving friends, some mere sprigs of eighty, came over. She soon resumed her lunch parties and the bridge afternoons she had enjoyed for most of her life, and then tea and sandwiches were produced by Norah. Susan pointed this out.

'Never mind. Let her see to it,' Mrs Warrington had said. 'It's what she was brought up to, and if it wasn't for us she'd have been in service all her life.'

It wasn't true. Resident domestic help had almost disappeared after the war, and Norah would have found her level in time, whatever she did.

It would be nice if she were at home tonight. Susan craved some cosseting, and Norah would provide it. Her wish was granted, for as she drove in, Norah heard the car and came out to greet her, just as George always did. He was out tonight, at a PCC meeting, Susan suddenly remembered. Of course Norah would not have gone out too, leaving her alone. They never did that.

'Have you had a nice afternoon?' Norah asked, taking a Jaeger bag from Susan when she had shut the garage doors. 'Had a good spend?' Susan occasionally went on a shopping spree and would then clear out her cupboards to make room for her new acquisitions, but this had happened less often lately. Norah suspected the reason was an economy drive.

'I bought George a new sweater,' said Susan. 'That old maroon one he wears is so shabby. I got one for myself, too,' she added.

Would it be black or beige? Susan wore too much black, Norah thought. It looked chic on younger women but depressing on the old unless they had high colouring themselves, or wore a bright scarf. Beige had suited Susan until ten years ago but now her fair hair was almost white and her face, when she masked her threadlike broken veins with make-up, seemed to tone in so that she looked beige all over. Norah resolved to buy her a rose-coloured sweater for Christmas.

'Good,' she said now. 'The Scouts are having a

jumble sale next weekend. I said we'd find something for them.' Susan's throw-outs were notorious snips at sales in the village.

'It's good to be home,' said Susan as she entered the house. She slid her coat off and let it drop on to a chair in the hall. Norah would take it upstairs later, when she drew the curtains and turned down the beds.

'Did you see Malcolm?' Norah asked.

'No. Why should I have done that?' Susan was instantly on the defensive. She had told no one where she was going.

'Well, you've been to Malchester,' said Norah. There was no branch of Jaeger's in Feringham. 'So it's natural that you'd look in on him. He wasn't there?'

'No. He was out on some business or other. There was a note on the door,' Susan said.

'You didn't go round to the house in case he went straight home?'

'No. I thought Brenda might not like it,' Susan said.

Thank goodness she'd had that much sense, Norah reflected.

'You could always telephone,' she suggested.

'Yes. Perhaps I will,' Susan said.

'George went off early,' Norah told her now. 'The vicar wanted to talk to him about old Mr Bernard's funeral. There's some problem about where he's to be buried. He'd fancied a place near the yew tree but he may not be able to have it, since there's so little space.'

'I hope the vicar gives him a drink,' said Susan.

'He will. George took a bottle along,' said Norah. 'You go and have one yourself while I see about dinner. George said he'd have his later, when he gets back.'

'Then he'll have indigestion, since the meeting is sure to go on for hours,' Susan said. 'Eating late doesn't agree with him.'

'I know, but he didn't want to have lamb chops at six, either,' said Norah, going off to the kitchen.

Susan went into the drawing-room and crossed to the drinks tray, where she poured herself a glass of dry sherry and then went to sit in front of the fire. George would be having a whisky at the vicarage; he'd need it; he was in for an arduous evening.

When had Norah started to call them by their Christian names? It had gone on for years, of course, and Mother had been shocked when she first noticed. George had told her not to be stuffy. He had always stood up to Mother, who had enjoyed sparring with him, but in this instance she had waspishly commented, 'Familiarity breeds contempt. You'll be sorry.'

But familiarity between Norah and David had developed a long time before that, and they had undoubtedly addressed one another by their given names: indeed, to the family, Norah had always been Norah.

Had they expected too much from Louise? Sometimes Susan wondered about that. Helen Cartwright had a theory that parents expected their children to succeed where they had failed as well as to emulate their successes. Put like that, it seemed a tall order and likely to daunt even the most able. Helen had made her statement when Susan had lowered her guard enough to admit to despair about Malcolm's inability to lead a normal life.

'By normal, you mean conventional, don't you? Wife and two children, job in town?' Helen said.

'Well – yes. I suppose I do.'

'I felt the same,' Helen had confessed. One of her daughters had become a television producer who showed no signs of marrying; the other was a zoologist who, at the time of this conversation preferred baboons to people and was exploring in some distant jungle. Subsequently she had married and produced children who were brought up with few rules but seemed very bright and happy. The producer daughter, now in her late thirties, had expressed the desire for a child and seemed likely to accomplish her wish without settling down with its father; indeed, Helen feared that the man would be selected for no other reason than good health and appearance and then dismissed. Her son had dropped out of university to pursue the hippie trail to the Himalayas. Some years later he had returned and was now a financial expert in the City. He lived in St John's Wood and keenly followed cricket, hoping that one of his two sons would play in a Test Match. 'Don't expect too much,' Helen had advised, from her own experience. 'He's got problems to sort out.'

'Lots of adoptions work out very well.' Susan, stung, had been on the defensive.

'I know. Probably most of them do, but my point is that all parents have these sorts of worries, and brothers and sisters are often jealous of one another. Malcolm may resent Louise because she's really your child. Does he harbour a grudge against his real mother for giving him up?'

'He's very fond of Louise,' Susan had declared. 'When they were small, they quarrelled a lot, but children do. Yours often did. That passed as they grew up.'

But it had been succeeded by something she pretended she had not noticed. He hung round Louise, teased her verbally but with an undercurrent of something more than mischief; it was almost malice. She had been relieved when he got married.

After he went to Australia and Louise came home, she had picked up old threads of friendship in the area and had sometimes played tennis or squash or swam. There was no pool at Selbury House but friends had pools and courts, and kept open house at weekends. On summer Sundays any young people who were around made the most of what was offered. The various mothers baked and roasted, froze and thawed, catered lavishly and spared no effort to provide for them. George had had the hard court laid, and Susan persuaded Norah to come down for frequent weekends at that time of year, for she was always a help when it was their turn to be the hosts, but Louise had never wanted to go to late parties, nor to give them.

Years later, when Norah was a permanent part of the household, Susan wondered what she had done at Christmas in the past. At the time, she had never thought about it. Of course, there was plenty going on in London, concerts and church services, and she must have made friends at work. Since Louise's disappearance, Christmas had become a time of anguish and for the last few years she and George had gone to Portugal, where they had found a quiet hotel which laid no particular emphasis on seasonal merrymaking. Norah, left behind, did not lack for invitations from her new friends in the village; in addition to Myra, she seemed on intimate terms with two families in the new houses, often baby-sitting for one and apparently spending hours with a boy from the other, trying to play computer games. Occasionally Susan felt resentment towards these people, incomers, who had a stake in Norah's life. Still, it seemed to amuse her and meant that she would not want to leave them. Sometimes, though it shocked her to acknowledge the thought, Susan felt that she would miss George less than Norah if either were to die before she did.

She wouldn't be too sorry to die, herself. When she allowed herself to reflect that her mother had lived to be over ninety and that she might have to exist for another twenty years, Susan felt real dread. Even Norah might not survive her, let alone George, and Malcolm would put her into a home where she would sit drooling in a chair all day, exposed to non-stop television with the volume on at full blast. The fact that her mother had never drooled for one day in her life, except possibly as an infant, did nothing to dispel this nightmare prospect.

If anything happened to George, she would look for an acceptable place where she might end her days in reasonable comfort, protected from the worst humiliations meted out to the old. Though she had eaten into her capital through rescuing Malcolm, what was left of it plus the money the sale of the Lodge House would bring should be enough to pay for such an arrangement. If not, there was always an alternative: you could give up and finish it yourself, if you had the means. She might have to do that, one day, if she could, faced with only Malcolm to take care of her.

But he would, wouldn't he? Didn't he love her? Hadn't he always turned to her when he was troubled? Or was it just for the money he knew she would find for him?

She had already accepted the answer.

6

Richard

Detective Superintendent Marsh instructed a young, ambitious detective constable to track down Richard Blacker, Louise Vaughan's sometime lover, according to her brother Malcolm. He would have to pursue the search in spare moments since the case was dormant.

Whitlock began on the telephone, first ringing various advertising agencies he found listed in the yellow pages. It was going to be a tedious task. He looked at the big boxed notices and dialled a few, but none had a Richard Blacker working for them. Then his gaze turned to the ordinary smaller entries and a name stood out: Blacker, R., with an address in West London. Could it be as simple as this? Was this the Blacker who had known Louise?

He telephoned the number and said he was a solicitor seeking a firm who had handled work for a deceased client. The client had manufactured an ingenious type of clothes-peg. The agent's name had been Blacker, and he lived in Essex. Unfortunately the client's records were incomplete, but it was thought that money had been owed to the agent and the executors wished to settle the debt.

'I don't think that's our Mr Blacker,' said the telephone voice. 'He lives in Oldington – has done for years. That's not in Essex.' She did not say where it was.

'Robert Blacker, would that be?' asked Detective Constable Whitlock smoothly.

'Oh no. Our Mr Blacker is Richard, like in Dick Whittington,' said the girl.

'Sorry. I must have got the wrong address,' Whitlock said.

He was very pleased with the result of this short interview and, in a gazetteer, soon located an Oldington in the Thames Valley, between High Wycombe and Reading. Directory Inquiries gave him R. Blacker's telephone number, and, when prodded, the name of his house.

'Let's hope it's the right Blacker,' said Marsh, when Whitlock reported the results of this swift bit of sleuthing. 'We'll follow it up and see. You go over to Oldington and mosey around a bit, find out the set-up and if there's a wife and kiddies – all that. And if it's a second wife or what. Then we'll decide what to do.'

Whitlock was pleased at the prospect of a day in the country. Oldington was about twenty-five miles from Feringham, reached, once he left the motorway, along narrow winding lanes edged with tall hedges that almost met overhead. He passed two horsewomen wearing hard hats and padded jackets, their mounts, one grey and one chestnut, jogging along the tunnel-like way at some considerable risk, he thought. But roads were originally made for horses and he liked to see them, though an alarmed animal hitting a car could damage itself and the vehicle severely. Whitlock, in his red Mazda, edged past, and the women nodded at him in thanks for slackening his speed. That was the life, he thought: fresh air and exercise. This was a welcome break from trying to find stolen cars and interviewing shoplifters.

He soon found Blacker's house, which lay in a valley between beech woods in an unspoilt piece of countryside.

'Nice area,' he observed over half a pint in the pub. 'Not much building going on.'

132

'No. There's big landowners here,' said the publican. 'They keep the speculators out.'

'Oh,' said Whitlock, nodding wisely.

'Just passing through, are you?'

'That's right.'

'We're not on the way to anywhere,' remarked the publican, though walkers and wayfarers often came to his inn.

'No. I'm going to Reading,' Whitlock volunteered. 'But I've time to kill before my appointment so I thought I'd go the long way round. The wife and I do a bit of rambling at weekends and I know there's lots of footpaths about here. It might be worth our coming over.' Whitlock was not married.

'Oh, it would be,' agreed the landlord. 'Thirsty work, rambling.' Too often the rucksacked groups that came this way were self-sufficient, laden with cardboard cartons of fruit juice and plastic-wrapped sandwiches. They even, sometimes, ate them in his garden at his picnic tables.

'I noticed a pretty house – Martin's, I think it's called,' mentioned Whitlock. 'What would a place like that fetch these days?'

'You're talking about a cool four or five hundred thousand,' said the landlord. 'But the fellow that lives there isn't likely to move. He's owned the place for years. He's in publicity of some sort. They have a lot of people down at weekends and he sometimes brings them in. All on expenses, you can be sure.'

'Not married, then?'

'Oh, he's married all right. Got two girls and a boy,' said the landlord. 'Pony mad, the girls are. This is a great area for horse-riding.'

'I met two ladies on the road, on horses,' Whitlock said.

'You should meet the hunt,' said the landlord.

133

'That's a pretty sight. Blocks the lanes up something awful.'

'I can imagine,' Whitlock said. 'Been here long yourself?'

'Six months,' said the man.

'Ah,' said Whitlock, who had picked up this useful response from Marsh, who often used it. He had better not show too much interest in Blacker, so he stated that he wouldn't mind moving into one of the smaller cottages if his number came up on the pools.

'You do that, mate,' said the landlord.

Some other people came in then, and his steak and chips arrived, served with broccoli from the freezer. Whitlock took his plate to a corner table and listened to the talk round him as the bar filled up. He heard nothing useful. Where did these people come from? There were young men in smart suits, business people doubtless working in the towns around; how could they spare the time out of their offices? They weren't all discussing deals. There were some older people, too, mostly grey-haired couples; the retired, presumably.

Later, he parked his Mazda at the entrance to a footpath and walked up a hill to a position where he could look down on Martin's. So late in the year, with the trees bare of leaves, he could see it clearly. It was an old house built of mellowed brick, with a tiled roof, and with various plants, none of them now in bloom, growing up the walls. A swimming-pool covered with a green tarpaulin stood a little apart, sheltered by a high wall. Lattice windows, all tightly closed, sparkled brightly, reflecting the winter sunlight. Whitlock could see the burglar alarm attached to the house. It was a secluded place; such houses, in their rural isolation, were an invitation to thieves who sped along the motorway, did a place and were gone again with scant chance of being caught. Those jobs were carried out by experts who would reconnoitre first, just as he had done. A few questions in the village shop or at the post office might establish if Mrs Blacker was likely to be at home, for instance, unless the people there were more discreet than the publican who had freely talked about his customers. He was new to the trade; experienced inn-keepers were more wary. Many of these large places needed two salaries to meet the mortgage, but Blacker had owned his long enough to have bought it relatively cheaply. He contemplated going up the drive, pretending to sell double-glazing, but that would exceed his brief and he could not support such a statement with any documentation. He settled for taking some photographs of the house before dusk fell; then he'd hang about, see if lights came on and whether there were visitors. He sat in his car near the gates to Martin's, and was rewarded by seeing a large blue Audi turn into the drive at five o'clock. After a shorter day than usual in the office, Richard Blacker had come home.

On his next day off, Marsh visited Blacker's London office. He had no appointment and Blacker's secretary was reluctant to admit him, so Marsh made it official.

Soon afterwards he was being ushered, with some deference, into a large room which occupied most of the second floor of an elegant Georgian house overlooking a small garden north of Hyde Park.

The secretary, aged about thirty, was attractive, fair and slim. She was much the same physical type as Louise Vaughan, Marsh noted, tabulating the information away in a file in his mind, to decide later if the relationship should be investigated in case it was continued outside the office. A man – or woman, come to that – who had played away from home once might do so again.

'Would you bring some coffee, please, Sarah?' Blacker requested before she closed the door.

'Not for me, thank you,' Marsh said curtly, and Blacker made a gesture to the woman before asking her to see that they were not disturbed.

'What's this all about, Superintendent?' he inquired when they were alone.

'You knew Louise Vaughan,' Marsh stated, and had the satisfaction of seeing Blacker turn quite pale, grip the arms of his chair, and stare at him in stupefaction. So this was the right Blacker.

His quarry had pulled himself together.

'Yes, I did,' he answered, wetting his lips, trying to keep his voice from shaking. In the face of such a confident assertion, it was useless to deny acquaintance. 'What about it?'

'You never came forward when she disappeared.'

'No. I hadn't seen her for over a year,' said Blacker.

'You had an affair with her,' said Marsh.

'I – yes. Yes, I did.' Wherever the superintendent had got his information, it was sound. Lying could only lead to trouble, but if he was frank, once the reason for this interview was known, his confidence might be respected. Richard Blacker had never had cause to tangle with the police and did not mean to do so now. 'I hope that admission need go no further,' he suggested nervously.

'Who broke it off?' snapped Marsh. He had taken a dislike to Blacker, and for no good reason since so far the man was cooperating, looked intelligent and pleasant, with dark hair greying elegantly, a well-tailored suit worn with a pale silk tie, and large brown eyes behind horn-rimmed spectacles.

'She did. She couldn't cope with the need for secrecy,' said Blacker. 'My wife, you see – ' he let the sentence trail off, implying that they were both men of the world.

'There was no question of you getting a divorce and marrying her?'

136

'No. Oh no. Mind you, she thought so for a while, but I promised nothing,' Blacker said. 'I couldn't break up my family. There were the children to consider. They were quite young then. I've got three – a boy and two girls. The eldest is at university and the second girl is doing A levels. My son is younger, just thirteen.'

Marsh calculated that the boy had been born during the year before Louise vanished. Had she known about him? Very likely; women often kept tabs on old flames, let alone former lovers.

'Has your elder daughter got a lover?' Marsh demanded.

'Probably,' said Blacker. 'But what's that got to do with Louise?' Or you, come to that, he thought angrily.

Marsh could see he was beginning to smoulder. Good.

'Only that Louise can't have been much older than your daughter when you started your affair with her,' said Marsh.

'But I was younger, too. It was years ago,' said Blacker. 'God, superintendent, she's been dead for twelve years.'

'Oh, of course that excuses everything,' said Marsh. 'You were a man of experience, not like the students your daughter mixes with. What if she has an affair with a married tutor?'

'Now look, superintendent, I don't have to listen to this,' said Blacker. 'I'm extremely busy, but I don't imagine you've come here to read me a lecture on my responsibilities to young women. Has poor Louise been found?'

'What do you think happened to her?' asked Marsh.

'I imagine some pervert or maniac got hold of her and dumped her in a river or quarry or under the concrete of a motorway,' said Blacker. 'It's too terrible to think about. I was badly shocked when I heard, I can tell you.'

137

'Oh, were you? I'm glad to know it,' Marsh said caustically. 'It's difficult to believe that a competent young woman, such as everyone agrees she was, would find herself, when in her own car, not on foot, in such danger in a town like Feringham, and so long ago, when we heard less about such cases.'

'What are you getting at, superintendent?'

'Suppose she met someone she knew? Someone she trusted? She'd let him into her car, wouldn't she? Even drive off into a quiet street where they could talk?'

'I suppose so. It's possible.'

'Was it really Louise who ended your affair or had you become bored with it?' Marsh asked. 'Had she pestered you to get a divorce? Was she pestering you again and generally being a nuisance – more of a nuisance than ever since you'd now got a son to carry on your name?'

'What are you implying?' Blacker's face had flushed. He shuffled some papers on his desk.

'You might have been meeting again,' Marsh suggested. 'She might have wanted to renew the relationship. You might have decided to put a stop to it, once and for all. You'd know about her regular singing nights if you'd been seeing her again. Where were you the night she disappeared, Mr Blacker?'

'I'm not sure. At home, probably,' said Blacker. 'How can I possibly remember after all this time?'

'I should have thought it would have been like it was when President Kennedy was killed,' said Marsh. 'People can still remember where they were when they heard that news. Your former mistress had disappeared in mysterious circumstances and the case made headlines for quite some time. I don't think anyone concerned would forget the date or what they had been doing at the time.'

Blacker doodled on his blotting paper. Upside down,

Marsh could see that he had drawn a gallows. What should he infer from that?

'No – well, I was at my flat in London,' Blacker admitted. 'I keep a place in town for when I have to entertain clients and am likely to be late. My real home is in Oldington, but I expect you already know that. I don't want to drive down there after a night out and have your chaps after me to test my breath.' He attempted a light laugh as he uttered this sally. 'It's just a tiny flat,' he added. 'Quite near here, as a matter of fact.'

Convenient for entertaining mistresses, Marsh thought sourly.

'Were you alone?'

'Of course I was,' said Blacker.

'Not with a lady?'

'What do you think I am, Superintendent?'

'Your wife might have joined you for an evening out,' Marsh stated.

'She couldn't. She can't come up often, she's tied up with the children, and she was especially then, when they were small,' said Blacker.

'I see,' said Marsh.

'If you're going on with these questions, I'm going to call my solicitor,' said Blacker, recovering some of his normal self-possession. 'Where was Louise found?'

'She hasn't been found, Mr Blacker. I wonder if you can suggest some likely place for us to search?'

'I know nothing about it,' said Blacker stormily. 'I was very upset at the time. I still am, when I think about it, which now you're forcing me to do. She was a lovely girl, very sweet and fresh – rather unworldly in some ways.' For the first time in their conversation a genuine emotion – or it seemed to Marsh that it might be genuine – sounded in his voice. 'I would have liked to marry her,' he added. 'But it just wasn't on. Those situations don't work out easily. It's so hard on

139

the children. And my wife's a wonderful woman – a perfect mother. The home and family mean everything to both of us; they're what I work for. A different sort of girl would have been content to let things run on as they were.'

'And miss her chance of marriage and children?'

'She'd make up for it with her career,' said Blacker.

'But Louise wasn't personally ambitious, was she? She had an interesting job but not anything very lucrative. It wasn't like a high-flying career in the city.'

'She was bright enough to switch.'

'But she preferred her books, didn't she? Her wild-life and natural history?'

'At that stage, yes,' Blacker agreed. 'But later she'd have seen the light and changed.'

'Yes – to compensate, when she saw she had little else going for her,' said Marsh. 'Well, Mr Blacker, her body hasn't been found but I have returned to Feringham. I was involved with the case as a young man. Now I'm in charge of the CID in that division and I am curious about all those concerned.'

'One of them told you about me. Who?'

'That's irrelevant,' said Marsh.

'Not to me, it isn't,' Blacker said. 'We were very discreet. No one knew.'

'People always know,' said Marsh, pitying Louise who had kept faith and told no one his identity, for if she had confided in a girl-friend, surely that girl would have spoken up at the time? Though one or two had hinted at an unhappy romance, no one had named the man. 'Someone did, anyway. Your wife may have suspected something but preferred not to have a showdown.'

'I hope you're not going to tell her now,' said Blacker anxiously. His pulse was racing. What about his blood pressure?

'Not unless I have to,' Marsh replied. 'Now, is there

140

anything helpful you can tell me? Anything that might bear on the case? What about her relationship with her parents?'

Blacker relaxed in his chair as the talk took this safer direction.

'She was devoted to them, but they stifled her. She was living in London to assert her independence, as young women do.'

'But she went back to live at home. Was that after you broke up?'

'Yes. They'd pleaded with her to return, and we both thought it would make things easier. The break, I mean,' said Blacker. 'She was quite unhappy,' he confessed. 'She may have felt she needed their support to see her through a bad few weeks. But it's possible that, when she'd got over it, she felt oppressed. They'd want to know where she was, who she was seeing, that sort of thing. Parents do,' he added wryly.

'So if she was meeting someone else she might keep it from them?'

'It would depend,' said Blacker. 'They were older parents, weren't they? They'd been married a while before she was born. That might have made them over-protective. Later motherhood wasn't as common then as it is now.'

'The mother had been widowed in the war. She had another child that died,' said Marsh.

'Louise never told me that,' said Blacker. 'There was an older brother. He was adopted.'

'Did she talk about him? How did they get on?'

'She didn't like him. In a way, I think she was afraid of him,' said Blacker. 'He tormented her when they were children – pulled her hair, that sort of thing. Kids can be terrible. She felt bad about not liking him – thought it reflected on her, as if she was in some way jealous of him, which she wasn't, or so she said. The mother seemed to dote on him.'

141

'Ah.'

'He got married. Then that went wrong and he came back to live at home. She was still living in London then.'

'But she went home later. He had gone to Australia by then,' said Marsh.

'So he had. I'd forgotten.'

'And she died soon after he returned,' said Marsh slowly.

The two men looked at one another across the desk. It was a long, brooding gaze.

'Coincidence,' said Blacker at last.

'He was living in Cornton. That's at least thirty miles away,' said Marsh. 'He was driving a taxi and had taken a fare to Heathrow that night. It would have been checked out.'

But had it been? He remembered little about the brother then, except that he had accompanied several of the search parties. Hundreds of officers had been working on the case but their reports would be on file. He couldn't sanction going through them yet; not without some evidence of one kind or another. He took a card from his wallet.

'There's where to reach me, if anything occurs to you,' he said. 'We talked to her flatmates at the time, and her colleagues at work, but they could tell us nothing useful.'

'She could be as close as a clam,' Blacker told him. 'But someone knew about me. Otherwise you wouldn't be here.'

How had Malcolm known about the affair? Marsh wondered about that as he left the building.

7

Malcolm

Marsh went round to Brenda's house the following Monday evening.

Malcolm was out.

'May I come in a minute?' Marsh requested, having identified himself, and Brenda, looking puzzled, stood back to admit him.

The house was very small with, he guessed, only two bedrooms. The living-room contained a plain dining-table and chairs in a pale wood. The walls were painted off-white with a pinkish tinge, and there were pink silk-covered cushions on the sofa which was upholstered in fabric matching the walls. Everything looked modern, new, and expensive, but might well be low-price from a discount warehouse.

'Your house,' he stated.

'Yes. Malcolm's been living here a while,' she said. 'How may I help you? Why do you want him?' His debts, she thought; there had been telephone calls from angry creditors wanting to know when he planned to settle. They must have been worried to track him down at her address and she did not like that; she had worked hard to establish her own business and she did not want her reputation tarnished by association with someone who might be about to go bankrupt, as he must unless he paid his dues.

'How long have you known him?' asked Marsh.

'A few months. Why? Nothing's happened, has it?' She knew a moment of stabbing anxiety and in the next second recognised that it was not dread of some accident he might have had, but of her own involvement if he was in trouble.

'Not to my knowledge,' Marsh replied. He went on to explain his interest in Louise Vaughan.

'Oh, I see. That was dreadful. Poor girl,' said Brenda. 'He was fond of her. He said it broke him up. He couldn't understand how such a thing could happen in a place like Feringham.'

'Such things can happen anywhere,' said Marsh. 'Does he talk about her much?'

'No. In fact, I didn't know about her until we went to see his parents. He wanted to warn me in case I asked who it was in a photograph or if they mentioned her at all. It happened before I came to this area. Didn't you have any idea of who had done it?'

'Not a one,' said Marsh. 'No leads at all. All the usual dubious characters were investigated but there was no reason to suspect any of them.' He did not mention Tom Francis and the tough time the police had given him. It had had to happen; routine procedure was to eliminate possible perpetrators close to base before a wider net was cast even if, in the process, the trail to the real villain grew cold.

'She was never found, Malcolm said.'

'That's right,' said Marsh. 'It happens, though not very often, I'm pleased to say.'

'She might turn up one day. Her – her body, I mean.'

'Yes. Some years ago a missing woman's body was found when a lake was dragged during a search for someone else who'd gone missing,' Marsh informed her.

'So that one was tidied up?'

'It was.'

'That could happen again.'

'Yes.'

'Malcolm wasn't living in Selbury then. He was just back from Australia and had a flat in Cornton.'

'Yes.'

Why had she told him that? She had answered a question he hadn't asked. Was it to reassure herself?

'I can't tell you where he is now,' she stated. 'Maybe selling a car.'

She would not suggest that he might be in a bar with people he thought of as his cronies, but who only hung round him because he was an easy touch for free drinks. He said it was a good way to pick up business. Much of his trade was with youngsters; they were the ones who bought used cars now, or women, Brenda thought wryly, for so many men had cars as part of their jobs. Some women did, too, she had to admit, and she ran her small Citroen on her company account.

'How's he doing?' asked Marsh.

'You'll have to ask him,' she said. 'We're not in business together. We're just friends.' She smiled at Marsh, a stocky man with dark hair receding above a creased forehead. It must be sad to lose your hair; she wouldn't like hers to fall out. With this reflection she tossed her auburn curls, which she wore tied back in the office but which now tumbled unrestricted about her shoulders.

The gesture unsettled Marsh. She was a good-looking lady. How had a failure like Malcolm Vaughan managed to make it with her?

'Forgive me – you've a mortgage?' he asked.

'Yes.'

'Does Malcolm Vaughan pay it?'

'Whatever gave you that idea?' She laughed harshly. 'Certainly not.'

So Malcolm had lied. What he had done once, he could do again.

'Tell him I called, will you?' Marsh asked her.

'Do you want him to come and see you?'

'No. I'll find him myself, another time,' said Marsh. 'There's no hurry.'

When he had gone, Brenda felt uneasy. Why this revived interest after so long? The poor girl had been dead, if not officially buried, for twelve years; the police were not going to discover new clues now, unless they found her body.

Malcolm couldn't have known anything more about it than he'd told her. He'd been driving a taxi then, a temporary arrangement till he started up some business of his own, he'd said, and he had taken a fare to Heathrow that night. You would remember something like that, she supposed: whatever you were doing while your sister was murdered.

She shivered. Murder! That wasn't an everyday thing at all, not something everyone had to cope with like work and marriage and money and sex.

There had been his marriage. Malcolm had told her nothing about it except that they had been too young to know what they were doing and were not right for one another, which was true of a good few couples. She had been sympathetic; her own husband had walked out on her, preferring someone else. But suppose Malcolm had knocked Gwynneth about? It wasn't impossible; he could be quite aggressive and she had sometimes found it exciting, but he'd gone too far once or twice and she had stopped him.

What if she failed, some time? What if he really beat her up?

He had a very jealous nature: she knew that. One night when they were out together a man she knew had chatted her up while Malcolm bought their drinks. Seeing the man put his arm around her, Malcolm had been furious; he had smouldered at her and squared up to the man, who had laughed and backed off. She'd been annoyed; she wasn't Malcolm's property. He'd taken quite a time to simmer down, and subsequently she had noticed that his face would redden if she exchanged more than a few words with another man; he

146

would start to speak aggressively and would move close to her, touch her, act the owner. She hadn't liked it and she had told him so.

What if he was jealous of his sister in some way? There could be dozens of reasons. For one thing, she was the real child of their parents, and for another she seemed to have been good at most things, where he had clearly failed to make his mark. In any case, jealousy need not be rational; often it was quite unjustified.

This was ridiculous. He'd had nothing to do with the death of his sister; such an idea was quite impossible and he had had an alibi for the time in question. She was letting that policeman's interest get to her and give her silly notions. All the same, when Malcolm at last came in, it was still on her mind.

By that time, she had begun preparing a meal for herself. Usually they ate together, often out, but her budget did not run to many restaurant meals. If Malcolm paid, it made up for the fact that he contributed nothing to the mortgage and very little to the housekeeping, so she had no qualms about letting him settle the bill, always charged to one or other of his credit cards. He had this grand way with him which at first she had rather enjoyed, as if he had a bottomless bank balance. It was the way to get on; she had begun her own business with an assumed air of confidence which now, since she was succeeding, had become natural. She had an increasing register of firms for whom she found employees; she took trouble to suit both parties and her name was good with staff and companies, but her continuing success depended on keeping everything going and she employed only one other woman, also divorced and with two school-aged children. Brenda allowed her to work flexible hours so that she was able to collect the children after school, and during the holidays let her go, engaging a temporary helper for that period. As a result, she had a loyal and contented

147

assistant but was very busy herself. She had recently embarked on talks with local firms about improving arrangements for working mothers, either by introducing child-care facilities or fitting in with school hours; it had to be done, for there was a shortage of skilled staff in the area where new businesses were opening all the time, and a vast supply of potential workers was restricted by such problems. Brenda herself did not like the idea of young children wandering around the town waiting for their mothers to return; some could be trusted to let themselves in, find something to eat, turn on the ubiquitous baby-sitter, the television, and remain in reasonable safety on their own. Others got bored and wandered out in search of something to do, and those were the ones at risk from other people, whether older youngsters leading them astray, or worse.

Brenda hoped to change things, and she meant her business to expand. If Malcolm had problems, whether debts or connected with his sister, she could, by association, be affected.

She'd have to think about it seriously.

Malcolm, when he arrived, had brought a bottle of burgundy.

'What's for dinner?' he cried, bursting into the kitchen exhaling whisky fumes.

'Well, I'm having chicken,' said Brenda. She had taken a chicken breast out of the freezer and was preparing it with the dregs of some white white left over in an almost empty bottle and a few grapes out of the fruit bowl.

'Surely there's some for me too?' Malcolm halted, his face falling into sulky lines.

'There was only one piece left,' said Brenda. 'And I didn't know your plans.' Then she relented. 'There's a lasagne in the freezer,' she said. Thank goodness for the microwave which came to the rescue at such moments.

'That'll do,' said Malcolm, genial again. He opened the bottle and poured two glasses of wine.

'You can lay the table,' Brenda told him.

'Done,' said Malcolm.

He was in a good mood; perhaps he had sold a car. This was how he had been when they first got together, full of charm and easy to please, but with a tough streak which appealed to her. She had not held out against him very long, for living without sex was frustrating. Brenda did not subscribe to the view that any partner was better than none, but when she learned that Malcolm's flat lease had expired – a less than accurate description of his accommodation problem – she was ready to suggest he should move in for a while. Now she was going to tell him to move on.

Malcolm had sold the Jaguar that afternoon. He whistled as he set the table and he even scrubbed a potato to add to his lasagne.

'A policeman was here today, asking about you,' Brenda reported when they were sitting at the table. His lasagne steamed beside the large potato and a pile of green beans.

'A policeman? Why?' Malcolm looked immediately alarmed.

'Why should you worry? Your conscience is clear, isn't it?' said Brenda, in a teasing tone. 'Or have you been up to something I don't know about?'

'It's not a joking matter. What did he want?' Malcolm leaned across the table and grabbed her wrist, squeezing it painfully. 'Tell me,' he said. His face had gone that ugly shade of red and he was glaring at her, his eyes turned to hard blue pebbles.

'Let go my arm,' said Brenda.

'Not till you explain.' He gripped it harder and as

she tried to wrench free, between them they knocked over one of the glasses of wine.

'Oh, hell,' said Brenda. 'Now look what you've done!'

'Leave it.' Still Malcolm held her wrist. 'Why did a policeman want me?'

'I'm not telling you until you let me go,' said Brenda. She picked up her knife and made as if to stab his hand. Before she could do so, he released her.

'Bitch,' he said.

Brenda was trembling. She stood up and fetched a cloth to wipe up the spilled wine. It had spread into a wide pool but it had not dripped on to the carpet. She mopped at it carefully, not wanting him to see that she was frightened and was very near to tears.

'It was Superintendent Marsh,' she said. 'He was asking about your sister.'

'Oh, that.' Malcolm sat back. 'Why couldn't you say so?' He tried to speak calmly; giving way to panic might lead to other revelations.

'What else could it be about?' she demanded. 'Is there another reason for the police to be interested in you?' There was no teasing in her voice now.

'Of course not. How could there be?' he blustered.

But there must be something; why else would he be so upset?

'He said he'd find you sometime,' Brenda said. 'It can't be urgent.'

Malcolm had resumed his meal.

'That's up to him,' he said, affecting calm.

Why had he reacted so vehemently? Had he been up to some trickery at work, fiddling his book-keeping, dodging the VAT? Brenda had parried Marsh's question but she knew his business was not doing well; she had gone round to the workshop recently to collect her own car, which he was servicing to save her a garage bill, and while he was just finishing what he was doing

150

to it, she had gone into his office to wait. Curious, she had opened a drawer of his desk and had seen the bills and threatening letters.

She had said nothing, going into his washroom to prink in the mirror, and flushing the lavatory so that he would not suspect her of prying. She didn't think the police served writs; those were civil actions and private detectives did it for their clients.

'Well, I've told you, anyway,' she said. She cleared away her half-eaten chicken, all appetite now gone. What should she do? She couldn't turn him out tonight, so late; that would be too harsh. Besides, he was so touchy, he might blow up and get really violent. For the first time she felt afraid of him and she went upstairs before the *News at Ten*.

This was no way to live. He had to go, and soon.

She contemplated locking the bedroom door, but he would be capable of knocking it down if she did. Stories she had heard from other women came into her mind to reinforce her fears. Her own former husband had not been violent, only unfaithful; in fact he was rather a gentle sort of person, too quiet for her, and his escapade into adultery had surprised her by its boldness.

Malcolm did not come upstairs. She lay cringing in the big bed, fearful that he would lumber in wanting sex, but he had had a lot to drink and might find the wish exceeded the performance, as someone had remarked. It had happened before and he got angry every time.

After a while she heard sounds from below and then the front door banged. A few moments later his car started up outside; there was no mistaking the Porsche as it roared away. Brenda went downstairs and locked the house, pushing bolts across and putting up the chain so that he could not return. Let him spend the night in his workshop; he'd done it often enough before he moved in with her; he had a folding bed and sleeping-bag.

Malcolm had been briefly frightened himself when he held Brenda's arm so fiercely and felt hate and rage welling up within him. This was how he had felt when he met Louise that last night. Brenda had made him very angry with her taunting talk of the policeman's visit. What were they up to? What did they know? He'd told them about Richard Blacker; that should have given them something to think about, a line of inquiry to follow. Wasn't that how they phrased it?

He'd often hurt Louise. He'd enjoyed it, grown excited when he saw that look of fear on her face. It had been the same with Gwynneth, and with other women, but tonight was the first time he'd seen Brenda with the same expression. Making women fearful gave him a sense of power, but he liked it, too, when they smiled at him, were impressed by the good manners and unbounded charm he could turn on so easily. He despised them for their gullibility.

He drove away from Brenda's house because he did not know how to play the next scene. To recover his self-confidence, he began explaining to himself that she had provoked him, leading him on, not telling him quickly what Marsh wanted, just as Gwynneth made him lose his temper when she looked at him with those large woebegone eyes spilling tears. A man liked a bit of spirit, and Brenda had plenty; meeting her, he had been instantly attracted, and when he discovered that she owned her own house and was living alone he made haste to let her know his feelings. She was a looker and available, and she posed a challenge. Malcolm thought he could have any woman he fancied; he had been successful enough to bolster this conceit, but he had never been capable of sustaining a relationship.

152

Look at Louise. What made her so po-faced about it? They were not related by blood, after all. If she expected preferential treatment from George and Susan because she was their own child, then she couldn't suddenly decide that getting together with him was against nature. Those were the words she had used, trying to fend him off, struggling as he tussled with her.

Well, he had got what he was after, not that it was anything so great, but it meant he had won, had beaten her.

Susan never suspected a thing. Even when she had caught him on the landing, she'd never given it a thought. That generation was so bloody ignorant, or people like George and Susan were, insulated by money and possessions from what went on in the real world. All her life Susan had been sheltered, living in that one large house for nearly the whole of it. She hadn't a clue.

With Louise out of the way, he'd expected her to turn to him all the more, and in a way she had. There was no one else in the running now, unless a ghost could be a rival. There would be her money, too, when she and George were dead. With that he could set up elsewhere, start again with adequate finance at last, open a leisure centre or a sports club; that was the coming thing, swimming-pools and gyms. In his mind he anticipated inheriting at least a million pounds.

Malcolm now owed over fifty thousand pounds on unpaid bills, his mortgage, and interest to money-lenders he had used to keep some of his creditors quiet. His bookie's account, seven hundred, was the least of his worries. He owed over a thousand pounds to a filling station. He used a lot of petrol, driving about as he did, picking up cars.

He decided to go for a drive, alarm Brenda by staying

out for a couple of hours. She'd be glad enough, after that, when he returned.

He drove over to Cornton where he went into The Bear and Ragged Staff, getting there just before it closed. He downed three drinks in rapid time, then drove around the town. It was too early to go home. No police car came up behind him as he weaved his way back to Malchester, and luckily no hapless third party crossed his dangerous path. By the time he reached Brenda's house his belligerent mood had gone and he was almost maudlin, ready to beg her forgiveness. Very occasionally he had done this with other women, not deliberately as a tactic but because it happened naturally. They had always come round, cradling him in their arms, acting the mother, but he hadn't tried it yet with Brenda.

He didn't want to break with her. Where was he to go? He'd be on his own again, and he had no money to rent a flat. Even he couldn't be expected to find someone else to move in with overnight. What a pity it was too late to buy her some flowers. Still, he'd do that tomorrow, an enormous bouquet, the best Bloomers could provide.

When he reached her house and blundered his way out of the car, he had difficulty opening the gate, focusing on it carefully, elaborately raising the latch, pushing. He met resistance, some obstacle that blocked the path. Malcolm leaned down and felt the hard shape of a suitcase. There was a second beside it, and a heap of carrier bags.

The bitch! The trollop! Malcolm called Brenda every name he knew, aloud, kicking at the bundles, as he took in the fact that she had packed up his things and left them on the path.

Upstairs, sitting with her hand on the telephone ready to call the police if he made a scene, Brenda listened to him swearing. Instead of returning to bed after she locked up, she had rushed round the house collecting everything that she could find of his, stuffing them into his cases and into plastic carriers, heaving them out on to the path as quickly as she could before he could come back. Then she had locked up again.

The swearing stopped. She heard the car start up again. He hadn't loaded his cases; there hadn't been time. But he'd gone; that was enough for now.

In the morning, very early, she ordered a taxi, and when it arrived she paid the driver to deliver Malcolm's possessions at his workshop, and to dump them on the forecourt if he was not there.

She thought he would be. Where else could he go? Even Malcolm wouldn't have run back to his mother in the night.

But he had.

It was after one o'clock in the morning when Malcolm arrived at the Lodge House. It was his true home, wasn't it?

There was a bed in the spare room; it should by right be his except that the room was too small for anyone other than a child. He might demand to live at home, see that Norah moved. But what if she really was his mother? What then? How could she be punished?

He drove out to Selbury in a mood that swung from maudlin misery to obsessive rage as he thought about the twists of chance that had ordered his existence. Some primitive sense of self-preservation kept him hugging the kerb and travelling at a steady pace, only speeding up when he came into the village. Luck, also, kept police cars off the roads that he was using. He was about to blow the horn when he turned in at the Lodge House gates, just as he always did arriving there in daylight, when the darkness of the house reminded him of the time. Well, he'd got his key. He'd let himself

155

in as he had so often done at the big house. He cut the engine and hauled himself out of the driver's seat; then, his bladder bursting, he urinated extravagantly against the wall beside the front door. There was more to the action than simply physical relief; the gesture made a territorial statement. Then he selected the appropriate key from the bunch which included those to the workshop and Brenda's place.

Norah, not yet asleep, heard the door open and at once knew who it must be, even as she picked up the stout stick she kept in her bedroom in case of intruders. She put on her dressing-gown and bedroom slippers and stepped out on to the landing, knocking on George's door and opening it, turning on his light.

'George,' she called softly. 'There's someone in the house. I think it's Malcolm.'

She did not wait for him to answer but went quickly down the stairs, her stick at the ready, just in case. Thieves could catch them out, because neither she nor George would ever suspect a nocturnal visitor of being anyone but Malcolm, so conditioned were they to his sudden unwelcome appearances.

He was in the drawing-room, pouring himself a large whisky from the decanter on the drinks tray.

'Well, what's happened now?' Norah demanded, dismayed to find that she was trembling. She must be getting old.

'I need a bed for the night,' said Malcolm. 'So naturally I came home.'

'Turned you out, has she?' Norah could not refrain from straight talk, but she managed not to add that she was not surprised. 'What's wrong with a hotel?'

'Costs money,' Malcolm said. 'And I've a cash-flow problem at the moment. Besides, where should a fellow go but to his mother?' He drained his glass and filled it again.

'Keep your voice down,' Norah said. 'Let Susan

sleep, if you've any feeling for her at all. You've brought enough worry to her, as if she hadn't plenty to cope with already.'

'I said my mother should help me,' said Malcolm and he lurched towards her, an odd look in his face. 'My real mother,' he added.

'Don't be silly,' Norah said. 'How can she help you? We don't know where she is.'

'Don't we?' Malcolm advanced further. 'What about you? You're my mother. You had a baby and he was adopted. You're my real mother.'

As he said this, he advanced further and Norah shrank away from him, horror on her face.

'Don't say such things,' she gasped.

'Good of the Vaughans, wasn't it?' he continued, snarling now. 'Rescued you, didn't they, taking me in when they were wanting a son?'

Norah regained control.

'You don't know what you're talking about,' she said. Would George never come? 'I had no son.'

'No, because you gave him away,' said Malcolm.

'God help you if you think that,' said George, coming into the room and moving close to Norah. 'Your mother's name was on your birth certificate; you know that. Jane Frost. Father unknown.'

'It's easy to give yourself a false name, registering a birth,' said Malcolm.

'She was a farmer's daughter,' George answered. 'You were born in Yorkshire. You can try to find her if you want to. There are societies to help you.' Poor woman, he briefly thought. They'd been told she came of good country stock, a healthy girl, and probably the father was some local married man; anyway, she wasn't saying. If Malcolm traced her now, he would truly be a chicken come home to roost.

'Lies, all lies,' said Malcolm. 'Norah had a baby.

157

I'm him. It all adds up – why she's kept so close to you all these years. Doesn't make sense otherwise.'

Norah had recovered, shock replaced by icy rage.

'I got pregnant,' she told him. 'I had an abortion. It was during the war, years before you were born. I was seventeen years old.'

'It's easy for you to say that,' Malcolm sneered. 'You can't prove it.'

'I'm not in the habit of lying,' Norah remarked. 'Who have you cast as your father in this fantasy of yours?'

'I don't know.' Malcolm's laggard imagination had not carried him that far. He looked at George and opened his mouth.

'No, Malcolm,' George intervened. 'I am not your father, but you have been my son in every way except biologically. You've had every opportunity in life, help when you've been in trouble; too much, perhaps, for your own good. You've made Susan ill with worry about you when she's had quite enough to bear already. I'm not going to allow you to disturb her now. I'm going to drive you back to Malchester, as you're obviously unfit to drive yourself, and I wouldn't wish you on that young woman in your present condition so I'll take you to your workshop. Give me your keys.'

He held out his hand and, faced with his authority, Malcolm crumpled. Like an automaton, he handed them over.

Norah, looking at George for the first time since he had entered the room, saw that he had put on trousers and a sweater. How sensible of him.

If Susan had heard them, she would have been downstairs by now; with luck she would not waken; she often took a pill.

'I'll follow and bring you back,' she said.

'Thanks,' said George, who had known that this was how she would react. A few things in life were certainties. 'A note for Susan, maybe? Just in case she wakes and comes downstairs? We're helping a motorist in trouble, perhaps?'

She nodded.

'Put on something warm,' George told her. 'I'll drop Malcolm and meet you at the Baptist Church.'

They would be gone some time; best part of two hours if the expedition went without a hitch. Norah watched George march Malcolm out of the house and then she went upstairs to dress. Before leaving, she listened outside Susan's door; all was quiet.

She left the note on the kitchen table. If Susan woke she sometimes made herself a cup of tea or a milky drink, refusing to have a kettle or a thermos in her room. She said that walking about the house settled her, and in the summer she would go into the garden, sitting in the stillness sniffing the jasmine or the night-scented stock and other plants she grew for their sweet smell. Poor Susan; she was one of the walking wounded.

But aren't we all, thought Norah fiercely, even Malcolm. She was glad that it was George who was tackling the Porsche, not her; she backed her own car quietly out of the garage and set off in pursuit.

She had to wait some time for George.

She parked, as arranged, outside the red brick Victorian church round the corner from the workshop. Posters exhorting her to put her trust in the Lord and fear no man and to walk hand in hand with Jesus frowned down at her from framed billboards beside the gate. Much good that did you if a gang of muggers went for you, she thought. The world had always been a savage place and turning the other cheek only invited fresh attack. What chance had Louise had, the night she was abducted? A good course of self-defence, taught to every schoolgirl, might save some, but not if they were out-numbered by an evil mob.

George would be talking to Malcolm, she supposed, trying to win something positive from this disastrous incident. Or perhaps Malcolm had finally passed out and George was putting him to bed; she knew there was a camp bed in the office. Susan was greatly troubled by thinking that he might sometimes have to use it.

Norah had a chronic dread that one day he would carry out some act so grave that no one would be able to protect him from the consequences. Maybe it would be the best thing: a spell inside Brixton or Wandsworth might pull him up, make him take a grip on himself, and at least it would keep him out of circulation for a time. But Susan would take it all on herself, see it as her failure, want to go prison-visiting.

She had been sitting there making herself thoroughly depressed by this line of thought for about ten minutes when a police patrol car drove slowly past her, stopped a short distance ahead and then reversed towards her. A youthful uniformed officer got out and approached.

Oh dear, thought Norah, winding down her window, ready to be ingratiating though she was committing no crime. Still, older women did not customarily park in urban streets in the small hours of the morning.

'Good evening, madam. Anything wrong?' asked the officer, shining his torch into her eyes and making her blink.

'No, not at all. I'm waiting for someone,' Norah answered.

At her age, she couldn't be a prostitute waiting for a punter, could she? The young officer pondered it, eyeing her, a woman of sixty, give or take a few years, with bright brown eyes and an alert face innocent of make-up. Still, you never knew.

'And who would that be?' Police Constable Perry inquired.

'My employer,' said Norah curtly. 'My name is Norah Tyler and I am housekeeper to Mr and Mrs Vaughan at the Lodge House, Selbury.'

Selbury. That was thirty miles away or more.

'I see, madam,' said the constable equably while he wondered what her employer was doing while she waited. 'May I see your driving licence, please?'

'I'm sorry, I haven't got it with me,' Norah answered.

'And where is your – er – employer?' Perry doggedly pressed on.

'Mr Vaughan has just driven his son home after a visit,' Norah said. 'He – the son – wasn't feeling very well.'

'Mr Vaughan junior does not live in the Baptist Church,' said Perry with some confidence.

'No, but we agreed this would be a good place for me to wait, near a light and where I would not be harassed,' said Norah firmly.

Enlightenment dawned on the constable.

'Would it be Mr Vaughan junior who runs the used-car business in Sebastopol Road?'

'That's correct,' said Norah.

'Hm. And he's unwell?'

'Yes, but it's nothing serious.' Norah did not want to prejudice the constable. 'Nothing that need concern you. I'm sure you've more important things to see to.'

'I'll just ask you to give me your full name and address,' said Perry, nettled by this remark. 'And you must take your driving licence and certificate of insurance to a police station within seven days.'

'If you say so,' Norah replied. 'But what offence am I committing? There's no parking restriction here.'

George came round the corner to see Norah standing on the pavement, breathing into a breathalyser.

Luckily she had been at home that evening and had had only a glass of sherry before dinner and one glass of light white wine; had she been to Myra's, she might have had a gin and much more wine. George had certainly drunk two glasses of wine, maybe a third; would there have been time for that to clear his bloodstream? It would be just like life for one of them to be clobbered for protecting Malcolm.

Perry had not meant to get in so deep over this, once he recognised that Norah was, apparently, harmless. After all, she didn't look like a car thief, and he could soon check out the vehicle which she had said was hers. But you had to stay in charge of the situation or lose face, and she had needled him. Besides, finding such a person in such a spot at such an hour was, to say the least, unusual.

Norah cast George a desperate glance as she exhaled into the machine. Perry carefully inspected the result.

'Good evening, officer.' George spoke calmly. 'Miss Tyler is waiting for me. I don't think the car is causing an obstruction, is it?'

'No, sir,' said Perry, now heartily wishing himself elsewhere for Norah's test showed her well below the limit.

'I hadn't got my licence,' Norah said.

'Well, I've got mine,' said George, taking his wallet from his jacket pocket. He had automatically picked it up before leaving; money might be needed before the night was over.

The constable scrutinised George's licence, a blameless document bearing no endorsement. 'Detective Superintendent Marsh, at Feringham, knows me well,' he added. 'And Miss Tyler, too. I'm sure he'll vouch for us when you make your report.'

'That won't be necessary, sir,' said Perry, daunted by the name of Marsh, whose area included this division. 'I'm sure everything is in order.'

'Do you still want me to bring my licence round?' Norah asked in dulcet tones.

162

'No,' said Perry, giving in. 'Not under the circumstances.'

What circumstances, wondered Norah: their acquaintance with the superintendent?

'Well, if that's all, then we'll be off,' said George briskly, holding the driver's door open so that Norah could resume her seat. 'Good night, officer.'

'Good night, sir,' said Perry, backing off as George walked round the car to the passenger's side.

'Let him go first,' warned George as the policeman strode back to his car, swaggering slightly to make himself seem the victor. 'He'll want to get away without making a worse idiot of himself, but if we do the least little thing wrong he'll be on to us like a hawk.'

'Have you no confidence in me, George?' asked Norah. 'I, who drove three-ton lorries in the service of His Majesty?'

'I've got two hundred per cent confidence in you, my dear,' said George. 'But none in our luck holding out until we get home. I won't offer to drive in case there's one of that young fellow's pals lined up to ambush us. We know you're in the clear, and I may not be.'

Their route lay away from the abbey and the old part of the town, not enough of which, people thought, had been protected from planners who tore down old warehouses and shops, and built fortressed towns to enclose new stores and supermarkets and covered malls. They went down residential streets, past sleeping houses veiled in darkness punctuated by tall street-lamps. The night was fine and clear with only a few wispy clouds occasionally crossing the sliver of moon, and, as they progressed into the country, dark trees stretched black skeletonic branches in silhouette against the sky. When the headlights touched them, boughs and hedges turned brown or grey, with the faded winter green of grass verges beneath. Their jour-

163

ney was uneventful; no police car pounced on them from a side road.

'What took you so long?' Norah asked at last.

'I had to clean him up,' said George. 'He was being sick. I couldn't leave him to choke on that. Difficult to explain to Susan. Or to the coroner.'

'I see,' said Norah.

'It's never going to go away,' said George.

'You mean Malcolm?'

'Yes. The worry of him. We can't wash our hands of him.'

'You can only do so much,' said Norah, as she had said to George on countless occasions, and even to Susan too.

'He's capable of doing something really dreadful.' George echoed Norah's thought. 'There's so much latent violence there, and his thinking is so warped. If he hadn't been so drunk tonight, who knows what he might have done?'

'Where did he get the idea that I was his mother?' Norah asked. It had been in her mind since he had made the accusation. 'How did he know I'd had a child?'

She had told George herself, in a weak moment after they became lovers over twenty years ago, when he took her out one evening in London. Often before, they'd been to a theatre together; this time they went back to her flat, and it set the pattern for their rare meetings afterwards, always when Susan was busy with something to do with her mother or the children. She had not told him who the father was; Norah still protected David, as his mother and sister had done. Why else was the child aborted?

If Susan had adopted him – or her – things might have been so different; Malcolm might never have entered the family. But the other Malcolm, Susan's brother, was still alive then; he was to have produced the heirs.

She had told George that the father was someone she had met and fallen for when she was young and silly; she knew Susan would never have betrayed her brother's secret, even to George.

'A random shot,' he had said, seeing no point in adding what he still thought: that it was a pity she hadn't had her child, for it might have inherited her spirit and, if adopted, have been a blessing to its new family.

'He must be very disturbed about his antecedents,' Norah said. 'Maybe he ought to find out all about them. Face his past.'

'He might have heard some talk in the village.' George was still beavering away at the source of Malcolm's allegation. 'There must have been some, after all.'

'I doubt it,' Norah said. 'I was in the factory then, though I still lived at Selbury. It was all over and done with before there was time for people to suspect anything. Susan and her mother saw to that, and I'm absolutely certain they would not have told a soul.'

'What a time you must have had,' George said. 'Poor little kid. Only seventeen.' He reached out and patted her knee with easy familiarity, wondering as he did so if they would ever go to bed together again. Neither could be said to be filled with ardour now, but some human closeness would be rather pleasant. He sighed a little, recognising that they were excellent friends.

Norah spared a hand from the steering-wheel to press his as it lay on her thigh. She was very fond of George.

What a ridiculous pair we would seem to anyone observing us, she thought; what an extraordinary way we have spent the best part of the night.

*

They were very quiet when they returned to the Lodge House, but Susan heard them.

She had woken as Norah drove away, mildly puzzled by the sound but soon settling back again. For some time after hearing the car start up outside she lay warm in bed, drowsy with sedative, seeking sleep. The radio that helped Norah during bouts of insomnia was no aid to Susan; she preferred silence. She cast her mind into the past, something she now did more and more, trying to evade the present, lying there half-dozing in the clean square room with its print curtains, its button-back chair and some of her mother's good furniture, pretending that she was a child and Mabel would come in with her hot water. Those brass cans and sets of washstand china – bowls and jugs and carafes – were collectors' items now. So much had changed, and not always for the better; Norah, for example, could not be expected to do all that once Mabel had done for Susan. Shopping, she thought, turning her mind in a less personal direction; no supermarkets then, but Mr Dobbs himself sitting in the kitchen writing down the order and delivering requirements several times a week. Now it was Sainsbury's for what could not be obtained from Mr Dobbs' latest successor in the village, where Susan still felt obliged to deal. There had been other sorts of shopping: trips to London with her mother, to Debenham and Freebody's, and Harrods where they went for gloves apart from other things; you rested your elbow on the counter while an assistant fitted on the glove, having first dusted it inside with talc and stretched the fingers with a type of tong. No one bought gloves like that now; indeed, people rarely wore gloves at all except in cold weather, and even Royal personages were to be seen with their hands in their pockets.

No one does things for other people now, Susan lamented; service has become a dirty word. We put our own petrol in our cars; machines perform functions once carried out by humans and thousands are out of work. Thousands more are isolated because they are denied trivial daily encounters, and at night people sit at home, often alone, watching television instead of going out because city streets are dangerous and it is difficult to park.

We help each other here, though, she accepted; or rather, George and Norah both help me. With the clarity of small-hour perception, she saw that she did little, if she ever had, for them.

This realisation shocked her into total wakefulness and she had to get up. That was another tiresomeness of being older; if you woke in the night, sooner or later you had to visit the bathroom. Afterwards she went downstairs, very quietly so that she would not disturb the others, not listening to the part of her mind which told her that the car she had heard was no passer-by but had left from here. She would make a drink and maybe take another pill; it wouldn't matter if she slept late in the morning; she had no appointment.

She saw Norah's note and, reading it, understood that they had both gone out, leaving her alone.

Susan didn't like that. She put the kettle on and paced about in her long quilted satin dressing gown with the warm lining. How had they got involved in a Good Samaritan act? It must have been someone from Selbury House who was in difficulties, and bossy Norah had dragged George into a rescue operation instead of leaving it to other people. Norah always had to be involved; she could never leave well alone. Cross, Susan found a cup and saucer, then a tiny teapot; let Norah clear it all away in the morning: that would show her. Only by degrees did Susan allow herself to deduce that the stranded motorist had been Malcolm and that they were taking him home, for it was the only solution that made sense. George would have made a different plan for a stranger.

167

What was wrong? Was Malcolm hurt?

She wrote various scenarios in her mind, sitting there at the table, glad of the warmth from the Aga, waiting for their return. She drank a cup of tea, and then another; finally, she admitted to herself the folly of her vigil, brooding like an avenging angel ready to expose whatever deception George had devised to save her pain. She would leave it till the morning, trap them with questions at breakfast, find out what Malcolm had been doing. She had a right to know; she was his mother.

Only she wasn't.

What would her own little Harry have been like if he had lived? She often wondered that, and it was easy to endow him with every virtue. He might have grown up confident and boastful, like her elder brother, or more like his father. She had scarcely known Hugh except as a charming, romantic figure who made her feel good because he was handsome and had excellent manners. In truth, what had they in common? He was a friend of the Spencers and it was there, playing tennis one summer's day a year before war was declared, that she had met him. They had met again at various dances and more tennis parties, and after that, as a Territorial officer, he had been called up. There had been many hasty marriages in the war, people snatching at what they thought was love from dread of what lay ahead, although everyone thought the war would be over in months.

Susan cleared away her tea-things to leave no trace of her recent presence in the kitchen. Then she went back to bed where the electric blanket had kept it warm and snug.

How ignorant we were, she thought, and remembered a visit she and George had made to Hugh's grave not so very long ago. It was George who had been the more overtly upset as they toured the long lines of symmetrical tombstones in the vast cemetery, a beautiful and peaceful place. Were they truly Hugh's bones under that particular patch of soil? An enemy soldier had doubtless given him his first swift burial, a man no better and no worse than Hugh but one opposed to him by a mere accident of birth. If he had lived, he might have returned from the war physically or mentally maimed, and how would she have coped with that? Or, if he had escaped all wounds, would their marriage have become an uneasy truce between two polite people preserving a façade, as was so common in their generation? Younger couples were not prepared to settle for so little and shopped about optimistically for other partners, often ending up no happier.

She did not want to know if George had ever been unfaithful. If so, he had been discreet. Their secure life together mattered to them both and they were bound by troubles shared.

While Susan's thoughts ran thus, Norah had turned the Golf in at the gate and driven into the garage. She cut the engine and the pair of them sat there for a moment, silent, collecting themselves. They got out of the car together and she waited for George while he closed the garage; then they entered the house together, very quietly, closing the door with barely a sound. George poured himself a stiff tot of whisky and Norah put a mug of milk to heat up in the microwave, so neither of them touched the kettle to discover from its warmth that it had been boiled quite recently. Norah's note was still on the table; Susan could not have wakened.

They stepped softly up the carpeted stairs past her door, parting outside George's, where he leaned across and lightly kissed Norah's soft, familiar lips. If Susan had witnessed that tiny moment, she would have been astounded and quite uncomprehending; the idea that George might feel anything other than a comradely affection for Norah, born of their long acquaintance, would never have occurred to her.

Glad they were back, sure they had resolved Malcolm's immediate problem in the wisest way and that it would be time enough for her to learn about it in the morning, she snuggled down under her duvet and, eventually, drifted off to sleep.

After parting from George and Norah, Police Constable Perry continued his patrol through the town. Officers usually went in pairs at night, but his station was shorthanded with two men off sick and another hurt in a fracas with drunken hooligans at the weekend, so he was alone. He had been right to question the woman. She could have been waiting for an accomplice who was involved in some felony in the area, or, more probably, in view of her age and appearance, she could have been having mechanical trouble with her vehicle. Their interview had got out of hand because of her manner, and it did not do to lose face.

Perry knew Malcolm Vaughan both by sight and by repute. One of Perry's colleagues had bought a Vauxhall Astra from him and it had been a success, fairly priced and in excellent order. Driving through the centre of Malchester, Perry brooded. He stopped two youths who were walking along the street and demanded to know where they had been and where they were going. They had been visiting friends, said the youths, and were on their way home. It was credible; they were not drunk. Perry told them to watch it and sent them on their way, feeling frustrated. It would have been good to find someone flouting the law, bring off a coup, restore his morale and earn a commendation from his sergeant.

It was odd that old Vaughan had taken his son back to the workshop, seeing that he was ill. Why hadn't he been put to bed at home or taken back to wherever he lived? Surely he did not reside at his business premises?

Perry completed a circuit of the shopping area where break-ins were easy because most upper floors, once flats, were now offices and deserted at night. As people retreated, crime advanced in city centres, and Perry was too young to remember a time when there were plenty of people about such streets after the working day was over. He turned off and went round a housing estate, emerging again near the Baptist Church but facing the opposite way so that it was easy to turn into Sebastopol Road and draw up outside Vaughan's Reliable Cars.

A number of vehicles were parked on the forecourt; Perry got out of his Escort and walked towards them. There was an old Triumph Vitesse, a blue Metro and a Maestro as well as a Porsche. All, except the Porsche, bore price tags. Perry touched the Porsche's bonnet. It felt cool, but the engine might still be warm. He circled it critically but could see nothing wrong, shining his torch on the tyres, which were good. The car bore a valid tax disc. He supposed the man Vaughan had trade plates to use if he took a car he was selling on the road, to cover its licence. He went up to the work-shop, an unlovely concrete building with galvanised folding doors, which he tried. They were firmly locked. Perry walked round to the pedestrian door let into a side wall; it had a Yale lock and was secure. There was a window beside it, a blind drawn down obscuring the glass. No light showed, and there was silence.

Perry banged hard on the door, reasoning that if Vaughan were inside and ill, an inquiry as to whether he needed help was only his duty.

There was no reply to his knock, so he thumped again, then went to the window and shone his torch on the blind, trying to peer past it, but he saw nothing. He rapped on the pane.

'Police,' he cried. 'Open up!'

After repeating this command several times and rapping again on the glass, a light went on and he heard bumps and bangs from within, then a groan. The blind went up with a snap and a man stood at the window, gazing out in a bemused way and blinking in the light from Perry's torch. Perry turned the beam towards his own uniformed chest and made gestures towards the door. After what seemed to him a very long time, and was, indeed, several minutes, it was opened, and Malcolm stood revealed, fully dressed apart from shoes and his tie.

'What's the matter?' he asked. He had sobered up considerably after his unpleasant interval in the washroom before George departed, but his head was throbbing and there was a familiar sour taste in his mouth. What did this bloody copper want? Had one of his cars been stolen? That was all he needed now.

'Are you all right, Mr Vaughan? I thought you might be ill,' said Perry. 'Seeing that you're still on the premises.'

How had the fellow known he was there? He hadn't left the light on. Malcolm was too fuddled to work out that he had been deliberately roused, only that something didn't quite fit.

'I'm quite all right, thank you,' he answered crossly. 'I'm entitled to spend the night here if I wish. There's no law against it.'

Perry hoped there might turn out to be some bye-law by which he could, on a future occasion, trap the man. He would leave the statement unchallenged now.

'I'll say good night, then,' he remarked, doused his torch and went back to his car. If he couldn't catch Vaughan over sleeping on the premises against some archaic rule or other, he'd watch out for him on the road; his breath had smelled horrible and the cause of his so-called illness was plain. His father had brought him back here because he was not fit to drive himself. It was an odd destination, though; the son must have a flat or a house somewhere, or at least a room. Perry would have to find out.

He cheered up at the prospect of discovering something which might not be quite how it ought to be, and the night was further enlivened when he was called to a break-in on the far side of the town, where he caught one of the miscreants trying to get away over a wall. Perry was young and fit, an advantage in a chase. He was elated with success when he took his captive into the station and charged him.

Malcolm had been in a stupor when the policeman woke him and now he had little memory of how he came to be spending the night in his office. Someone had put up the camp-bed and had found the sleeping bag, laying it over him. Someone had removed his shoes and his tie. Could it have been George? He seemed to remember a male voice, icy with anger that was being controlled by iron effort, directing him to move here, do this, do that, but it could have been a voice from the past.

He made himself some strong coffee and laced it with brandy. The hair of the dog, he thought, swallowing. The clock on the wall showed half-past three. What a time to be having a brush with the law, and what an extraordinary hour to be here. Why wasn't he tucked up warmly with Brenda in her comfortable bed? And why had that damned copper come nosing round?

Slowly, fuzzily, the night's events began to come back to him. Brenda had locked him out. Then he'd gone home to his parents. Confused images of Norah confronting him, then George, came into his mind. They'd turned him out, too; that was it. George had brought him here. The drink Malcolm had swallowed

173

rose in his throat as he remembered just making it to the lavatory, George pushing his head over the pan. He did not recall George sponging his face with cold water and helping him on to the bed, covering him over, finally leaving.

Sitting alone in his office chair, Malcolm was conscious of silence around him. A distant lorry changed gear, the sound a welcome break in the absence of noise. How could he bear to stay here until morning?

His radio stood on the desk. He switched it on and twiddled the knobs until he found speech, then lumbered back to his bed, lying there with the voice droning on in a foreign tongue until he lapsed into sleep again.

Next morning he showered and shaved and felt better, but he had no clean clothes to wear. Never mind. Brenda would have come to her senses by now and be ready to apologise for her conduct the night before. He'd pop round to give her the chance to do so before she went to the office.

He was searching for his keys, which George must have used both to drive the Porsche and to get into the office, when he heard a car draw up outside. He went out to find a taxi parked on the forecourt, the driver depositing two suitcases and a pile of carrier bags: his belongings.

Malcolm tipped the driver the last pound he had in his pocket, thanking him in a grand manner as though the man had done him a favour, then heaved the baggage inside. He was very angry.

So she'd done it. Damn her! Now he was really alone. Well, it wasn't the first time, but such periods had to be kept as brief as possible. Meanwhile, he couldn't stay here; it was uncomfortable and far too oppressive at night. He'd soon find another woman, and until he did, he'd check into a hotel. No need to pay with money; he'd use one of his plastic cards. Or perhaps not: there were other ways to evade the reckoning.

Malcolm found his keys in the top drawer of his desk among the pile of threatening letters and unpaid bills. He wondered if George had seen what they were, not that it made any difference; there would be no help from him. If only he could get himself straight, Malcolm thought for the umpteenth time; that was all he needed, just to have his debts cleared and the slate wiped clean, then make a fresh start without the fates turning against him, as, in the end, they always did.

Now, at last, he remembered why he had gone to the Lodge House and what he had said to Norah. Was she really speaking the truth when she denied being his mother? There was only her word for the fact that she was so young when she was pregnant. Of course she would give out that story, but somewhere in among her things there would be papers to prove what had really happened. She could have given a false name when she registered his birth; she could have agreed to the tale that she had had an abortion to maintain the fiction. All he had to do was get her out of the way and go through her possessions. Women were tremendous hoarders; look at all the stuff his grandmother had kept, piled into drawers and boxes. It had all been transported from the big house when she moved to the Lodge House; she had refused to destroy a thing. After her death Susan had had a colossal bonfire. She might not have burnt it all, however; there might be a diary or some other document which would prove the truth of his theory. Somewhere at the Lodge House there would be information he could use. The word blackmail did not come into Malcolm's mind as he slowly worked things out, but the prospect of money did; knowledge was money; people did not like old scandals being raked up and would pay to keep things quiet. When Norah was pregnant, abortion was illegal and so she would have had the child; he was sure he would find some way to prove it if he went through the papers he was certain to find at the Lodge House.

He'd go and search. He would have to find a time when they were all out, a day when Susan was at a lecture and George at a meeting. He could deal with Norah alone. In his scheming, he did not define what method of dealing he would employ, but she was not a large woman and he was strong. He would not allow her to stand in the way of his getting the evidence he had convinced himself existed. He forgot that even in nightdress and dressing-gown she had outfaced him during the night. He could lock her up, bind her and gag her, while he hunted for what he required. He could pose as a thief, wear a stocking mask and leave her tied up until George or Susan came home to release her. He had never liked her; now he would have his revenge.

He needed some breakfast. By rights he should be at Brenda's, drinking freshly perked coffee and eating toast and marmalade, though it was true he didn't fancy food at the moment. He made himself more instant coffee and poured in a further slug of brandy, and he was drinking it when a thin man in a fawn suit came to the door and served him a writ, another one, for an outstanding debt. This was from a finance company he had turned to when he had to keep other creditors quiet.

The money raised by selling the Jaguar had instantly gone to a solicitor who had succeeded in delaying two summonses. He had to lay hands on some more real money, in cash; not promises.

The Vaughans should provide it. They would pay anything to preserve their precious reputation. A few thousand would stave off the immediate crisis. Malcolm ignored the fortune which Susan had already invested in his various ventures and the pay-off to Gwynneth as, in his mind, he endowed her with a bottomless purse and resolved to act without delay. He could not wait for an opportunity to present itself; he would create one.

He set off in the Porsche to book himself into the Manor Hotel, newly opened on the outskirts of Malchester, one he had not yet visited, so no one there knew him. As he entered he saw on a board the names of two firms holding conventions there, and he said he came from one of them, a late entry, and that was why his room had not been booked in advance. He used all his charm on the blonde receptionist in her trim uniform and accepted a room on the ground floor, registering with a false name and address.

He would need the room for only a matter of days. He would soon be in funds again and able to rent a flat while he started a new business. Used cars were a busted flush now; he would cash in on those he had got and avoid laying out on others, then set up something else though at the moment he had not decided quite what that would be. Still, there were always needs to be met and this time he would pick just the right opening. Malcolm was quite used to starting off in a new direction, and the resolve to do so always improved his spirits; by concentrating on the future, he could forget past failures.

He had run out of cash and was unable to tip the porter who brought his bags to his room. He patted his pockets and shrugged, and promised to see the man later.

He would have to get some money at once. Would anyone take a cheque? He could not try the hotel, for he was not Malcolm Vaughan here.

He had given his name as Edward Tyler.

*

Susan had drowsed off towards dawn, and she began to dream.

She saw Hugh, still young and handsome, not dead at all but walking along a country lane, wearing his uniform. In her dream she knew he was going to post a letter, and it was to tell her that he had been killed.

'But you haven't,' she struggled to say, in the fearful dream compulsion of an action devoutly desired but impossible to perform. 'I can see you, Hugh. It was all a mistake and you're still alive.' But as she said the words her feet seemed to be immured in the ground and she could not make him hear her. Now, though, he must learn that their baby had not survived and he would blame her for that. Yet Hugh had died before the baby was born. Past and present were confused in her dream, and there was joy because after all Hugh had been spared; she must waste no time in spreading the news. George must be told, and that would be sad for him because it meant that their marriage was null and void. In her dream, her paralysis at last came to an end and she ran to catch Hugh before he mailed the letter while George stood waving sadly in the background. She was, however, her present age in the dream, with her blonde hair almost white and faint brown specks already beginning to show on the backs of her sinewy hands, while Hugh was as young as when she last saw him and unscarred by any wounds. Now a schoolgirl Norah appeared, wheeling a pram in which sat a laughing infant whom she knew as Harry, although he had died before he could sit up. For a moment, in the dream, she questioned his identity: was it really Harry or could it be Malcolm? No, it was Harry; and beside the pram walked a fair-haired little girl: Louise. The fact that Louise was born years after Harry died was of no account in this happy scenario.

Suddenly it began to rain and the figures dissolved, Harry vanishing into a hole in the ground and the

178

others dispersing like smoke, yet their disappearance was not distressing. She had been with them and it was bliss.

She woke feeling rested and content, more peaceful than for years, and was able to recapture calmly what had seemed so real. There was Hugh, young and strong, and the smiling child, and Norah before her fall from grace; horror had been banished and innocence restored. All recollection of Norah and George's nocturnal adventures had gone and Susan came down to breakfast smiling and happy until, seeing the others heavy-eyed and gulping down strong coffee, she remembered.

Would they tell her what had happened or would she be forced to ask?

George rose and kissed her cheek; it was soft and cool.

'Slept well, did you?' he asked.

'Yes,' said Susan, thus making it impossible to admit that she had heard them moving about in the night. 'I had the most wonderful dream.'

'Oh? What was that?' George had sat down again and picked up *The Times*, which he always read at the breakfast table. He peered at her over his half-glasses, giving her his full attention.

How old he looked, compared with Hugh in her dream. How lined he was, with deep furrows creasing his cheeks. His thick eyebrows were almost white. He was a kind, good man, and she felt thankful that she was not compelled to desert him for the situation provoked in her dream in order to return to Hugh, as she had chosen then.

If she told him about it, the memory might vanish; if she kept silent, the dream might return another night.

'I can't really remember now,' she said. 'Just that it was sunny and warm and no one was dead.'

179

'Perhaps it was all about heaven, then,' George suggested.

'Yes,' she agreed. 'Perhaps it was.'

Later that day Detective Constable Whitlock, who had been sent to Malchester on another inquiry, went round to Vaughan's Reliable Cars to find out how Malcolm had known about Louise's affair with Richard Blacker.

The place was locked up, with no sign of its proprietor, which, thought Whitlock, was tough on anyone wanting to buy a car. He took a look at those on view and decided his own Mazda had been a most judicious purchase.

While he was strolling about, feeling that Malcolm Vaughan was sure to turn up soon for work, the man himself was just settling in at the hotel where, to fill time before attempting to make new friends among the businessmen who were in their conference rooms, he had decided to have a sauna, which he saw was available, then a swim in the hotel's indoor pool. He found his swimming-trunks in one of the bags Brenda had packed, brightly patterned ones he had bought in Rhodes where he had gone with some girl whose name he could no longer remember.

The hotel's pool was part of a leisure complex used as a sports club by local people as well as hotel guests. When Malcolm went in, two elderly women and a grey-haired man were sedately swimming steady lengths, while in the gym women of varied ages, wearing leotards, laboured away on treadmills and stationary bicycles. Malcolm marched out of the changing room and dived into the pool between the two women swimmers; he made a considerable splash and a large displacement of water. He scraped the tiled floor of the pool, which was shallow and where diving was forbidden as stated on notices clearly visible to anyone entering the enclosure, but as he had gone extremely flat he did not damage himself except for stinging the whole of his chest and stomach. He swam angrily up and down. He was a strong swimmer and used a powerful crawl, breathing heavily, making a big wash and occupying the centre of the pool.

The three other older, regular swimmers, who normally progressed in silence, concentrating on maintaining their rhythm and counting their accomplished lengths, exchanged irritated glances as they drew level with each other, and formed an avoiding column in file to continue with their exercise. Such things happened sometimes. Inconsiderate hotel guests ignored the rights of others in the pool.

Malcolm behaved as if they were not there. He swam up and down until he tired, which was soon for he was far from fit and quickly became out of breath. He left the water, patting his chest, sleeking down the wet pelt of hair that covered it, trudging off towards the changing rooms. The three other swimmers adjusted their positions and carried on. They could all keep going indefinitely.

Malcolm felt refreshed and ready to give of his best when, afterwards, he met the conference delegates in the bar. Soon he interested one of them in buying a used car for his wife. He had led the conversation round to cars by asking what the various delegates drove. One company supplied their executives with Sierras or Granadas, according to status; the second ran mainly Montegos, with a few Rovers for the higher operatives. Malcolm found a man from the Montego range who expressed interest in something for his son, just down from university. That afternoon, when they broke for the day, the two potential customers met him at the workshop and he took them for spins in the Maestro and the Vitesse, hoping to sell them both, but the men

181

were only amusing themselves and Malcolm was left with no sale.

He was about to follow them back to the hotel where he could charge a good meal to his account and look for new faces in the bar, perhaps even an available woman with a place of her own, when Detective Constable Whitlock arrived for a second attempt at catching him on the premises.

At first Malcolm thought his call was connected with the uniformed officer's visit during the night.

'I'm not sleeping here now,' he said, 'if that's why you've come, though there's nothing to stop me, if I've a mind to.'

'No, I'm sure there isn't,' agreed Whitlock, baffled at this line of talk. 'You've been living here for a while, have you?' he asked, trying to tune in.

'Only last night,' said Malcolm. 'I told that copper so. I'd decided to move from where I was and hadn't had time to make other arrangements. I'm fixed up now.'

'So where are you staying?' said Whitlock, for he might need to know.

Malcolm named the hotel, forgetting that he was registered there as Edward Tyler. 'I'm only there for a night or two,' he added. 'Just till I find a new place of my own. You can always contact me through my people, they live in Selbury.' This was supposed to reassure Whitlock as to his impeccable standing.

'I know that, Mr Vaughan,' said Whitlock. 'It's a family matter I want to discuss.'

'Oh?'

'About your sister,' said Whitlock.

'But I talked to someone the other day about her,' said Malcolm. 'That's all over and done with now and I mentioned then that I couldn't help.'

'Oh, but you did, Mr Vaughan,' said Whitlock. 'You

182

told Detective Superintendent Marsh about Richard Blacker and we've traced him.'

'So?' Malcolm waited. What had they dug up? He had only mentioned Blacker to get the police off his own back.

'Oh, he confirmed what you said but denied seeing her that night,' said Whitlock, not adding that Blacker had no alibi.

'She might have gone to him afterwards,' Malcolm suggested. 'It's possible.'

'After what?'

'After she – after whatever happened to her,' he added, and went on more confidently, 'After she was attacked.'

'So she was attacked. You're sure of that?' Whitlock said carefully.

'Well, wasn't she? It's the only explanation,' said Malcolm. 'And she got away from the area. Or was taken.'

'You're suggesting she wasn't killed in Feringham, but was able to get to London?'

'Well, there was no blood in her car, was there? Or so it was said at the time,' Malcolm declared.

'How would she get to London without her car, unless someone took her?' asked Whitlock.

'There's a train,' said Malcolm. 'She used it every day to get to work. It's possible.'

'But she had no money. Her handbag was in the car.'

'A lift, then. She hitched.'

'But why? Why should she want to get away? Wouldn't she want to go home, if she'd been assaulted?'

'Maybe she didn't want to face them. They fussed over her all the time, as if she was made of china,' said Malcolm, and there was bitterness in his tone even twelve years later.

'If that's so, why didn't whoever gave her a lift come forward?'

'Well, would you, if you were the last person to see her alive?'

'Yes, if I had nothing to do with her death,' said Whitlock.

'Maybe he was the bloke who did for her,' Malcolm suggested.

'Will you tell me about your own trip to Heathrow that night?' Whitlock invited.

'Oh, I can't remember the details now,' said Malcolm irritably. 'I told the police at the time. I was living in Cornton then, and I had to pick up these Americans at the Star Hotel and take them to catch a plane. It was about nine at night – their flight, I mean.'

They would have had to be there long before take-off. Malcolm would have had plenty of time to get over to Feringham after dropping them and meet his sister when her rehearsal was over.

'How long does it take to drive from Heathrow to Cornton?' Whitlock wondered aloud. 'Or rather, how long did it take then, before the M25 was built?'

'Less than two hours,' Malcolm said. 'Though you'd need to allow that in case of delays.'

'So you could have dropped them and driven to Feringham by nine or nine-fifteen. The choir practice ended at around ten-fifteen that night.'

'What are you getting at?' Blood rushed into Malcolm's face as he spoke.

'You could have met your sister. You could have been the man who attacked her,' said Whitlock.

Malcolm's face was almost purple. Veins bulged on his temples and his slightly protuberant blue eyes glared at Whitlock who recognised, then, his potential for violence. Whitlock's nose for the hunt sharpened.

'Is that what happened?' he asked, very quietly.

A pulse worked in Malcolm's jaw and he clenched his fists to prevent himself from lashing out at the man.

'What a suggestion,' he said, almost hissing the words. 'Why should I want to hurt my sister?'

'But she wasn't really your sister, was she? You might have felt something about her that wasn't in the least brotherly,' Whitlock pressed him. 'As you weren't true kin, it wouldn't have been incest.' He used the word bluntly.

'There was nothing like that,' said Malcolm, his tone flat as he bit back the expletives he felt like uttering. 'She – we didn't get on all that well,' he added.

'You never said that at the time,' Whitlock pounced.

'No – well, I wasn't going to say anything bad about her, was I?' said Malcolm. 'After all, she was dead, or so everyone seemed to think.'

'Suppose you did meet,' said Whitlock. 'Suppose you saw her by chance that night.' He decided to leave for the moment the point that Malcolm could have travelled to Feringham on purpose to see her away from their parents. He would have known about the choir and where to find her. 'Suppose you quarrelled and she ran off?'

'Well?'

'Did you run after her?'

'What do you mean, did I? This is all your idea. It isn't what happened,' said Malcolm.

But as he made the denial, Whitlock knew he had hit his target. He could see the iron effect Malcolm, not a man notable for his self-control, was putting into keeping his temper. It was not a natural reaction to what was being alleged.

'Did you catch her, Mr Vaughan?' he said softly. 'I think you should let me know.' For an instant he wondered about cautioning Vaughan, then let it go. The moment might pass and he had no evidence. That could come later.

But Malcolm was holding on.

'I never saw her that night,' he said.

'I think you did,' said Whitlock. He waited, but Vaughan said no more. 'You quarrelled and she ran off, leaving her car. You moved it later.' That would account for the seat being pushed back to accommodate longer legs than Louise's.

'You've got a vivid imagination,' Malcolm replied. 'You should try writing a thriller. You'd do well.' He stared at Whitlock, swaying a little, determined to out-face him.

'Truth's often stranger than fiction,' said Whitlock tritely. 'And I mean to get at the truth of this, but it's waited a long time and it can wait longer yet.'

He must tell Marsh about it, see if Vaughan could be brought in and given as much of a hard time as was possible now, under PACE. If he was feeling inner guilt, he might confess, but there was not a shred of evidence to use against him, nor any new light on where to search for some.

'I'll be speaking to you about this again,' he said, and left. The question about Blacker could wait; this had priority.

Afterwards, Malcolm sat at his desk in a turmoil. If he told the truth, he would not be believed, any more than he would have been at the time. Only two people knew what had really happened that night and one of them was dead. Protection lay in silence.

He would have to leave. That detective had been like a terrier with a rat, determined to shake something out of him, the merest admission on which to build a case, however circumstantial it might be, and he would be able to do it for want of proof to the contrary. Malcolm had no illusions about the police; they would fit him up if they chose.

He had intended to seek some proof, at the Lodge House, that there was a connection between him and Norah, force her to pay him, if not his due, certainly money for keeping quiet. His intention, then, had been to stave off court action over his debts; now there was more from which he must escape, and it was urgent. He must act without delay.

Canada, he thought: it was far away, required no entry visa, the language was the same and he could soon be absorbed into the country, losing his pursuers. Unless Louise's body was found, they would have no grounds for attempting to extradite him, and she had lain hidden so long that only a fluke would deliver her up to them now. He must raise all the cash he could at once, which meant selling the cars he still had, cutting his losses, making what he could out of them without wasting time looking for profit. And he would go to the Lodge House to see what he could achieve there. They wouldn't want a scandal to break over their greying heads.

He went back to the hotel where his possessions were stashed away in his comfortable room. A good dinner would restore him, give him the strength he would need for what lay ahead, and he'd let his new friends there know he was going to Canada very soon and he would undertake commissions. Then he'd make a plan for tackling the three at the Lodge House. He needed to know the truth about Norah and the child she had had, still convinced that she had lied, perhaps about dates, and that he was that infant, for it explained everything, her links with the Vaughans, her authoritarian manner. She'd been so strict on her visits, always defending Louise against him, and making him stand in the corner for lying when he denied taking a pound from his grandmother's purse. The fact that he was guilty did nothing to mitigate Malcolm's sense of resentment, as strong now as it had been then, when he was twelve.

Women, he thought: too many of them had been around in his life, messing things up. First his mother, conceiving him carelessly and then not standing by what she had done but selling him to the highest bidder; then Susan, and her mother who was ruthless when Susan was always conciliatory; then Louise, who was George's pet and who would not submit. He had almost forgotten Gwynneth, his wife, and the women between until Brenda, the latest, had failed him.

There would be women in Canada, bold frontiers-women used to an outdoor life, thought Malcolm, who hated that sort of existence himself, or business women needing a man to run things. Either type would suit him. Cheered by this positive thinking, he had a good evening at the hotel. The delegates were, in the main, used to all sorts and listened with tolerance to his tales of success in Australia, and he generously stood unlimited drinks all round, charging them to his account.

In the morning he used guile.

He went to his office and dialled the Lodge House. When George answered the telephone, he did a trick he had been shown by an Australian con man; he put two fingers into his mouth, between his teeth, to affect his articulation, and he pitched his voice into a Cockney timbre, such as he had sometimes attempted in jest, lowering the tone to make it sound deeper. He said he was speaking for Superintendent Marsh, who had something important he wished to show Mr Vaughan, something that had come to light out of their area but near the railway embankment just outside Reading. Would Mr Vaughan meet the superintendent at Sonning, where a police car would convey him the rest of the way? Malcolm was pleased with himself for using that word; the police always used words like convey and proceed. The superintendent further suggested, Malcolm went on, that at this moment in time it might be best not to mention the purpose of his journey to Mrs Vaughan but to make some excuse.

George's voice was level and calm as he replied that yes, that would be quite all right, he would set off at once and be there in about an hour.

Malcolm chortled with glee at the ease of this deception. He thinks they've found Louise, he congratulated himself; it would be at least two hours before George realised that it was a hoax, and longer before he returned to the Lodge. Malcolm left the Porsche, so clearly identifiable, on the forecourt and got into the Metro, not clipping on the trade plates which would be an instant giveaway. He drove towards Selbury planning how to get Susan, if she happened to be at home, out of the house so that he could search through the drawers at his ease. He'd dig up some sort of dirt, for sure, enough to make them finance his departure. They'd be glad to see him go, he thought bitterly, just as they were when they sent him off to Australia. Well, they need not think they had seen the last of him; he'd be back when things died down, or he'd find a way to go on bleeding them from a distance.

Driving on, he remembered stories he had been told about various confidence tricks successfully played by men he had met in prison. People were gullible, he had learned; they wanted to believe messages relayed in a confident manner or persons who appeared at the door well dressed and carrying credentials which at first glance appeared to be genuine.

George and Malcolm passed on the road, but George barely noticed the Metro going the other way; Malcolm, however, had been looking out for the Volvo. George was gazing straight ahead, concentrating on the road and his mission. Malcolm laughed aloud.

Two miles from Selbury, he stopped at a callbox and waited there for twenty minutes. It was agony to waste time, but he must let enough elapse to make his next story credible. By now George had been gone from the house for about forty minutes.

Malcolm dialled the Lodge House again, and this time Susan answered. He put on an American accent, pitching the tone higher this time, and said he was sorry to trouble her but her husband had been involved in a road accident near Henley-on-Thames and was on his way to hospital in Oxford.

'Which hospital?' snapped Susan, her voice almost a scream. 'The John Radcliffe?'

Malcolm had not foreseen the complication of several Oxford hospitals. The one she mentioned would do for his purpose.

'Yes,' he agreed, and added, 'He's not badly injured.' He had never wanted to hurt Susan. 'A broken leg, and some cuts,' he elaborated. 'I was just passing by and he asked me to call you.'

Susan's voice was still shrill with fright as she thanked him. He hung up before she could ask any more questions. Then he drove on to Selbury and parked in the village square where he could watch who emerged from the road that led to Selbury House and the Lodge. No one would recognise him in the Metro. There was an old cloth cap in the glove compartment, one he had used when taking the car to a prospective customer a few days before; he put it on and crouched down behind the wheel as if he was having a snooze.

Ten minutes later Norah's Golf, not Susan's car, paused at the road junction, then pulled out and headed off towards the Oxford road. The two women were in the car; of course, Norah would never allow Susan to set off after George alone. Now the coast was clear at the Lodge; he would have plenty of time to ferret about and find what he could, steal Susan's jewellery and any money that was lying around, leave the impression that they had been deceived by some outside thief, not their son taking only what was his own.

By the time he reached the Lodge House he had forgotten that his original aim had been blackmail of a sort. He had forgotten, too, Mrs Gibson, who had come in daily to clean for his grandmother and now came twice a week to help Norah, for even Susan did not expect her to undertake every domestic task.

Malcolm parked his car in the garage, whose doors were open. Susan's Opel was not in sight; it was, in fact, being serviced, but Malcolm did not wonder about it for long as he closed the doors so that no casual caller or passer-by could notice the Metro. Then he let himself in with his key.

Mrs Gibson had heard his approach and was in the hall as he entered, one hand on the vacuum cleaner which she was about to use in the drawing-room.

'Oh Malcolm, why didn't you get here sooner?' she exclaimed. 'Your poor mother – you've just missed her. She's gone off to the hospital. It's a terrible thing, your father has been in a car smash.'

'Oh,' said Malcolm. He was astonished to see her. 'I've come to collect some papers they've left for me,' he said, thinking furiously. 'It's important or I'd come back another time. I wonder if they've left them ready. I'll just have a look. Then I'll go after them,' he added. That was a good touch: Mrs Gibson would expect it.

'Right,' said Mrs Gibson.

She would not query his presence, but she would tell George and Susan later that he had been to the house. If she did that, they would know the identity of the hoaxer, especially when things were missing. He would have to see about this complication but he put it to the back of his mind while he dealt with what was, at the moment, his main task.

'I'll make you some coffee,' said Mrs Gibson, abandoning the sweeper and padding off towards the kitchen. She was old, now, and shapeless, her body a wedge above sturdy legs in warm tights. He had known

191

her for most of his life. While she was out of the way, he went to Susan's desk in the drawing-room and looked inside. It was tidy, quite unlike his own; a few bills, all paid, were held in a clip. Envelopes and headed writing-paper were stacked in pigeon holes; there were files to do with her charity work and her art interests in the drawers, but no diary, no evidence from the past. In the bottom drawer was a file full of cuttings about Louise's disappearance and an envelope.

'Found it, dear?' asked Mrs Gibson, returning with a cup of coffee and two custard creams.

'No. Perhaps she went off in such a hurry that there wasn't time to leave it out,' Malcolm said. 'I'll just make sure.'

Inside the envelope was a copy of Susan's will. Malcolm read it carefully after Mrs Gibson had left the room, murmuring that she would leave him in peace and get on elsewhere.

It was dated the previous week. He saw that only when he had read, with disbelief, its provisions, and turned to the signatures on the final page. The witnesses were the vicar and his wife.

Susan had carried out one of the most positive acts of her life and had virtually deleted him as her heir. Everything was to go to George, with no trusts or restrictions of any description. If they died together, or he died first, the beneficiaries were his sister's children. Apart from that, and a legacy to Mrs Gibson, five thousand pounds were to go to Norah Tyler, and a further five thousand to Malcolm.

Five miserable grand! Why, she would be leaving hundreds of thousands! The Lodge House alone must be worth two hundred thousand or more.

The truth was that, by helping him so much over the years, Susan had depleted her capital to such an extent that apart from the house there was not a great deal for George to inherit.

Malcolm closed the drawers of the desk. He went upstairs to Susan's bedroom, and was taking the jewellery out of her red leather case – her engagement ring from Hugh – she always wore George's – her mother's rings, two of them very valuable, one set with diamonds and sapphires and the other a large square emerald surrounded with diamonds; her diamond drop earrings; several brooches and clips – when Mrs Gibson, carrying the sweeper, came into the room and stood staring in amazement at what he was doing.

'Why, whatever are you up to, Malcolm?' she exclaimed, and before she could say any more he had rounded on her and caught her by the neck, shaking her, squeezing the life out of her. Her horrified eyes stared at him above her purpling face as she made little choking sounds which soon ceased as her gaze went blank. She was dead.

As he strangled her, Malcolm cursed her, calling her a silly, interfering cow and many worse epithets, not consciously intending to kill her, merely wanting to silence her and protect himself and, at the same time, hurt someone for what had been done to him by denying him, as he saw it, his due inheritance.

When he let her go, he flung her across Susan's bed like a stuffed doll and she fell limp, her head to one side, her arms spread out.

He was shaking. He took some deep breaths to steady himself, then put the jewellery in his pocket, wrapping it first in some handkerchiefs of Susan's. He had time now; no one else would interrupt, and he looked in the bedside cabinet to see if there was anything useful there, in the end tipping the drawers on to the floor. There was a volume of poems by Walter de la Mare in one, and as it fell a faded envelope that might have been marking a place dropped out. It was an old letter addressed to Mrs Hugh Graham, and Malcolm couldn't think who that was at first; then he remembered that it had been Susan's first married name.

There was a letter inside the envelope. It was very short:

Dear Sue,

You'll only receive this letter if I don't come back some night or other. If that happens, please see that Norah is taken care of. She's a darling girl and she thinks she loves me, so she'll be sad, but there's no commitment between us and I'm not sure if she'll feel the same when she's older. Besides, what would mother say?

Lots of love,
David.

The letter bore a date in August 1943. Two weeks later, David had been reported missing, believed dead.

She'd had it off with David, then, the filthy slut! But did that mean that he was David's son? If so, he truly was a Vaughan. For a moment Malcolm felt quite dizzy, until he took in the date and saw that it was seven years earlier than the one on his own birth certificate. The letter didn't mention a baby, but surely David knew about it? Surely that was what was meant about taking care of Norah?

Malcolm did not work out that David would probably have worded his letter differently if he had known that Norah was pregnant. All he knew was that what he had imagined was untrue: Norah was not his mother. The baby Norah should have had had been got rid of so that it would not bring disgrace to the respectable Vaughans.

Malcolm put the letter in his pocket, along with the things he had stolen. Then he looked at the body of Mrs Gibson.

He would have to conceal the fact that she had been strangled, and any trace of his presence in the house.

He hadn't worn gloves; his fingerprints would be all over this room.

Hurrying now, for George might already have discovered that he had been lured out on a false trail, and Susan and Norah would soon make a similar deduction, Malcolm ran downstairs and out to the shed where petrol for the mower was always stored. He brought the can into the house and poured the contents over the floor in the hall and up the carpeted staircase. Then he lit some crumpled paper and flung it down to start up the blaze. He had used fire before to vent his rage; now it fulfilled a more useful function.

It was only twelve o'clock as he drove away.

PART THREE

1

Carol

Carol Foster read about it on Thursday in the *Daily Mirror*, which Eric's mother bought every morning from the newsagent's on the corner. It was on the kitchen dresser when Carol called in after work to collect Joanna and William. Her mother-in-law always picked them up from school, took them home with her and gave them tea, amusing them until Carol arrived, when she, too, would be given tea and a slice of home-made cake to tide her over until she and Eric had their meal together later.

BODY IN BLAZE, she saw, in banner headlines, and below, in large black print: DOOMED FAMILY LOSE HOME IN FUNERAL PYRE. She did not pay attention, for she seldom bothered with news of any sort; there was plenty going on in the world which she could not influence and which she preferred to ignore. What concerned her was the destruction of the environment and how it would affect succeeding generations, more particularly her own children. One day, she hoped, they might be able to move into the country, but property was expensive everywhere and especially outside the town; here there were the conveniences of urban living: good schools, buses, a leisure centre with a splendid swimming-pool, and work for her within easy reach of home. Eric ran a car, an elderly Citroen, cherished because he saw no prospect of ever affording a replacement, and he had the permanent drain on his finances of supporting his first wife, Frances, and their daughters who were now in their teens.

'I never liked that Frances,' her mother-in-law had confided, some time after she and Eric were married. 'Gave herself too many airs, she did. Eric's better off with you.'

Carol knew that Frances had locked Eric out of the house one night and never allowed him back, and for no apparent reason; she had simply tired of the married state. They had divorced discreetly, without rancour, on the grounds of desertion by Eric of Frances, and ever since that time Eric had paid her mortgage and an allowance, regularly increasing, for the girls.

'Terrible thing, that,' said Ethel Foster, seeing Carol glancing at the paper. 'As if they hadn't had enough to put up with, poor things. I remember that case well.'

'What case was that?' asked Carol, adding, 'More tea, Mother?'

Hearing that she was an orphan, Ethel had insisted that she be thus addressed when Eric announced that they were getting married. Ever since that day she had made Carol feel truly loved, seeing her through the births of both children, their subsequent mumps and chicken-pox and other mild disasters, and Carol loved her in return.

'Please, dear.'

Carol poured out more tea for Mrs Foster and a second cup for herself. The children were sitting in front of the television set watching *Neighbours*, like almost every other child in the land. Carol thought it a wholesome programme; she had called it the Enid Blyton of the soaps to Eric, who, unlike his mother, understood exactly what she meant. During its span, she and Ethel had a chance for a quiet chat. She enjoyed these interludes, when she felt safe and sheltered in the small semi-detached house where Eric had grown up. Ethel had lived there nearly all her married life and throughout her widowhood, and Carol knew

200

she had a secret dread of being forced to leave it through old age or some infirmity.

'I doubt if you'd remember it,' Ethel was saying, 'It'd be before you came back to England. They lost their daughter years ago. Murdered.' She lowered her voice to say this, nodding towards the children who were engrossed in the doings of Charlene.

'Read it, dear,' said Ethel, frowning, with a finger to her lips. Murder was not a topic for her grandchildren's ears.

Carol kicked off her shoes, sank into the dilapidated armchair beside Mrs Foster's blazing coal fire and tucked her feet up under her, taking a bite of chocolate cake as she did so. Mrs Foster regarded her with sharp, affectionate interest as she read the front-page outline, then, putting her cake down on the worn velour of the chair-arm, turned the page to follow the more detailed story within. She was an odd, quiet girl and had seemed a little lost at first when she joined their family, but it had been a lucky day for Eric when he met her in the library; she suited him, and he adored her.

'Well, they're all right, at least,' Carol said at last.

'Who, dear?'

'The – the parents. The Vaughans.' Carol was surprised to hear her own voice sound so steady in her ears.

'Yes. What a thing to do – lure them away by hoax telephone calls and then rob the place. That poor woman, though, the cleaning lady. I don't suppose he expected to find her there.'

'No, I suppose not.'

This was not brilliant deduction on the part of Ethel, merely an echo of Detective Superintendent Marsh's words at a hasty press conference held on the night of the crime.

'He'll have cased the place, known they had plenty of stuff after moving out of such a big house,' went on

201

Ethel, who like many kindly people enjoyed following lurid and gruesome crimes at second hand and regularly watched police series on television. 'Someone local, it was, you mark my words, or someone who'd made a study of their habits.'

'Just as long as they weren't hurt themselves,' said Carol. She had been quite shocked, Ethel noticed with surprise; her face had turned quite pale. But then she had a tender heart; she salvaged wounded birds attacked by cats and had kept a lost hedgehog through a winter's hibernation.

'The woman would have recognised him, you see,' Ethel went on. 'Could have described him, if he'd let her go.'

'Yes.' Carol unfolded her legs. 'May I have another cup of tea?'

'Of course, dear. You don't have to ask,' said Ethel comfortably. She loved these sessions, her little gossip with her daughter-in-law, the children stretched out on the floor on their stomachs, eyes glued to the screen. After they had gone, she always missed them; the house felt lonely and cold, even though in fact it was always warm and snug.

Carol and Eric lived twenty minutes walk away, in a modern house on an estate being built as they were married; Eric had taken out a large mortgage to obtain it, but Carol too was working then, in the office behind the scenes at Boots. She had carried on until six weeks before Joanna was born and, as soon as the baby was four months old, she had found evening work in a hotel nearby, serving drinks and snacks in the bar. Ethel had known that Carol hated it, though she never complained. It was the only way she saw then to bring in some income. After William was born, she took in typing and translating for an agency; it seemed that she was very good at French, which was a surprise, but she talked so little about the past.

202

She told them that her parents had been killed in a road accident when she was very young. At that time they had lived in the south. After this, she had gone to live with her only relative, her mother's sister in Australia. When her aunt died, Carol had decided to return to England. She had had various jobs, she explained, moving about the country, wanting to learn about it; then she had met Eric.

Carol had thought it out carefully, devising it in such a way that she could not be caught out easily, and hard to check unless anyone grew suspicious. She'd used it to account for why she had no official papers – no National Health card, none of the documents necessary for a normal life. She had done temporary work for several years, work which was paid in cash. Then she'd found a way to confirm her new identity.

'Terrible, that, to lose their daughter. Never to know about her,' Ethel said. 'Murdered, of course, that Louise.'

'Yes,' said Carol faintly.

It was true. Louise had been done to death, but by her own hand, and here she sat, twelve years later, reborn as Carol, owner of official marriage lines.

On the way home Carol bought two papers for herself, all that were available as they passed the newsagent's on the way to the bus-stop. She bought the children sweets to keep them quiet; she had never bought them comics. Had she read any as a girl? She didn't think so; pony books were what she had liked at ten. Suddenly, crystal-clear, she remembered her father reading the *Eagle*, which he had ordered for Malcolm, and saying to her mother that it was a pity the boy wouldn't read it as it was fun.

The memory pierced her with an agony that was like an arrow wound.

Such things rarely happened now, but sometimes a chance word, some phrase overheard, brought back the days of childhood as if they were only yesterday. Most of the time she successfully blanked out the past, except occasionally in dreams. She had her new life with Eric and the children. Meeting him had been the turning point, for he had offered her a future, and he must never learn how she had deceived him. All she wanted was here, in Tetterton, two hundred miles away from Selbury. Never mind that she had been the one to leave, while Malcolm, the outsider who had caused her flight, had remained.

She kept her emotions in check in the bus, listening to the children, joining in their conversation. Later she would read the papers carefully, savour every detail they disclosed about her parents and their present circumstances. Now she knew they were both alive; she had often wondered if one of them had died. How they must have suffered when she ran away! At the time she had known they would grieve, but since she had had children of her own, she had understood more personally the pain she had inflicted on them; the worst thing that could happen to her would be for harm to befall either Joanna or William.

She could have escaped from the claustrophobic trap she felt her parents weaving round her by a different means; she could have gone to work abroad, in Paris or Geneva, say; or even in America. People did that sort of thing to get away from mothers who wanted them to make safe marriages and repeat the pattern. She'd gone a bit mad, she realised now, flipping when Malcolm got into her car that night in Feringham. But after what he'd done to her, she lost her head completely.

You don't scream when your adopted brother gets into your car. You don't run through the streets yelling 'Rape!' even if that's what he did to you only a few

204

nights previously. And you don't tell your parents about it, because your mother might not believe you, and if your father did, he would be furious enough to kill Malcolm. Besides, she had felt so guilty; she should have been able to protect herself, not let it happen, only Malcolm was so strong and she had felt unable to call out. He'd known that, banked on it, his hand over her mouth as they struggled in the silence of the night. It had all been over very quickly; he couldn't have had much pleasure from it, but he had destroyed her, and that, she thought much later, was really what he meant to do. He hated her.

During the subsequent nights she had scarcely slept and at the choral society practice was barely aware of what was going on around her. No one seemed to notice; she supposed she looked much as usual, and one of the delights of singing was that it took you right out of yourself so that you thought about nothing else. She had managed her job without making any serious mistakes; obviously someone else had finished editing the books that she was working on, and the series had been completed by a colleague for she had seen the resulting publications in the library and had felt a pang of envy.

Thank God she hadn't got pregnant. She went on feeling soiled for years; in fact she'd never fully recovered her self-esteem though things were easier as Carol, who was another person.

She bathed the children and they came downstairs in their dressing-gowns to wait for Eric's return. He would be late tonight, for there was a training session at the store. Eric was head of the furnishing department at a big branch of a nationwide department store in Flintham, twenty miles away. When they met, he was an accounts clerk in a china works; then, due to a take-over, he lost his job and had to start again. He had crawled slowly up the ladder in the store, learning new ways, coping with new sorts of colleagues, determined to succeed, and she admired him. It was all so different from anything she had known before and that made it easier to forget Louise. She trusted Eric, and his mother, and she supposed they trusted her, which made her all the more resolved never to fail them, or her children.

She had a good job now, herself, as secretary to the managing director of a plastics firm, the sort of job that Norah had. Carol had not thought about her for years. She must have retired by now and probably was living in a retirement flat in Eastbourne or some other coastal town. That had been her plan.

The children had sandwiches and milky drinks for supper. While they ate their meal in front of the fire – a gas one, there were no open fires in this house – Carol put the casserole she had prepared that morning in the oven, spread the papers on the table and read through their reports of the killing in Selbury. She remembered Mrs Gibson, a plump middle-aged woman who had cleaned for her grandmother. Of course the old lady must be dead; she would have been ninety-four or so by now. They'd sold the big house, it appeared, and were living in the Lodge. It must seem very small. Why had that happened? Had they lost their money? She couldn't imagine her mother enjoying lowered status in the county.

In one of the papers there was an old photograph of her when she was Louise, with her straight blonde hair framing her thin face. She looked very young and solemn.

Carol had dark hair worn in pre-Raphaelite curls, a style that had come in not so long after she ran away. At first she had dyed it black, but gradually she had lightened it to a nondescript brown and perhaps by now it would have faded anyway. She rinsed it regularly, hiding the bottles of colouring from Eric, just as she hid so much from him.

There would be more in the papers tomorrow. She bundled today's together, folded them and took them upstairs to hide beneath her sweaters in a drawer.

She was just dishing up the vegetables when Eric came in, looking tired. He had been learning a new computerised system for operation in the store; supposed to make things easier, it was, in fact, quite complicated and susceptible to human error. Once he had mastered it, it would be his task to train new entrants to his department.

As always when he came home, his heart gave a little lift of happiness: here she was, his lovely, strange, secretive girl whom he could never hope to understand completely, but then how could any human totally understand another? He loved the homely scene, the children, clean and smelling sweet of soap and Johnson's baby powder, playing some childish game and waiting to wrap themselves around him with adoring hugs. They loved him now but they might not always feel the same; his older daughters had once seemed to think him wonderful, but now he thought he simply had their toleration.

Since his promotion to head of department money had been easier, and they could afford to do things outside the home. Carol took the children swimming once a week, and she went to evening classes on a Thursday, studying the History of Art, which she found absorbing. She had also joined Tetterton's Choral Society, a long-established choir which performed at Christmas and at Easter. She liked that, and always returned from practice looking happy. Eric was out two nights a week as well; on Tuesdays he went to German lessons and on Fridays he helped at a youth club. On the few evenings they spent together they got on very well. Eric was kind, and had been badly hurt by his first wife's rejection. Carol was grateful for his gentleness and the shelter of his name; she tried to be all that a good wife should, so that he might never regret their marriage. She could never make amends for cheating him, but she could be loyal. What she felt for him was a deep and calm affection, peaceful after the pain of her affair with Richard and the terror Malcolm had inflicted on her. Eric was never angry; he was sometimes rather quiet and would go off for a solitary weekend walk or even before breakfast in the morning, but that was because he had things on his mind, not because he was angry with her or the children. He worried a lot: about money and the children's future; about his older daughters over whom he had so little influence and whom he saw only once a month when they spent Sunday afternoon with him and his new family. These were difficult times; Carol feared that the girls would be bored and then they would cease to come at all.

They were nice girls. She had suggested various expeditions as her own two grew older, trips to the country to watch wild-life or look for rare flowers. Eric was amazed at how much she knew about these things and her ability to discover where to see them. They went for walks beside canals and rivers, and once had a rare weekend on a barge, a big success, with the older girls cheerfully helping with the cooking and glad to operate the locks. The weather had been glorious and they had seen all sorts of waterside creatures. In the evening Carol had read them *The Wind in the Willows*, and William had spent the next day vainly looking for Mole and Ratty. For a girl who had grown up in Australia, she knew an extraordinary amount about English natural history.

Carol felt nervous about the old photograph of her that appeared in the press. There were likely to be more, unless some other case stole the headlines. Would anyone think she looked like Louise Vaughan?

'Oh, do I?' she planned to say, if someone mentioned it. 'How peculiar.'

But no one did. Only Eric, some days after the first reports, reading the latest instalment and a résumé of Louise's disappearance, had wondered who the photograph of the missing young woman with her fair, straight hair, reminded him of, failing to glance across the room at his small daughter whose own fair, straight hair, at that moment, was caught back in a single plait.

Carol carried on with her established routine.

Mornings were busy, with the children to get up and ready for school after Eric had finished in the bathroom. She made sure he had plenty of time to shave and prepare for the day and saw him off, in his dark suit with his spotless shirt and a restrained tie, well before she and the children had to go. She had always risen early, so that was no new challenge for her, and she made preparations for the evening meal before leaving the house. Long ago she had left Selbury House at seven to catch her train to London; her father had followed an hour later, travelling first class. When she first returned to live at home he had said it would be nice if they travelled together, but she had refused to let him pay the difference on her fare and she didn't like watching his discomfort as their train filled at stations along the line. So she had said she must go earlier and he had taken the hint.

Poor Daddy. She really loved him, and Mummy too, but they had made her feel too precious. It was easy to understand but it had laid a burden on her, and had provoked Malcolm's jealousy. Norah, on her visits, had noticed a lot and understood more than she let on. She had saved Carol, when she was Louise, from some of Malcolm's torments and she would certainly have believed what Malcolm had done that dreadful night. Carol had thought about going to see her in the flat in Pimlico, telling her about it, seeking her help, but what could Norah do? Telling their parents would only cause worse trouble, and it was impossible to involve the police; the scandal and the shame would be unbearable.

She had been so feeble. She saw it now. She should never have come home, but it had been a simple solution to her problem over Richard, making the break easier. That was when she should have struck a blow for independence and gone abroad instead of taking the easy way, and if Malcolm had been around she might have done things differently, but he had been safely in Australia. Besides, she enjoyed her job and did not want to give it up; seeing the series through was interesting and she liked liaising with the authors and the artists.

She had had no plan, that night, jumping out of the car in terror and running down the street. In fact, she had not thought at all when Malcolm suddenly opened the passenger door and got in beside her, laying his hand on her leg. She'd braked and leaped out, regardless of whether any other car was coming up behind, but in fact the traffic lights where she had stopped were at the junction of four residential streets, busy by day but quiet at night, and by chance there was no one about. It seemed, from later reports in the press, that she had not been noticed. She realised afterwards that he had known the route that she would take and had lain in wait for her at this spot. If the lights had not been red, she would not have stopped, but he'd have chased her, waylaid her in the country, maybe overpowered her once again.

If her car door had been locked, she would have been safe, but the passenger's side was faulty. He knew that.

She'd run and run through the steady rain that was falling, dashing down an alley when she heard Malcolm start up the car to follow her.

The alley – a narrow footpath between two rows of houses – emerged quite near the station. She had not been reasoning at all when she rushed towards it, but as she ran into the booking hall, she realised that this could be a safe place because there would be staff about.

But the station was deserted. At that hour, the booking office was closed and if you caught a late train you paid the guard, if there was one, or at the other end.

She had hidden in the ladies' room, which was unlocked, bolting herself into a lavatory. There was less vandalism then; today even such a sanctuary would have been denied her. She did not know how long she crouched there in the darkness, afraid to turn the light on, hardly breathing, expecting at any moment to hear footsteps in pursuit. At last, after what felt like hours but was more likely thirty minutes, she thought it would be safe to telephone her father from the station call-box, tell some tale about her car being stolen and ask him to come and fetch her.

Nervously, peering about lest Malcolm was lurking in the shadows, she approached the red cubicle which smelled of stale tobacco smoke and worse, only to find that the instrument had been pulled from its fixture and she could not make the call. If she walked to another box, Malcolm could be waiting for her somewhere in the streets of Feringham. She stood there, helpless, wondering what to do. Then she heard a train approaching.

There was a scarf in her raincoat pocket. She put it over her wet hair and tied it under her chin. Then she walked to the end of the platform where the last coach would draw in, hiding against the buildings, hoping the driver would not notice her.

No one left the train as she dashed across and got into the empty last coach.

She had not thought then of disappearing; in fact she had not thought of anything except avoiding Malcolm. She had no money, and no plan for when she reached the terminus. Shivering, she put her hands in her pockets, shrinking into the corner. What would she say if a guard came along? Would she be arrested?

She was trembling, and she shook and shivered through the first half of the journey. The train stopped at quiet stations. No one entered her coach. When she reached London she would explain to the ticket collector that she had lost her handbag. She would suggest they telephoned her father who would guarantee her fare; then she would return on the next train, even if she had missed the last one and might have to wait until morning. Her father would meet her. When that happened she would decide how to explain her flight. He and her mother must already be wondering where she was, since she was never so late home after the choral society meeting. She might have to explain her actions, but she'd somehow do it, even if it made her sound as if she'd lost her wits. She had, she told herself; of course, she had.

Then she saw the purse. It was tucked down the side of the seat facing her, where, unnoticed, it had fallen from its owner's capacious bucket-bag. It took her nearly ten minutes to overcome her scruples enough to pick it up and open it. Inside was some change and nearly fifty pounds in notes, as well as an Access card and a driver's licence. It also contained a rail season ticket between London and a station two stops beyond Feringham. The owner of the ticket might not have needed to show it, either because she was well known to the collector or because the station was, like Feringham, imperfectly manned, and had possibly still not discovered the loss of the purse. The train had started back without it being noticed; at this hour, no one would look through the coaches.

If I leave it here, someone else may steal it, Louise reasoned. I can take it, use the ticket to get off the platform, borrow some money for the night and return it to its owner when I've decided what to do.

She laid the purse back on the seat opposite, staring at it, her talisman to freedom. Should she use it? Was fate dictating what she ought to do?

As the train drew in to the terminus, she picked up the purse and removed the ticket. Showing it at the barrier, she walked through unchallenged and went straight to the station hotel, which had an entrance from the platform. She had often used its first-floor cloakroom in the past, and she went there now, though without a comb or make-up, while she decided what should happen next.

She never once considered going round to Richard's flat, asking for help or, at the least, shelter for the night. She did think of taking a taxi to some friends, then dismissed the idea. Something strange had happened to her; she was letting events manipulate her, not her own free will.

The name on the driver's licence was Carol Mount. That was who was sheltering in the ladies' cloakroom in the station hotel, washing, smoothing her hair, doing what she could to freshen up. Instinct, though, told her to lie low, not make herself conspicuous by wanting a late meal or occupying a seat in the lounge. She had a lot of money; fifty pounds in 1976 was more than enough to pay for a room for the night and have a great deal over, but she had no luggage and, if a search were made for her, the desk clerk might remember her if questioned.

She moved off down the corridor and tried a few doors. All the rooms were locked, but eventually she found one that yielded, opening into a housemaid's

213

cupboard. Fatalistic now – if she was caught, she would say who she was and plead loss of memory – she went inside and closed the door. There she spent the night, curled up on the floor, chilly, sleeping a little now and then. When first light came she went back to the cloakroom and, eventually, left the hotel unchallenged.

Even then she could have gone to the office, somehow resumed normality, but instead she crossed London by tube and went to Euston station. There, she had some food and wondered where to go. It must be somewhere north, to Scotland, maybe?

There weren't enough people in Scotland. She had been to the Highlands with her parents, on a touring holiday years ago. Malcolm was with them, bored and bad-tempered, and it had not been a successful experiment. By a loch they'd hired a boat; Malcolm had tried to push her overboard. She wouldn't think about him; she'd go somewhere where he'd never been.

In the end she walked along the road to King's Cross and caught a train to Leeds, which was large and might offer anonymity. York, more interesting to her, would be smaller, more Louise's choice; Carol Mount was setting off for Leeds.

Though she had intended to repay the money she had used to the real Carol Mount, whose address was on her driving licence, she had never done so. She owed her everything, in fact: her name; her fresh start; her liberty, for that was what, despite the insecurity and the fear that haunted her during the first months, she had ultimately gained.

Every day, now, she bought the papers to read about the Selbury case. It soon faded from the front pages because its real interest lay not in the murder of an elderly cleaning woman but in its link with her own disappearance, where there had been the inference of a sexual crime. Violence sold newspapers; so did sex, and a combination of the two was both common and

214

compelling. Mrs Gibson was no sex object, though one reporter did a piece about her husband, an invalid suffering from a chronic bronchial condition, and the fact that their only child, a daughter, lived in Minnesota. *Neighbours rally round grieving widower*, ran the text, and, reading it, Carol could imagine what was going on in the village that seemed, now, to be light years away.

Her parents would be besieged by the press. She wondered if they still thought about her. Perhaps they did; she hoped so. It would be sad to be totally forgotten. How could they ever forgive her for what she had done, for the grief and pain she had caused them, if they found out about it? They could never understand; she did not understand herself, completely, only that after a time it seemed impossible to undo the deception and she had no wish to do so.

At the office, Carol did her usual work. She dealt with all the normal things. She had done well, she supposed, to get this really quite good job with very little to offer as credentials. What had the real Carol Mount done? Had she a degree, or been computer trained? The real one was a little older than Louise; she had realised that when she worked her age out from her driving licence.

At first, arriving off the train in Leeds, Carol had secured casual work as a waitress in a cheap café. She had found a room to rent, walking the streets where vacancies in boarding-houses were advertised, picking one at last. She stayed for a month in a small room at the back, sharing the bathroom with the other tenants, going then to Sheffield. She felt it was vital to keep moving while the papers were full of the investigation into her disappearance. She picked up work successfully, answering advertisements. It might not be so easy now, with high unemployment, but she had not been over-choosy. Her fear was that if she took on something permanent she would need papers, and as she had none she devised the story about coming from Australia. She knew a bit about the place, for her mother had been interested in the country when Malcolm went there, though his letters did little to satisfy her curiosity. Carol, in the evenings, read about it in the public library.

Somehow the weeks and then the months slipped by. She contemplated going to the DHSS, making herself official, even signing on, but that would be the way to get caught out. They would check on her. If she truly was who she alleged, a woman born in England who had, as an infant, gone to Australia, her birth would be registered in England and she would have a certificate to prove it. Without a birth certificate, she could not prove her identity; with one, she would be safe.

She had read *The Day of the Jackal*, learned how the assassin equipped himself with false identities from studying tombstones and applying for the certificates of those born near his own birth date but dead as infants. She even went to graveyards, studying dates and names, wondering if she could do the same. But you needed more: you needed to know the mother's name and the place of birth. She found that out by asking on the telephone.

She had Carol Mount's identity. Carol was four years older than herself. She knew Carol Mount's address.

It took her a long time to find the courage, but at last she did it, convincing herself that all she had to lose was the cost of the telephone call.

She had been working as a cleaner for a while. It was hard work, but she enjoyed it because it could be mindless and it was entirely free from hazard, as cleaners were paid in cash and stamped their own cards, or didn't, as the case might be. She answered advertisements in shop windows, and soon was going out five days a week to various houses in an up-market residential area. She told her employers that she was a single mother – divorced – with a child at school. It was easy to lie once you began, she had discovered; the first time was the hardest. She invented Billy, her little boy aged six. Her employers were impressed by her neat demeanour, though not all of them admired her wildly waving hair. She spoke nicely, in a soft voice without any sort of accent, and she wore a navy skirt and sweater. Carol had done some shopping at an Oxfam shop after her first purchases of washing things and a change of underwear. She liked being in the large, comfortable houses, and two of her employers were often out when she was working.

She used the telephone at one such house to make her call to Carol Mount, for if she used a call-box the fact would be obvious when the telephone was answered. Pollsters did not use call-boxes, and that was what she would purport to be.

She knew that Carol Mount went out to work for she had owned a season ticket. Therefore, it must be an evening call, and she might not catch her in the first time.

She took to baby-sitting for the Boxes, telling them that her mother would always sit with Billy if they wanted her. The Boxes, a prosperous couple with two lively children, liked dining out; they gave dinner parties, too. Carol came and washed up several times, for now that she had invented her mother, she was stuck with her. She did not mind the work; it kept her busy and she was well paid; in fact, looking back, that time was very therapeutic for she was working physically hard.

Carol Mount did not answer the telephone the first time the imposter using her name tried to speak to her. The second time, just as she was about to dial, one of the children in the house woke and came wandering downstairs in search of company.

217

Ten days later Louise, now Carol, made a third attempt. Her quarry must still live at that address, or directory inquiries would not have been able to provide the number.

This time a woman answered.

Using a brisk voice, the new Carol said she was speaking for a research organisation conducting a survey into the movements of people away from their birthplaces. Would Carol Mount, whose name had been selected at random from the electoral roll, mind disclosing where she was born and on what date, and how long she had lived at her present address? Would she mind also revealing her mother's maiden name and some details about her and her father?

Carol Mount did not mind at all. She gave the answers readily and said it was an interesting project.

From the digs where she was now living, her usurper wrote the following day to the Registrar of Births and Deaths in the area where Carol had been born, easily discovering the correct address from the telephone directory in the library, where volumes covering the whole country were available. She enclosed a postal order for the fee.

Not long afterwards she received a copy of the real Carol's certificate. Now she was equipped, and legal, but she was apprehensive until she realised that what she had done would only be detected if someone grew suspicious, and that wouldn't happen.

What about a passport? She didn't need one at the moment, but who could tell about the future?

Someone checking up on her, if she were to become suspect for another reason, could detect the fraud, but they would have no cause to do so for she would make certain that, apart from this major deception, she would not defy the law.

She worked for Mrs Box for several months; then she left and moved to Manchester, where at last she equipped herself with proper documents, unchallenged.

She moved away again. The more you moved, the less likely you were to be traceable in the event of any query. She had been in Tetterton for a year, in her first permanent job, when she met Eric in the library, where she always spent a lot of time.

If she were to meet her parents now, would they even recognise her? She'd sometimes imagined, when money was short, or she was ill, or when she was in cold, uncomfortable digs, going back and pleading for their forgiveness, but she had always managed, thanks to Carol Mount's original bounty, and she got a sort of satisfaction out of having done so. It was strange, however, to recollect that once she had been an editor, commissioning work; now she was content to have limited authority. What mattered was the money she contributed to the family budget and she was lucky to be in an airy office overlooking the canal, with agreeable colleagues. She'd hated the night-time bar job she had done after Joanna was born; she'd got so tired and she had loathed the smoky atmosphere and the occasional sexual overtures made by customers. Some women liked it and thought that they were failing if they did not attract flirtatious back-chat and attention. Sexual harassment, people called it now. Carol had developed a chilly manner and a glacial smile. The manager had asked her to try to be a bit more friendly, there's a love, but she had not been able to comply. She was efficient, and he did not want to fire her; he kept her in the background when he could, making up the buffet meals.

She never complained to Eric, but he did not like her working there; however, there was nothing else she could find in the evenings, the only time that she was free. Eric's mother was still working herself then, and couldn't be expected to retire to mind the children; she had her own security to think about and must qualify for a full pension. Most of the time Carol deferred to Eric, who was never assertive or unfair, but just occasionally she held out for something whose importance to her he could not always understand.

'I must do my bit,' she insisted when he said he did not want her to take on evening work. 'I must make a contribution to the budget. We all cost you such a lot.'

'But you're my family,' he protested. It was almost as though she considered herself and the children burdens who had nothing to do with him.

Carol, in fact, hated the feeling of having not a penny of her own but what he gave her, and, because she had cheated him by not telling him the truth about herself, she felt a weight of guilt which was slightly eased by effort. Working gave her back some self-respect.

They had been married in the register office, with Eric's mother and father there, and a few friends, mostly his, but several of Carol's colleagues came to the buffet lunch they had afterwards at Eric's flat. Carol wore a navy dress with white trimmings, and a wide-brimmed white straw hat; Eric wore his best suit. That morning, when she got up in the spare bedroom at her friend June's where she had spent the night before, she had thought about her mother and father and of the very different wedding her mother would have chosen for her, given the chance. Then she put them from her mind, she hoped for ever. She had given up her own bed-sitting-room and moved her possessions into Eric's flat, where she had spent only rare nights before the wedding. Observing the conventions mattered to both of them, but for different reasons. Eric wanted no breath of gossip or scandal because he aimed to give Frances no cause to twist things round and imply that he was unfit to have access to his daughters. Carol, who had believed that she could never face a sexual relationship again, was anxious to be beyond reproach wherever possible because of all the secrets she was hiding.

Both of them meant to keep their vows, and they had succeeded. Carol, to her surprise, was even happy. It had been a lucky accident that had caused her to knock into Eric accidentally in the library, pushing back her chair as he was passing with a pile of books. When he saw her there a few nights later, he had smiled tentatively and said, 'Good evening.' Then one evening they had gone off for coffee together after leaving the library. Two weeks later they had supper at a new wine bar in the town. Next it was a concert; then a cinema, and at last a day out in the country one weekend when his children were away and he couldn't see them.

He had explained his circumstances, making it clear that he was no catch.

'But you've got a good, safe job,' she said. 'We can't all be Einstein.'

He had laughed at that, and as she got to know him better, she had enjoyed finding ways to make it happen again. His worried face would lighten and his large grey eyes would twinkle; she saw that he could be fun. She'd almost forgotten how to laugh herself, busy being Carol, living from day to day, looking ahead only to paying the rent and subsisting.

He introduced her, at last, to his daughters and, not accustomed to the company of children, she treated them as contemporaries, playing games she remembered from her own childhood, introducing them to Scrabble, which she bought for them. They were too old for the children's version and she and Eric introduced deviations from the adult game which made it easier for them to score. Much laughter arose over this as Hazel invented words she said were the names of exotic beasts and Rowena put in the names of her hamster and its progeny, which it had an unfortunate habit of eating.

Carol still got on well with the girls. She had never felt possessive about Eric and had no grounds for resenting them and their earlier life together. For him she felt a gentle affection and a wealth of gratitude; her deep emotions only came to life after the children were born, and the intense, primitive love she felt for first Joanna, then for William, her fictional Billy brought to life, was unlike any feeling she had ever known. It obliterated the unresolved trauma of her past and gave her life new meaning. Now she had more for which to be grateful to Eric, and her affection for him deepened. Theirs was, by any standards, a successful, happy marriage.

Sometimes at night, even now, she would start awake with sudden terror that she had talked in her sleep, used some name or expression or in some other manner given herself away. She would lie, heart thumping, listening to Eric's even breathing – he never snored – calming herself, remembering that her offence had been against her parents, not against him, except for her deception. She had no black past to conceal, no terrible crime, only the theft of Carol Mount's money and name. And the fact of her desertion.

She had had to sell her gold watch in those early days when she had needed money, but she kept the locket she had worn. It had been mentioned in the description of her in the papers; if she tried to sell it, an alert jeweller might identify it. She had it still, an aquamarine set in pearls, once her paternal grandmother's. She had worn it since her marriage, but now she kept it in a drawer in case it figured in the new reports from Selbury.

When Eric lost his job, things had been hard for them. At first he could find nothing, and he stayed at home caring for the children while Carol gave up her translating and went back to full-time work. She soon found an office job, one which paid quite well, and then Eric's father died, suddenly, of a heart attack. That was a bad time, but they got over it, pulling together as true partners should. Eric found an opening at the department store; it wasn't the sort of job he had had before but there were prospects. He took it on, made a success in various departments, and finally he was awarded his own small empire.

'You deserve it,' Carol said, celebrating with a bottle of sparkling wine she had bought at Marks.

They'd talked about a holiday in France, but so far they had only been as far as Scarborough, where they rented a self-catering cottage near the beach. The children loved it there, and Carol thought it perfect for them at their present ages. She found North Yorkshire very beautiful, with its unspoilt countryside and the wide, light skies.

She could safely get a passport, if they really did decide to go to France. She had the necessary certification. The sooner the better really, before everything went on to computers and it might be simple to run checks, find that another Carol Mount already had one.

Lately, she had become interested in ecological disasters, shocked by Chernobyl and realising that her children would be threatened if the rain forests were destroyed, the ozone layer filled with holes, the seas contaminated. She read a lot about these things and even spoke of joining Greenpeace. Eric was faintly amused by the passion she showed about withering greenery and soil erosion; wistfully, he wished she would display the same intensity in their more intimate moments. Still, she was always loving and tender, and that was all that really mattered. She had never mentioned past lovers but of course there had been one, at least. At first she had been nervous and tentative; he knew she had been hurt by some unhappy experience and he did not probe. He hadn't told her all that had happened in his marriage, nor about his other romance with a girl called Phyllis. That was in the past. What mattered was the present and they did not need to talk to be happy together. Their whole way of life was proof enough.

Sometimes he wondered at the complete absence of any Australian accent in Carol's speech, but then her aunt had been English, and she had been back in England for several years before they met. She once said that her aunt had not cared for Australian vowel sounds and had sent her to elocution classes.

He accepted everything she told him as the truth, and she had learned that it is frighteningly easy to deceive, especially where there is both love and trust.

Her routine, since the new crime in Selbury, was to read the paper in the lavatory at work, putting the lid down on the toilet seat and sitting there to study the reports in privacy. Conditions for the female staff were very good, with a large cloakroom containing roller towels that worked and a rack of paper ones as well. There were big mirrors all along the wall behind the basins, and copious hot water. People changed there, even washed and dried their hair, for there was a power point, before going out on evening dates. The factory workers, too, were well catered for, with still more spacious facilities for their far larger numbers. Carol knew that some of her office colleagues, and many of the machinists, went home to poky rooms in grimy streets, much less pleasant than their work environment; for years this had been her own experience. She knew that many children, too, must find their modern school with its bright classrooms and big gym and playing-field a sharp contrast to their homes.

People came and went outside as she read the various accounts of events in Selbury. She was dimly aware of movement and voices; someone tried the door. Carol took no notice and read on. The reporters, referring to her disappearance twelve years before, made capital out of the fact that lightning had, it seemed, struck twice, though this time in another form. Reference to Greek tragedy was made, and finally she read of Norah's involvement.

Miss Norah Tyler, 62, housekeeper to the Vaughans, accompanied Mrs Susan Vaughan, 70, on her journey to, as she thought, her gravely injured husband's bedside, ran one text. There were pictures of her parents, even one of Norah, looking much as she had always done, but none of the dead woman; her fate was lost in the bigger story.

So Norah had been absorbed into the family. When had that happened? Carol digested the information and drew comfort from it, for Norah would support her parents now. She was a shrewd woman who saw through cant, and Carol had always admired her.

Photographs of the burnt-out Lodge House made it look bigger than she remembered it when her grand-mother was living there, supported by the larger house with its home-grown vegetables and other resources. When had Norah thrown up her job? Was it after the disappearance of Louise? Carol felt guilty at that thought. What other repercussions had there been from her flight?

You did something, took some drastic action, and at the time your first thought was only of what it meant to you, not of how it would affect a host of other people. Even at the time, her own immediate problems of sur-vival had overshadowed her awareness of the pain her parents must be suffering.

What about Malcolm? At last she deliberately let herself remember him. Where was he in all this latest furore? He was not mentioned in the papers. Had he been sent abroad again? Surely even her mother would finally tire of making excuses for him? Perhaps he had found some other wretched girl to marry.

Carol had once passed the scene of a bad fire when

she was living in Leeds. A house near her lodgings had gone up in flames one night, the occupants escaping thanks to the prompt arrival of the fire brigade. For days the area had smelled of smoke, an acrid odour quite unlike the scent of autumn bonfires which she remembered with nostalgia. Now that bitter smell would be lingering around her parents' house. All their possessions would have been destroyed, and with a pang she knew that meant their photographs of her, the albums crammed with snapshots of her life, her small biography. Louise had been truly killed at last, all traces gone.

What would they do about clothes, tax returns, papers, all the bureaucratic clutter of modern life, the things that she had slowly acquired in her renaissance?

She shed some tears, sitting there in the small cubicle, and when at last she emerged, choosing a moment when she was sure there was no one in the outer cloakroom, she took time to pat her face with paper towels wrung out in cold water, and to put on lipstick. She looked at her hair in the mirror; she might have to add some grey streaks soon, to mark the extra years she was supposed to have lived.

When she was pregnant with Joanna the doctor in charge of her expressed surprise at her recorded age, saying he would have thought her several years younger. Luckily she had been officially young enough to avoid extensive tests, but she would doubtless be a freak with a late menopause. It was too soon to start worrying about that, and maybe no one but Eric would notice. And his mother. Not much escaped her sharp eye. Still, even she wouldn't be here for ever. At this thought Carol felt a pang. She depended on Ethel; so did they all. Ethel had truly been a mother to her.

She had deprived her own parents of their grand-children. After they were born, she had wanted to send photographs to them, had even contemplated doing so, but had pulled herself back from making such a stupid, self-indulgent gesture which might bring ruin to them all. They did not know that she was still alive; they did not know their grandchildren existed; the idea of them, if they had one, would be like the ghost child in that Barrie play – *Dear Brutus*, that was it.

She kept the relevant newsprint pages, throwing the rest away in the waste-bin before returning to her office.

Each day Ethel, too, had read the latest instalment and was eager to discuss it.

'Shows money can't buy happiness,' she tritely said. 'I suppose they're well insured and can rebuild, but it won't bring that poor woman back to life.'

'They'll have to live somewhere in the meantime,' Carol said. She had been wondering about that. Where would they go? Their friends all had large houses. Maybe someone like the Cartwrights would take them in, if they were still alive.

'They won't be homeless on the streets, sent to bed and breakfasts by the council,' said Ethel.

George and Susan had spent the hours immediately after the fire at the Vicarage, which was close by, while Norah made some arrangements. The vicar and his wife, both kind, good people, had three children and only a small modern vicarage, the old one having been sold for enormous sums to a company director who travelled to London and back each day in his huge Mercedes.

'We can't possibly stay,' Susan whispered, while their hosts pondered which child to move from its room in order to house their homeless parishioners, and worried about the inadequacies of their single bathroom.

'I'll think of something,' Norah had said, and had booked them a room at The Crown in Feringham. It would do for the moment, until a more permanent plan could be devised. Meanwhile, she accepted Myra's offer of her tiny spare bedroom for herself for as long as it was required.

Next, she rang Malcolm's workshop and, as he was out, left a message on the ansaphone telling him what had happened and that they were all safe, and his parents would be at The Crown from that evening. She rang Brenda, too, at her office, in case Malcolm went straight home from wherever he was. Brenda, told about the fire, expressed shocked dismay but told Norah bluntly that Malcolm and she were no longer living together.

'My decision,' she added, to make the position perfectly clear.

There was a lot to do. The police took statements about their movements during the day and the telephone calls that had sent them all out. The address of the insurance company had to be traced, since no one remembered it perfectly, for it must be notified. Luckily all three had had their money and bank cards with them, the two women taking their handbags on their trip to Oxford and George with his wallet in his pocket, so there was no problem over the actual cash needed at once to buy toilet things and some clothes. Norah dealt with this, going off to see what she could get at Boots and Marks and Spencer to tide them over, the same priorities Louise had discovered twelve years before when she, too, had only the clothes she was wearing.

There was no word from Malcolm until Thursday, the day after the fire, when he came to see them at The Crown.

'You took your time,' said George.

'I've been away,' said Malcolm. He had driven to Coventry, well away from his home area, where he had sold the Metro for cash. He thought about selling the jewellery there, but it was unlikely that any dependable firm would pay him the large sums it was worth in cash, and to demand it might arouse suspicion. If he tried to open a bank account under a false name and pay in cheques from such sales, he might be caught out on an identity check. That had happened to him in Australia.

The jewellery was his insurance for the future. If he could get it out of the country, he could use it to make a fresh start. Meanwhile he had two other cars to dispose of, and they could soon be turned into money. This gave him assurance, facing George's reproof.

'I knew you were safe. Your message said so,' he replied. 'So I didn't worry.'

'So I see,' said George grimly. 'I suppose it didn't occur to you that we could have done with some help? That we had to find somewhere to stay? That Susan was very shocked? She'd been told I was hurt in a road accident. That was a lie to get her out of the house.'

'I read that in the paper,' said Malcolm, who had turned with interest to the reports of the incident.

'You haven't even asked how she is,' said George.

'Well, she must be all right or she'd be in hospital,' Malcolm said. 'She'd got Norah to see her through, hadn't she? Good old Norah.' He said this with a sneer.

'Yes, she had Norah, thank goodness,' said George, who was still shaken himself though he tried to conceal it from this boorish, ungrateful man who bore his name. I'm getting too old for this sort of thing, George told himself.

'So you'll be staying here for a bit?'

'Yes.'

'Lucky you didn't lose one of the cars,' Malcolm said. 'Though I could have sold you one of mine at a special price. I'll go up and see Susan, then. Which is her room?' The interview had been taking place in the hotel lounge, to which George had descended when the desk clerk rang to say that Malcolm was there.

229

'You won't,' said George. 'She's resting. I'll tell her you came round.'

He looked at Malcolm closely. The younger man's eyes were glittering. He had looked like that once before and George had no difficulty in remembering when it was: just after Louise had disappeared.

'How did you know none of the cars was damaged?' he asked.

'It said so in the papers, or on the news,' Malcolm answered glibly.

He'd made a slip but it wouldn't matter.

'Well, if I can't see Susan, I'll be off,' he said. 'I've a customer to attend to.'

He was going back to his own hotel. On the way, he stopped at a florist's and spent twenty pounds of his profit from the Metro on ordering a huge bouquet of flowers to be sent round to Susan at The Crown, with a message which said: *From your loving son Malcolm.*

When Susan received it, she burst into tears, for hadn't she only just virtually cut him out of her will?

Malcolm himself had a swim when he reached his new base. The activity of the last twenty-four hours had stimulated him and he felt elated and energetic. He tried chatting up one of the leisure club attendants in her white shirt and short pleated skirt, but she, in training, had been warned about people like him; besides, she was going out with one of the under-managers and was no longer available.

Detective Superintendent Marsh had a weird sense of *déjà vu* as he drove out to Selbury following news that a body had been found in the smouldering remnants of the Lodge House.

He spoke to the chief fire officer in charge of the men who had put out the blaze and who had managed to save part of the building. An old man who walked round the village every day, exercising himself and a dog that was mostly collie and keeping both of them out of his wife's way, had seen smoke and flames behind one of the windows and had rushed in to the nearest house to make an emergency call, so the first fire engine had arrived very soon after the blaze took hold. The surviving structure had been saturated with water from the hoses and everything inside was very badly damaged; little would be salvaged. Mrs Gibson had been found on a sodden bed and at first it was thought that she had been overcome by smoke, but she lay on her back, stretched out like a victim of crucifixion. People who died in fires were usually found collapsed close to doors or windows where they had fought to escape; they did not lie down to die unless asphyxiated in their sleep. Until the results of the post mortem were revealed, judgement as to the manner of death must be reserved, but whoever had set the fire was guilty at least of manslaughter.

There was no doubt that it was arson. A petrol can was found in the hall and the way the fire had caught made it certain. A likely reading of events indicated that the fire had been started to disguise the killing and the fact of the burglary, for it was obvious that the cupboards and drawers in the room where the woman was found had been ransacked.

When he reached Sonning, sent there by the bogus telephone call, George had discovered no police car waiting to meet him. He had waited only half an hour before driving on to a call-box to telephone Marsh, for this was the sort of appointment which would be punctually kept. It was soon clear that the message had not come from Marsh's office and a malicious prank was suspected; nothing more. George had turned back for home whilst meanwhile Susan and Norah were on their way to Oxford.

When they arrived at the hospital, it was some time

before they were convinced that George had not, in fact, been admitted. He might have been still in the Casualty department. Various calls and checks were made.

While this was going on, Norah had decided to call the Lodge House. If there had been a mistake in identity, George might be home by now. He had been distinctly cagey about his mysterious errand, saying it was to do with the council, but if so, why had he not explained, and why had he looked as if he had received a blow to the solar plexus?

When she dialled, the line went dead. She tried several times with no better result; then she rang the operator who confirmed that the telephone seemed to be out of order and volunteered to check, then call her back.

Norah did not wait for that; she rang the local police. If George had had an accident, surely they would know?

It was some time before the truth filtered through to the two women and meanwhile they waited at the hospital, for there was no point in going home only to find that George had been sent to some other place, one more suited to his injuries. Various appalling possibilities ran through both their minds as they sat there trying to preserve some calm. Eventually, when the local police could tell them nothing beyond saying that they were unaware of an accident involving George Vaughan, or his car, whose number Norah had given them, she telephoned Detective Superintendent Marsh.

She learned that he was out of the office, already, as it transpired, at the scene of the fire, but when Norah explained why she was calling, a sergeant came on the line and told her that Mr Vaughan was safe and was with the superintendent at Selbury where there had been an incident. Pressed, the sergeant admitted that there had been a fire at the Lodge House, but Mr

232

Vaughan was not involved as he had been the victim of a hoax call which had lured him away from the village. The sergeant did not mention that though he was safe, a body had been found.

Obviously they had been tricked, too. Norah and Susan drove home relieved but sombre, unaware of how serious the fire had been. It seemed they had all been dispersed to leave the coast clear for an arsonist.

Both women remembered Malcolm setting fire to the hay in the pony shed years ago, and the episode of the games pavilion at his school, but neither mentioned them to the other.

George had returned from his bogus mission expecting to find Susan and Norah at home. It was a day when Susan had had no plan for a lecture or other distraction, and had said she was going to sweep up the last of the fallen leaves.

He arrived in the village to find the road cordoned off near the Lodge House and three fire-engines and their teams engaged in trying to extinguish a blazing inferno. He knew total terror, thinking the two women were trapped inside, and when there were murmurs about someone being found upstairs he felt sick with dread. It was a mention from one of her acquaintances among the spectators who had swiftly gathered that made him realise, with shamed relief, that the victim must be poor Mrs Gibson. He asked if there was a car in the garage and learned that it was empty. So the two had gone out: where?

A police officer eventually brought a message that they were on their way back from Oxford.

Whatever had they been doing in Oxford? They'd had no plans to go there; they preferred shopping in Malchester for what could not be bought nearer home, unless they went to London. And why should the police know what they were doing?

Until he saw them, he could not know the answers. He waited for them at the end of the road, anxious to prevent Susan from seeing the wreckage of her home until she could be prepared for the shock, and as they approached, the vicar was walking to meet them, ready with his offer of sanctuary.

Later, Norah was with George when he spoke to the first reporters to visit the scene, saying very little. When they parted, he to take Susan over to The Crown at Feringham, she for Myra's flat, he said, 'They're sure to rake all that up again about Louise. You'll see.'

She did not contradict him. She knew that it was true.

2

Malcolm

Malcolm made his plans fast. After leaving George at The Crown – he had driven over in the Porsche which he had picked up from the workshop when he returned by train from Coventry – he took the Vitesse to an area of Malchester where there was a pub frequented by men with whom, before now, he had done deals. He had picked up bargains there, and he had sold cars which had proved hard to shift. He had also provided one or two for undertakings about which it was prudent to ask no questions.

He sold the Vitesse for a wad of exceedingly tattered notes from a man who knew he could make at least two hundred more by selling it on. Then he took the Maestro to a used car lot on the edge of town where again he sold at a loss.

Now he had only the Porsche left. He'd sell that near Heathrow.

He had dinner at his hotel, and some drinks in the bar later. A new group of businessmen had checked in for another conference and there were fresh faces to talk to; Malcolm swopped stories with them and bought rounds of drinks in his usual free-handed manner, and went to his room only when the last of them left the bar. He had a bath and shaved: appearances were important and he had a long night ahead of him. Then he packed his bags and, when the hotel was quiet, heaved them over the windowsill on to the lawn outside, then followed himself. He had earlier parked the

Porsche as close as he could to the end of the block containing his ground-floor room.

The night staff never heard him move from the lawn to the tarmac to reach his car. He padded to and fro with his load of belongings, taking only what was essential; the rest he left behind, and he rumpled the bedclothes so that it might be some time before anyone realised he had gone. The hotel was soundproofed and the night porter, dozing behind the desk, did not hear him drive away. Malcolm did not switch on his lights until he was clear of the gates. Then he set off for Heathrow.

He checked in at a hotel near the airport. The place was accustomed to people arriving round the clock and found nothing unusual about his request for a room in the early hours of Friday morning. He paid cash in advance, saying he simply wanted to sleep for a few hours after driving up from Plymouth, before catching a plane later on.

He lay on the bed and slept for three hours, after which he went off to sell the Porsche. It was a wrench but it had to be done, and again he was forced to accept a lower price than he might have got in a different way, but he now had several thousand pounds in cash; enough to get him across the Atlantic and launched into a new life.

The post mortem report on Mrs Gibson was through by Thursday morning and it confirmed that this was a case of murder. There was no smoke in her lungs and there was firm evidence of strangulation, with bruising on her neck indicating that the assailant was probably right-handed. Door-to-door inquiries in Selbury, begun on Wednesday and completed the following day, yielded reports of two people who had noticed a blue Metro in the village square on Wednesday morning. There had been a man in the driver's seat. He was there during the time one witness was in the post office mailing a letter to her cousin in Zimbabwe, and was still there while she had a conversation with two friends she met in the grocer's shop. She remembered it clearly because the talk, about the possible closure of the school in the village, had been important.

'With all the building here, you'd think we could keep our own school,' the witness had stated. Pressed by the interviewing detective constable, she had not been able to describe the man.

Neither of the witnesses had ever met Malcolm; they could not have named him even if they had had a good look at him, and neither was paying particular attention. Both said the car was not among those they might have recognised as being regularly parked in the square while their drivers visited the shops.

The priority, now, was to trace the Metro and find the driver, in order to eliminate him from the inquiry. Nobody else seemed to have seen anything that could be construed as suspicious. No one had seen any caller arrive at the Lodge House.

The firemen reported that the front door had been closed and locked on the Yale but the back door was unlocked. Mrs Gibson would have been going in and out, taking rubbish to the dustbin and putting the mat out while she mopped the floor. With everyone out, she would have locked it before she left by the front door.

At that stage no one suggested that the visitor might have been Malcolm Vaughan. Those in the village who knew him would not expect to see him behind the wheel of a Metro, for he always drove sporty, even flash cars. Those who knew his taste for a blaze kept quiet out of dread of what might be exposed if they spoke.

Detective Constable Whitlock had been working on

various cases concerning petty theft, trying to avoid bringing charges in a shoplifting case where the goods the store detective declared had not been paid for cost less than a pound – two small tins of baked beans. Meanwhile he turned over in his mind the fragments of information about Louise Vaughan's disappearance which had surfaced during his recent interview with her brother. The scenario Malcolm Vaughan had postulated about someone getting into her car and so alarming her that she had leaped out and run off had convinced him that Vaughan knew much more, but now the investigation into the fire at Selbury and Mrs Gibson's death, to which he had been assigned, took precedence over hypotheses about the missing young woman, however intriguing. But the cases were linked by location. It might be simply coincidence, but was there any such thing? Could it not be defined as fate?

When mention was made of a blue Metro, something nagged at the back of Whitlock's mind; some such car he had noticed not too long ago, but he could not immediately call to mind where it was. However, irrespective of that, Malcolm Vaughan must be interviewed as routine and told what had happened at his parents' home.

A constable from Malchester was sent round to the workshop. The place was deserted when he called on Wednesday, the day of the crime, at about five o'clock in the evening. Outside on the forecourt a Porsche, a Maestro and a Vitesse were parked. A note was made to find Vaughan later; he might have already heard about the fire and be on his way to his parents' side.

Police Constable Perry, who had subjected Norah and George to what could be called harassment, or alternatively extreme attention to duty, heard about the blue Metro in which the CID were interested as soon as he came on shift. By this time efforts to trace local blue Metros were being made and officers were instructed to stop any they saw and question their drivers about where they had been at the time of the incident. Perry had been driving around looking for trouble for some time before he remembered that there was a blue Metro outside Malcolm Vaughan's place on Monday night.

He drove past the workshop and saw that the Metro had gone: so Vaughan must have sold it. He'd sold the Vitesse and the Maestro as well, it appeared, and, as there were no lights and no one answered when Perry banged on the door, had no doubt driven off in his Porsche to wherever he was spending the night.

Perry saw no need for haste in reporting Vaughan's past ownership of a blue Metro. It could not be the one in question. Coming off duty early on Friday morning, he mentioned the matter, information that was thought important enough to be sent through at once to the Incident Room in Feringham.

Whitlock, who had been put on the case partly because every available man was needed for the preliminary inquiries and partly because Marsh himself made sure that he was on it, since he already had knowledge of some of the history of those concerned, was in the Incident Room when the information came through. He remembered himself, then, that he too had seen the car. Perhaps Vaughan had sold it to the thief.

He also remembered where Vaughan had told him that he was staying, and saw that he had not yet been interviewed regarding the crime; not that he could be considered a suspect, for he would not steal from his parents or murder their daily woman. Or would he?

Marsh had been home for only a few hours' sleep and on Friday, when he came in, he was told that Detective Sergeant Newton was proposing to question Vaughan about the Metro to find out who had bought it, as its connection with the crime must be established or dismissed. Marsh found Whitlock hovering, anxious to speak to him.

'I know where Vaughan is,' he said. 'He's got some explaining to do.'

Marsh looked at the young man's thin, sharp-featured face, his eager expression.

'You think he knew more about his sister's disappearance than we gave credence to at the time, don't you?' he said.

'He used the words, "She might have gone back to him afterwards", referring to Blacker,' Whitlock reminded him. 'And I asked him after what, and he suggested she'd been attacked and had then run away. He didn't like it at all when I suggested that he could have been the attacker. I told him I'd be speaking to him again. That was on Tuesday evening. Is there anything in from Australia yet?' After his interview with Vaughan, Whitlock had asked if a check could be run in Australia; it was unlikely that a result would be through so soon, he thought, but Marsh surprised him.

'Funny you should ask,' he said. 'Our pals down under turned him up right away. He did two years for fraud. Got out and came straight back to England. No money, of course.'

'Fraud,' said Whitlock slowly. 'What if he's in debt now?'

'Yes. I'll see what the banks will tell us. Probably nothing, but we'll soon know if he owes money around.'

'There might be stuff in his office. Bills and so on,' said Whitlock hopefully.

'I think it might justify a search warrant,' said Marsh. 'Meanwhile, Detective Sergeant Newton is keen to pick up Vaughan to interview him, and as you know where he's staying, you'd better go with him.'

Whitlock's face lit up.

'Even if he's not our man, he's got questions to answer,' he said happily.

'Yes,' agreed Marsh.

At the moment they had no concrete evidence to connect Malcolm Vaughan with the latest events at Selbury, only their own suspicions and the circumstantial link of his having had a blue Metro for sale.

Whitlock and Detective Sergeant Newton set off for the Manor Hotel. The journey took forty minutes and when they arrived it was to find that there was no record of a Malcolm Vaughan staying there.

Whitlock described their man, adding that he might have checked in on Monday. Then he mentioned the Porsche which he knew Vaughan drove.

'We get so many,' said the reception clerk. 'We've got conferences all the time. But it sounds rather like Mr Tyler; he had a Porsche. He didn't check out with the rest of his group. I wonder if he's up yet.' The hotel, being new, used plastic cards instead of keys to admit guests to rooms, so there was no instant check on possible absence. 'I'll ring his room,' she said, and did so.

'Don't tell him who we are,' Detective Sergeant Newton instructed. 'Just say he's wanted in the lobby.'

'I hope he's in no trouble,' said the girl, but of course he was if the police were after him and if he had booked in under a bogus name.

'He's not if he really is Mr Tyler,' said Whitlock.

He was not altogether surprised to learn that there was no reply from the room, and further inquiries revealed that Mr Tyler was not in the restaurant having breakfast.

The hotel had a note of his car's registration number, accurately filled in on Mr Edward Tyler's form. A check soon proved that this was, indeed, Malcolm Vaughan's Porsche. It no longer stood outside in the parking area. After this, the two men were let into room number fourteen, which had a *Please do not disturb* sign hanging on the door.

The empty room, with the unwanted trappings abandoned and the hastily dishevelled bed, confirmed the identity of the guest, and, in effect, his guilt.

'Don't touch a thing,' said Newton, including the under-manager who had let them in with Whitlock in this instruction.

'But what's happened?' asked the young man. 'What's he done?'

'Left here without paying, for starters,' Newton replied and turned to Whitlock.

'Bag everything,' he said, and to the under-manager, 'I'm afraid you can't use this room till it's been gone over for prints.'

'Well, as he hadn't checked out, no one else will have been booked in,' said the under-manager. 'What chance have we got of getting our money?'

'Not a lot, I'd say,' answered Whitlock.

'He didn't work for that firm, did he? He said he was with them.'

Whitlock shook his head.

Now there would be a man-hunt. He and Newton began to set it in motion.

Marsh telephoned Norah Tyler that morning.

Myra answered the telephone, and handed the handset over to Norah, mouthing 'The police.' Myra, in an exotic silk kimono acquired on a trip to Hong Kong, was sitting at her kitchen table smoking a cigarette, an activity from which Norah was resolved to wean her while she lodged in the flat. Norah herself, in the tweed skirt and dark sweater she had worn on the journey to Oxford two days before, had been clearing the breakfast dishes.

'Yes, Mr Marsh, I'll be here,' she said, after listening

to her caller. 'I'll expect you in about half an hour, then.' She replaced the instrument and looked across at Myra whose expression betrayed extreme interest. 'Something's happened,' Norah said. 'He sounded very serious. I hope it's nothing dreadful to do with George or Susan.'

'Why should it be? You worry too much,' said Myra, who, by escaping from her native Estonia in 1939 ahead of the Russian invasion had also avoided the later German one and saw no point in anticipating further catastrophe, despite recent events in the village.

'The shock might have been too much for one of them,' said Norah, fretting.

'If anything had happened to either one, the other would have got hold of you, fast enough,' said Myra. 'They can't manage without you. You know that.'

'I've known them a long time,' said Norah.

Myra had often told her that they took advantage of her and that she should escape, that she wasn't too old to start her own business, as Myra herself had done, and have some rewarding years before age forced her to curtail her activities.

'Forget the dishes,' she said. 'The little girl you found for me comes today, remember? We must leave her something to do. She can start by washing-up.'

'Oh, does she? I'd forgotten,' said Norah, thus indicating that she was more upset by what had happened on Wednesday than had, at the time, appeared. Norah never forgot arrangements she had made.

'The Orams are delighted with Mrs Jennings,' said Myra, referring to the couple who lived in the largest flat in the house. 'You've a genius for finding these cleaning ladies.'

'It's not genius. It's contacts,' said Norah. 'But you're right about the dishes. Daisy should do them as it's in her contract.'

Norah had suggested an agreement between Myra

243

and her new, youthful employee, to avoid misunder-
standings and for the protection of both. Myra had
wanted to make certain that the girl would wash up
on mornings after she, Myra, had had people to dinner.
She often had friends in for extravagant meals.

'You go and get tidy for your policeman, if he's
coming to see you,' said Myra. 'And don't worry. They
may have found out who did those terrible things. That
poor Mrs Gibson, it's really dreadful. If you're anxious
about George and Susan, why not ring them up?'

Norah would not do that. It was still early and they
might be sleeping late. She took herself off to the sitting-
room to make sure it was tidy enough for the forth-
coming interview. She was a great one for plumping
up cushions and tidying round when visitors were
expected, a habit that Susan found irritating because
the Lodge House was rarely in need of such extra
attentions since it was always so well maintained.
George, speaking very solemnly, had told his wife that
Norah had not got Susan's inner sense of security in
social situations, since she acquired her polish through
experience and not by osmosis.

Now, finicking about, Norah worried that Daisy,
when she arrived, might overhear what Marsh had to
say for the flat was very small, and she also hoped that
Myra, who was incurably curious, would put on some
clothes before he came.

Daisy's parents ran the village post office, which also
sold stationery and sweets; she was waiting to start her
nursing training and wanted work meanwhile. She was
very punctual, and Norah heard her and Myra discussing the day's tasks which included cleaning the silver.
Over the years, Myra had bought quite a lot as an
investment and she used it all the time. The thief would
have found plenty to take if he'd called here.

Marsh arrived twenty-five minutes after his call, and
Norah let him in. She was apprehensive about what

244

she was going to hear, and began to talk as she showed him into the sitting-room.

'It's an awful mess, isn't it? The Lodge, I mean,' she said. She had been to look at the damage the previous day, when George had met someone from his insurance company at the site, and had found her eyes prickling with tears at the thought of Mrs Gibson perishing in that appalling blaze. She had been so loyal both to Mrs Warrington and to Susan and George, and though she was getting stiff and slow, she had remained a wonderfully thorough worker of whom Norah was fond. Coming up to the Lodge House got her out of the claustrophobic atmosphere of her home and the claims of her husband who, unable to do much for himself, had become rather demanding. What would happen to him now? Would his daughter whisk him away to Minnesota, or would he end up parked in an old people's home? A neighbour had taken him in while the daughter made plans to come over, which she had said she would do when she heard what had happened. George had wanted to pay her fare, but Norah had advised him to wait and see what her circumstances appeared to be before making such an offer. Mrs Gibson had always implied that her son-in-law was a prospering merchant, and certainly the daughter sent generous presents to her parents. The old man's future was not Norah's problem, but she knew that George would make it his.

Marsh had scarcely taken his seat on the sofa when Daisy came in with two freshly made cups of coffee neatly arranged on a tray with sugar and cream.

Marsh, who had been up for hours, was grateful, and he appreciated the excellence of the brew. Myra always ground her own and bought beans newly roasted every week.

'I'm afraid there's something extremely tricky to be faced,' he told Norah, having agreed that the house was a shambles although much of the original structure had been saved. 'I need your help,' he continued. 'The Vaughans will have to be told that there's a call out for their son. We think he may know something about what happened and he seems to have disappeared.'

'Malcolm? Oh no!' Norah stared at him, setting down her cup, but her protest was a reflex for she felt no surprise, rather a confirmation of her deepest dread. Malcolm had come to the Lodge House on Monday night in a very disturbed frame of mind. He would have known where to find the jewellery. He would have known how to get Susan and George out of the way and he could have disguised his voice so that they did not recognise him when he made the hoax calls; she remembered him adopting various accents in some game or other years before. If Mrs Gibson had seen him, when the things were later missed she would have said he had been at the house, so she had been silenced, and as a final typical touch he had resorted to fire.

The thought made her feel quite sick, but she knew that Malcolm was capable of committing such a crime.

'Well, we can't be certain yet,' said Marsh. 'But he's got some explaining to do. He had a blue Metro for sale, and one was seen in the square on Wednesday before the incident, with a man sitting in it, wearing a cap. And we believe that he's badly in debt.' Even now an experienced detective sergeant and a detective constable were at the workshop inspecting the files.

Marsh told Norah that Malcolm had been staying at the new hotel and had skipped, leaving his large bill unpaid, and that he had booked in under a false name. He did not tell her that Vaughan had used her name; an odd quirk, that. Plenty of prints that were probably his had been found in his room and would be matched with those in his office before obtaining confirmation from Australia, if he were not arrested first. Any found at the scene of the fire, however, could be explained away by a clever barrister as being lawfully there.

'But to kill Mrs Gibson,' Norah said, still reluctant to accept that. 'The robbery – yes, I can believe that, dreadful as it is. I can believe he made the fake phone calls, too. He would know how easy it would be to lure Susan away if she thought George had had an accident.'

'And he would know you'd go with her.'

'Yes. But to get George to leave – to deceive him – that wouldn't have been so easy.'

'Mr Vaughan thought it was something to do with Louise. He thought we'd found her. That was the impression he got from the call which he believed came from me.'

'Was that what happened? Oh, how cruel!' No wonder George had been evasive about the message.

'I'm afraid so,' said Marsh. 'And there's more. Miss Tyler, it's beginning to look as if he may have known something about his sister's disappearance.'

'What?' Now Norah really was shocked.

'Well, you know that since I've been back in the area I've been ferreting about a bit. I've had a bright young detective doing some legwork for me, asking questions. It's not been official, you understand, but simply because I don't like unfinished business. Vaughan mentioned an affair his sister had had with a man named Blacker. Did you know about it?'

Norah shook her head.

'I had an idea there was someone and it ended in tears,' she said. 'No details. Louise kept very quiet about it, but I sometimes saw her in London and I picked up a few hints.'

'He was married – the usual story,' said Marsh. 'But her brother knew about it and he made some odd remarks when my young officer went to talk to him. He suggested that on the night she disappeared, Louise had been attacked and ran away, perhaps to this Blacker. But Blacker never saw her that night. I'm fairly sure of that, though it hasn't been proved.'

'But Malcolm didn't – he wouldn't – he couldn't – ?' Norah's voice trailed off as she stared in horror at the detective superintendent. Then, more robustly, she asked, 'Well, what did he do with her, then?'

'We'll find out, when we arrest him,' said Marsh. 'But her parents will have to be prepared for some shocks.'

'Oh.' Norah twisted her hands in her lap. 'And I'm to do the preparing?'

'Well, if you could tell them that we're looking for Malcolm in connection with the robbery. Just to help us with our inquiries,' said Marsh. 'I can't let them find out from the press or some other way. Not after what they've been through already.'

'You just want to talk to him to eliminate him. Isn't that how it's put?' said Norah.

'That's it,' said Marsh. 'We don't add, "Or not, as the case may be." '

But he'd done it; he'd killed Mrs Gibson and started the fire, and both of them knew it.

Malcolm was too late for the ten o'clock Air Canada flight to Toronto. He had gone straight to the airport in a taxi after concluding the deal over the Porsche.

British Airways had a flight leaving at three-fifteen, fully booked in the economy class but with a first-class seat available. Malcolm hesitated. It meant hanging about at the airport, leaving time for something to go wrong. Should he flit quickly across the Channel, then fly on?

He must make up his mind. There was no reason for anyone to suspect him of the crime in Selbury; all the police could do was talk to him because he was related to the family.

But he wasn't. He was a separate individual, one who did not know who he really was.

Standing there on the busy concourse, his bags beside him, Malcolm knew himself to be rootless and alone, and an emotion he had known before but never identified by name swept over him: sheer, blind fear. He must get out, and quickly, and he must not risk too many customs checks. He asked about flights to Montreal and found there was a first-class seat on the British Airways eleven-fifteen departure. He could catch the shuttle from there to Toronto, said the helpful girl, if it would be worth his while to save the time involved, very little in the long run and he would have to hurry or he'd miss that.

Malcolm dared not risk trying to pay by credit card, for he owed on all his accounts. Hating to part with it, he counted out the cash and took his ticket, then set off to catch the bus to Terminal Four. The girl had said she would let the departure desk know that he was on his way.

He checked in his cases straight away, using his charm on the clerk, agreeing that he had packed them both himself, paying without protest the extra due because they were overweight. Then he went through passport control, the point of no return, and immediately felt safe. He had made it. He had no hand luggage, not even a razor in a toilet-bag to put through the machine. Everything was in his cases, the jewellery dropped into socks and packed inside his shoes.

He'd need a shave before landing. Maybe the hostess would be able to find him a razor. It might be wise, ultimately, to grow a beard, just for a time, but arriving with a day's growth would be no disguise, merely untidy.

A striking-looking man, tall and well-built, his pockets full of banknotes, Malcolm went off to the bar. He'd find someone there to talk to.

Norah did not care for her errand.

She found Susan fretty and restless, hating her enforced stay at The Crown, which was a pleasant enough place with some genuine beams among the later additions, and a friendly staff.

'We can't stay here, Norah,' she said, when Norah knocked on the door of their large room on the first floor and had been admitted by George.

'No. Well, Helen Cartwright has been trying to get hold of you, but without the phone it hasn't been easy. She found me via Myra,' Norah said. 'She's in Scotland just now, with her daughter, but she says you can go to the house and stay there for as long as you like. She wants you to ring her. I've got the number.'

'Oh, bless her,' said Susan. 'I'll do it at once.'

'Before you do, there's something else,' Norah said, and cast a glance at George, who could see that she had more on her mind than Helen Cartwright's kind invitation.

'It can wait while I ring Helen,' Susan declared, springing up from the chair where she had been sitting. 'What's the number?'

'Susan – George – please sit down,' Norah said, standing in the middle of the big room which contained two small armchairs and a desk as well as the two beds. The room had been made up while George and Susan were having breakfast and everything was tidy, but the pair had no belongings to spread about, only what they had been wearing at the time of the fire and the things Norah had bought to tide them over. 'I'm here as a messenger not only for Helen but also for the police. I've got something horrible to tell you,' she continued.

250

'Nothing can be more horrible than what's happened already,' said Susan. 'No one else can be dead, unless poor old Gibson's died of shock. Is that what it is?'

'No,' said Norah. 'No one else is dead. It isn't that.'

'Well, I can see you're determined to tell us before you let me ring Helen, so get on with it, there's a dear,' said Susan, and sat down again in her chair.

George pulled up the stool in front of the dressing-table and sat on that, leaving the other chair for Norah. She took it, for her knees felt weak. She was not going to tell them about Marsh's suspicion that Malcolm might have been involved in Louise's death; that could come later, and she would warn George first. She looked at his haggard face. How would he cope with what he was about to learn? What if all this proved too much for him and he had a stroke or a heart attack? Such things happened.

But not to George. He was needed too much. He would find the strength from somewhere. She turned her mind away from these grim possibilities to give them her message.

'It's Malcolm,' she said, and plunged. 'The police think he may have done the robbery.' It therefore followed that they suspected he had killed Mrs Gibson too; there was no need for her to spell that out.

'What?' Susan, her face already pale under its network of fine thread veins, went whiter still and her eyes looked enormous, shadowed by deep hollows beneath them. She put a hand to her mouth and whispered, 'No, I won't believe it.'

'They've probably got it all wrong and he'll be able to tell them where he was on Wednesday,' Norah said hastily. 'But he had a blue Metro for sale and it's gone. So has Malcolm,' she added. 'He was staying at the Manor Hotel and he isn't there now.' She decided not to mention his unpaid bill.

'He's not at the workshop.' George's remark was a

statement, not a question. He was remembering that Malcolm had known no cars had been damaged in the fire, knowledge he should not have possessed.

'No, and there aren't any cars there, either,' said Norah.

'But that means nothing,' said Susan. 'He's off somewhere on business, probably buying something else if he's sold what he had. And he'll have the Porsche with him. He won't sell that.'

'You're telling us that the police think he made those bogus calls to lure us out,' George said slowly. 'It didn't sound like his voice.'

'No, but he could probably disguise it,' said Norah. 'Don't you remember how he used to mimic accents when he was a boy? There's more,' she went on, speaking quickly while her courage lasted. 'He was in prison in Australia,' she told them. 'For fraud.'

'How do you know?' The swiftness of Susan's response startled Norah.

'Mr Marsh told me,' she said. 'They did a check.'

'But why? Why should they do that?'

Norah shrugged. How could she answer?

'It must be to do with Louise,' George said. 'They've been looking at her case again, haven't they, Norah? Marsh wasn't just making contact. He's been poking about in the past. But why ask about Malcolm? He was miles away at the time. He can't have known anything about it.'

At this Susan suddenly burst into a torrent of hysterical tears and began to mutter incoherently. Disconnected words escaped between her sobs. 'Her room – he wouldn't – no. It's impossible,' they heard.

George put his arms round her and stroked her hair, soothing her as one would a child. Norah got up and fetched a glass of water from the bathroom. After a while Susan grew calmer but she would not explain her words. She would never tell anyone what she had seen that night in Selbury House, and the hideous fear with which she had been filled at the time, and ever since when she let herself think about it.

'He's not violent,' was what she said.

But he could be, and they all knew it, and if it could be proved that he had killed Mrs Gibson, then he would be sent to prison for a great many years.

And quite right too, thought two of them, while the third blamed herself for past, unidentified sins of omission.

Malcolm's flight had been called and he was sitting in the lounge at his departure channel when the police found him.

He had been battering the ears of a new acquaintance with details of the insurance business he claimed to be running in Toronto, believing it all himself as he spoke, and he had not noticed the three men who came in, glanced quickly round and then went up to the clerk who would check the boarding cards as the passengers filed out to the aircraft.

They were being called forward in groups, with the first-class passengers left till last, and the three men waited quietly until Malcolm handed over his card for inspection. Then they closed in on him. Few of the other passengers realised that anything was amiss, so neatly was it done. One of the three was Whitlock, who knew him by sight; the others were Detective Sergeant Newton and Detective Inspector Blake.

Malcolm struggled, but they put an armlock on him, soon followed by handcuffs, and he was borne away. He began to protest and bluster, but stopped when he felt the pain in his arm, and when the locks snapped he knew that he was beaten.

They found wads of banknotes distributed among his various pockets, and more in his cases, together with Susan's jewellery. Airport police, in response to a message, had intercepted his baggage before it was loaded on to the plane.

Carol read about it in the paper the following day.

How could he be so evil!

But he was: she knew it. Back into her mind came the memory she had successfully banished for many years, the sight of his red, vengeful face. There was no love in his attack upon her. People said rape was a crime of violence and she knew it was true; Malcolm hated women and he was bitterly jealous of her.

This might kill her mother.

Carol could not get it out of her mind, and Ethel's keen interest in the case kept it alive as a topic between them.

'Imagine! Their own son!' she exclaimed. 'Well, not really, of course, as he was adopted. How ungrateful.' She went on to tell Carol of other adopted children she knew who had turned out very well, one girl becoming a doctor to the amazement of her adoptive parents whose ambitions for her had been more modest. 'I suppose cuckoos in nests, some of them are,' she sighed. 'As if they hadn't had enough to bear, losing their daughter like that all those years ago. It's too bad.'

'Yes,' agreed Carol. 'It is.'

It died out of the news after the first reports of Malcolm being remanded in custody, charged with the robbery and with murdering Mrs Gibson. Now, until his trial, it was *sub judice* and the reporters could not air their theories about how and why it had happened. All that would come after the trial and the sentence. Ethel thought he would get off with manslaughter, if he had a clever lawyer.

Even she at last dropped the subject as another case arose to catch her interest. Carol had been avid for details about her family; she bought several daily papers while it was in the news, and she began having dreams in which she saw her mother weeping and wringing her hands, and her own image, ghostlike, in the background. If she hadn't run away Malcolm might never have done this and Mrs Gibson might be still alive. But if she hadn't run away, she would not have had her lovely children.

She made huge efforts to put it all out of her mind until the trial, which might not take place for a year or more, Ethel said; she knew about these things, declaring that it would take the police months to prepare the case and the defence more months to get theirs ready.

'They'll dream up extenuating circumstances,' she said. 'Plead provocation to get him off. As if that poor cleaning lady ever harmed him. Probably she let him in. They forget about the victims at a time like this. Even the police do. All they think of is getting their man.'

Even allowing for her racy way of putting things, Carol thought that Ethel's comments were justified; sentencing seemed to be a lottery, with some judges allowing men who had killed or attacked children or women to get off with short terms in gaol.

Carol lost weight. Eric had noticed her poor appetite. He worried. She must be overdoing things. Perhaps the Christmas break would put her right. Like most of the country, her firm closed down for the full holiday period until after the New Year. He began to talk about the summer holiday. What about France this year? She'd like that, wouldn't she, since she spoke such good French?

With difficulty, even after all this time, Carol remembered that officially she had never been to France, but had learned the language at the good school she went to in Australia and by having lessons with a French woman who was a friend of her aunt's.

Why not, she thought, and said she'd get some brochures.

They had a happy Christmas. Later, Eric often thought of that. Joanna and William loved their well-filled stockings and their other toys, and Ethel came to spend the day. There was a plump turkey and Christmas pudding, with ice-cream for the children. The weather was fine and dry and on Christmas Day they took the car out of town to the hills and went for a long and healthy walk. During the week that followed, he took the children swimming while Carol went to the sales.

She began to look better and happier, and her choir gave their concert, singing *The Messiah* in a large hall. Eric took Joanna along to listen, while Ethel stayed with William who was too young to sit through it.

The New Year came and went and the Fosters' lives went on in the normal way. Only Carol still had nightmares. She knew that she would do so until Malcolm's trial was over.

3

The Company

He would not confess to Louise's murder, nor to anything else.

They asked him endless questions, after charging him with the robbery and with killing Mrs Gibson. He sat mulishly silent while they suggested he account for the presence of Susan Vaughan's jewellery in his luggage. She had refused to identify it because to do so would condemn Malcolm, but George had no such scruples, and there were photographs taken for insurance purposes.

The Metro had been traced to the dealer in Coventry. Malcolm's prints were in it, and by painstaking effort forensic scientists found on a pair of his trousers a thread from the dead woman's sweater. Though saturated by the firemen, the garment was in good enough condition for the comparison to be made. Methodically the police built up their case.

They had automatically notified the airports on that final Friday morning, and when Malcolm, who had had to travel under his own name because of his passport, had checked in at Heathrow, there he was, logged on the computer. If the team from Feringham had not arrived in time to arrest him, other officers would have detained him, but Whitlock was delighted to have brought him in.

The Porsche was found at the used car sales place near Heathrow.

When Malcolm's belongings were checked at the police station, a faded envelope was found in one of his pockets. The name of the addressee mystified Marsh until he looked inside and saw the letter from Susan's brother David to his sister. When it was shown to her, she admitted that it had been tucked into a volume of poetry he had given her; she had once liked reading poetry, she explained to Marsh, who had brought it to her at the Cartwrights', where she and George were on an indefinite visit.

'Why did he take the letter?' she asked George.

George himself had received an enormous shock at the revelation that David had been Norah's partner in her early tragic love affair. Why had she never told him? Why hadn't Susan explained?

At last George told Susan that Malcolm had had some idea that Norah was his mother.

'That's too easy,' she replied. 'Stupid boy.' She was silent. Then she added, 'How we failed him. Or rather, I did.'

'You didn't, my dear. You did more for him than he had any right to expect. Too much, perhaps. It was he who failed, not just us but himself, his true parents – everyone.' And Louise, he thought, but did not dare to utter. What about her? What had he done to her?

'But I never really loved him,' Susan said. 'That was why I tried so hard. I'd used him to replace Harry, you see, and you can't replace one person with another. They have to make their own mark with you, individually.'

The relief of making this confession was enormous. As Susan spoke, she felt a sudden extraordinary release. George did not at first realise the significance of what had happened to her. He thought that she would want to visit Malcolm in prison, but she expressed no such wish. She seemed to have put him completely from her in a curious divorcement.

George went to see Malcolm, for he could not totally abandon the man whom he had brought up as his son.

Their interview, however, was not a good experience for him.

'Come to gloat, have you?' said Malcolm, who had at first considered refusing to see George but his solicitor advised against such conduct. 'Must make you feel great, seeing me here, considering that you're responsible.'

'Oh, Malcolm,' said George, nearly in despair. 'Why must you always blame other people for your own mistakes? You've done a dreadful thing.'

'I'd a right to that stuff,' said Malcolm. 'It was to set me up in Canada.'

'You'd no right to what wasn't yours, and what had Mrs Gibson ever done to hurt you? You killed her.'

'She shouldn't have been there,' said Malcolm sulkily. 'She got in the way.'

He made no such admission of guilt to the police, staying stubbornly mute when interrogated until at last his solicitor pointed out that by confessing to theft and manslaughter he might avoid conviction for murder and so escape a life sentence.

When he was interviewed about Louise, he did utter. He was asked how he knew about Richard Blacker and he said he had seen her with the man in London, more than once. He did not reveal that he was obsessed by her in a way he did not understand and had followed her, spying on her, long before his marriage and his sojourn in Australia. His absence had not cured him. He consistently denied having seen her on the night she disappeared, declaring that the words Whitlock had found significant were just a throwaway suggestion. After this lapse of time it was useless to look for anyone who might have seen him in Feringham that night, just as trying to trace the people he had taken to Heathrow had proved impossible.

'It's because there were none,' said Marsh. 'I know it. He knows it. We all know it.'

'He may crack after he's sentenced,' suggested Whitlock.

George took Susan to Switzerland for Christmas. They stayed in a comfortable hotel among mountain peaks which had failed to attract their usual depth of snow, so that bare rock was exposed and skiers had to travel some distance to find a piste. They walked around the town and on the lower slopes, and the pure air did them good. When they came home, they had made a plan for the future, and the Lodge House, still awaiting repair, was put up for sale.

Susan could not bear to live there again, nor to face the rebuilding programme. A developer bought the land and applied for permission to knock down what was left of the place and build four maisonettes on the site, allegedly for young couples, but Norah said she was sure they would work out too expensive for most. She told the developer that if the scheme went ahead, she would be interested in acquiring one of the units. Perhaps she could afford one.

The Cartwrights had friends with a holiday house in Cornwall. It was comfortable and well heated, and they willingly agreed to let it to George and Susan until they should need it themselves later in the year. George and Susan both assumed that Norah would go down there with them, but she said that the time had come for a change and that she was going to start a business offering a domestic cleaning service to local house-holders. She had already found help for various people in the past; now she would employ staff herself, fitting the cleaner to the job, offering both sides the support of contracts and rules. As part of a team you were less easy to exploit than an individual, and the same applied to the householder who need not pander to too idiosyncratic an employee lest she leave. It was the coming thing, Norah explained.

This was her final chance to break away. If she did not take it, she would find herself supporting Susan through the rest of her life. She had done that for long enough.

She went to Cornwall for a visit, and George said that they had decided to look for somewhere permanent in the area. New surroundings were benefiting Susan; she liked the sea and the clifftop walks they took in fine weather, and she did not mind the strong wind, which he found a little trying. He never went out without his new tweed hat. There was a Fine Arts group Susan could join and it welcomed husbands if they were interested; George said that he might try it. He had resigned from the council and was relieved to be free of his various duties though he knew he would eventually take on others. He might get a boat, he said; he had liked sailing and had done a lot as a boy, when he had lived not so very far from here. They had seen his sister several times and he was blossoming, Norah saw, at being permitted a life of his own again.

'You'll come and stay,' he told Norah.

'Oh yes,' she said. But they both knew that her visits would be rare and might even cease in time.

'Do you think they'll rake up Louise's death when Malcolm comes to trial?' George asked her. 'What does your police chum say?'

Norah had seen quite a lot of Detective Superintendent Marsh. She sometimes wondered if he was compensation to her for the child she had never had; he was about the same age as it would have been by now.

'Malcolm won't confess,' she said. 'Won't discuss it except to say that he never saw her that night. Without evidence, they can do nothing, even though they're convinced he knows something about it.'

'Susan thinks so, too,' said George. 'She won't tell

me why. Something must have happened to make her so certain. Maybe he said something which gave him away. I don't ask her about it. It's better left, except that if we could find her we could give her a proper funeral.'

'It might lay your poor ghost,' said Norah. 'Malcolm might confess when he's been in prison a while. He'll have to see psychiatrists and so on, David says.'

'David?'

'David Marsh.'

'So he's David too. How strange,' said George, and added, 'I never knew, you know. Susan never told me.' He wondered who she had been protecting. 'Poor Norah.'

'Poor David Vaughan. I adored him,' Norah said. It did not hurt now. 'It would never have done, you know,' she added, mimicking old Mrs Warrington's regal tone.

How ruthless the old woman had been, George was thinking. But she'd paid for it when her elder son was lost at Monte Cassino.

'I'm sorry about it now,' Norah said, answering the question George had not asked. 'But I was very young and panic-stricken. One forgets how awful it was then, to get caught like that. He might have been a lovely man by now.'

'Or a lovely woman?' suggested George.

'Yes,' she agreed. 'Funny – I'd never thought of that.'

The Tetterton Choral Society's Christmas concert had been a big success, with every ticket sold. Now they were rehearsing Schubert's *Mass in G* for Easter.

Carol forgot past, present and future while she sang. Your voice joined with those around you, blending or in counterpoint, making a melodious whole, and while

262

she sang she lost her sense of isolation. She travelled into town on the bus and often got a lift back from another member of the choir. Eric could not drive her over because he could not leave the children, and she could not drive herself because this was one area where she had decided not to take a chance. On marrying, she would have had to surrender her old driving licence to obtain a new one in her married name and the licensing authorities might detect the fraud. She told Eric that she could not drive.

There had been plans for her to learn; she could apply, now, for a provisional licence in her married name, but she had not done so, saying that there wasn't time, that she was happy as things were but she'd do it one day.

'I thought everyone drove in Australia. All that outback,' Eric once remarked, and she had smiled at him and patted his hand.

'My aunt didn't,' she declared. 'And we lived in town.'

Easter was early that year and the winter had been very mild. Spring arrived weeks sooner than was usual, even in the north. On a mild night Carol set out for the final rehearsal before the concert, which was to be a week before Easter.

As usual, Eric gave her the money for a taxi back. Each week she returned it to him, grateful for his thoughtfulness but determined not to waste it when she could take the bus if there was no lift available. That night a group of singers went to a pub near the rehearsal hall after the practice ended, but Carol said she must go home and that she would catch the bus. Another woman, not the one who often dropped her on her way, said that she must get home too and would take Carol as far as Milton Road.

They parted on a corner, and Carol, with a little more than half a mile to walk, took a short cut down a footpath between a school playing-field and a wall backing on to a row of houses.

He came over the playing-field fence, running up behind her on silent feet, his arm closing round her throat from behind, stifling her scream. She tried to bend forward, buckling her knees to make him lose his balance, and she tried to jam her elbow backwards into him, but she had no time before her strength gave out.

Eric began to listen for her ten minutes before her usual time. He always did that, putting on the kettle for a cup of tea, looking at the children to make sure they were asleep, so that he could ask about her day and reassure her that they did not need her while she answered him. When she was five minutes late, he went to the gate to look for her. After ten minutes he rang the woman who often brought her back to learn from her husband that she had not yet returned either, so he then relaxed. Twenty minutes later, he rang again, and this time was told that Carol had come straight home, brought back by a different person, Mary Bly. After a little delay, Mary's telephone number was provided and Eric immediately called her.

She had dropped Carol at the corner of Milton Road nearly an hour before.

Eric rang the police at once. It did not take them long to find her.

Carol's death made headline news.

UNKNOWN RAPIST STALKS SOPRANO, said one paper. A veteran reporter mentioned the similarity between this crime and the presumed murder of Louise Vaughan more than twelve years before, the difference being that in her case no body had been found. Both victims had been on their way home from a choral society meeting when they met their fate. It turned out later that they had been of similar build, but one was only in her twenties while Carol was over forty. One victim was fair, the other dark. Much later came the information that Carol's hair was dyed, perhaps to hide the fact that she was prematurely grey, one reporter hazarded, giving her piece the heading SECRET VANITY OF MURDER VICTIM. This journalist had caught Ethel unprepared and asked her if she knew that Carol dyed her hair. Ethel's spontaneous denial was all the eager writer needed to devise her new slant on the story.

After that, Ethel was more cautious, saying nothing.

Norah read about the murder in *The Independent*, which was delivered daily to the cottage in Selbury which she had rented for a year while its owners were abroad. During that time the Lodge House would be renovated and she would make a long-term plan. She had begun her cleaning business in time to catch the spring enthusiasm for thorough operations, and had bought equipment which her team of workers, growing steadily, would take with them to their clients. One of Norah's customers was Brenda, who had hired her to maintain both her house and the office.

The Independent did not give much space to what had happened in Tetterton but later, when she went to Feringham, Norah saw headlines in the tabloids which were much more graphic and she bought one out of what she recognised as a sick sort of curiosity.

Later, she talked to Marsh about it; her team cleaned his wifeless house now and she often saw him.

'It might have been a copybook,' he told her. 'Mention of what happened to Louise might have sparked off someone, but I think the choir angle is coincidence. Carol Foster should not have taken that short cut along the footpath, late at night, alone. And ideally the friend should have dropped her at her door. I expect she'll regret that for ever.'

'Will they catch this one?'

'Who knows? There will be clues this time,' said Marsh, not putting into words the reason: because there was a body. 'There may have been other attacks on women in the area, or there may be more, and if they can't get a line on anyone, they can blood-test all the men in the district. Expensive, but it gets results.' He hesitated, then added, 'As she was raped, there would be evidence of the assailant's genetic fingerprint, you see.'

'Oh yes. That new discovery. I remember,' Norah said.

'It's been used already several times, successfully,' said Marsh. 'It's going to make it much easier to convict rapists in future – and other attackers, too, if the victims have been able to scratch them, draw blood even, leaving traces.'

'And it will exonerate the innocent,' said Norah.

'That too, of course,' said Marsh.

Carol was buried on a bright day at the end of April. The inquest on her had been opened and adjourned, the coroner eventually allowing the funeral to be held. Eric wanted a grave to visit, and a week later he went there alone, with a bunch of tulips picked from the garden. He stood gazing at the patched turf fitted in over the new mound.

In her drawer, sorting through her clothes before sending them to Oxfam, he had found a pile of newspaper cuttings referring to the recent case of arson and murder in Selbury, for which crime Malcolm Vaughan, the adopted son of the house, was awaiting trial. He read about the disappearance of Louise twelve years before.

Eric was alone in the house. His mother had taken the children to the cinema to see *The Lady and the Tramp*, leaving him free to deal with a task that would be more difficult the longer he delayed.

He took the pile of cuttings down to the sitting-room and sat there reading them carefully. Afterwards, he burned them. Then he completed his packing up, putting all her clothes into bags, setting aside a tiny pile of other items – the ring that he had given her, her watch, and a pretty locket that he had not seen her wear for weeks.

Afterwards, he went to the library and, in old newspapers, read about the original case when Louise Vaughan had disappeared. Then he saw the resemblance between his own daughter and the young Louise; he learned about Louise's work in publishing and the type of books she helped produce. In one photograph she wore a locket round her neck.

'Why?' asked Eric, aloud, staring down at the quiet earth beneath which, in her simple coffin, she lay.

Could it ever be proved? There were tests, these days, and the parents were both alive. It might be done.

He thought about them, but what good would it do them now to discover what she had done? And why had she done it? She hadn't wanted even him to know.

She was Carol, beloved wife and mother, and he would put that on her tombstone. Let her keep the secrets she had not wished to share.

He gave Joanna the locket.

'I think that possibly it may have been your grandmother's,' he said.

'I wish that we had more of them,' said Joanna in reply.

'More of what?'

'Grandmothers and grandfathers,' she replied.

There was no answer he could give.

267

(Ext)

Yorke, Margaret.

Admit to murder

$16.95

DATE			

SEP   1990